To John

TANGIER

BOOK ONE: THE KING'S ARMY

Alex Janaway

Best wishes

TANGIER

Published by Browncoat Books 2014
Copyright © 2014 Alex Janaway
Map illustration by Trace Price
Author Picture by Claire Moir
All rights reserved.
ISBN: 0992813743
ISBN-13: 978-0992813741

DEDICATION

This story is dedicated to all who serve – past,
present and future. And to their families and friends who
endure it all with love in their hearts.

ACKNOWLEDGMENTS

Several years ago my old friend, Jim Beach, lent me a history book to read. It was called *The Army of Charles II* by John Childs. I found a story about an army, almost forgotten, that had fought in a distant land in the name of their King. What happened on the shores of North Africa did indeed give birth to the modern British Army. I am grateful to John for inspiring me to write this story. I am also incredibly grateful to SSAFA for giving me the opportunity to give something back. It is the least I can do.

Also by Alex Janaway

Redoubt
The Coming of Night

Go to www.alexjanaway.com to find out more
about the author and his upcoming releases

TANGIER AND FORTIFICATIONS

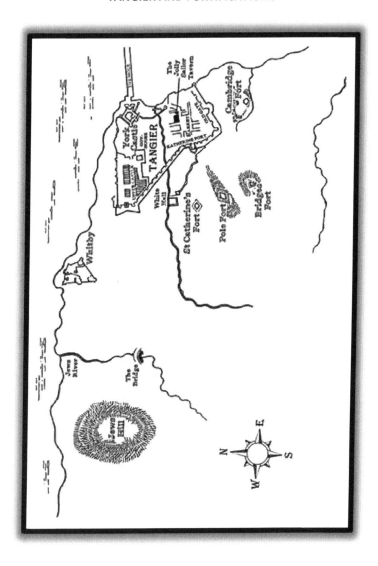

14 June 1658
Dunkirk – The Battle of the Dunes

"Bloody French," said John Fitzwilliam. He tried to push himself up, but his hands could find no purchase in the shifting sand. "Bloody Cromwell."

He fell back and propped himself up on his left elbow. He placed his right hand to his stomach and experienced a wave of pain, the like of which he had never thought possible. He felt a surge of nausea and his vision blur. He closed his eyes and took deep breaths. The sickness passed but the pain remained. He pulled his hand away; it was covered in blood, so much so that droplets fell back onto his jerkin. Damn it all, but he hadn't expected to take shrapnel in his stomach. It was an unlikely place to be hit when mounted on his horse. The poor thing had taken most of the blast as it was; its entire flank had been shredded. Damn piss poor bloody luck.

The Duke of York's cavalry brigade had barely begun their charge towards the French lines when their batteries had opened up. The Duke had taken one look at the forces arrayed ahead of him and turned tail. The cream of

Charles's Royalist army had given up the fight before it had begun. Fitzwilliam had been pulled out from under his animal by retreating comrades and deposited to the rear of the Anglo-Spanish lines to await his fate.

"Father!"

John looked up at his son, James. The lad was scrambling down the dune, his legs creating small waves as he tried to maintain his balance. Sixteen years of age, gangly and lean, he had yet to put on the bulk and muscle that was the physical trait of the Fitzwilliams. Centuries of hard Highland living had ensured it was part of their blood. The lad dropped to his knees before him.

"Well, son? How goes it?"

James bent over, his breath laboured.

"The Protectorate soldiers are right in front of us! They went and smashed the Spanish line and now the centre is in retreat."

Once more the red-coated soldiers of the Lord Protector, Cromwell, had come to fight against them. And once more it was they, not Charles' army, who would win. John felt himself thinking back to his holdings up near Fife. He hadn't done that for years, not since the day in the year 1650 when he had exiled himself to continue the fight for Charlie's cause. He had left everything, his fortune, his land and the grave of his wife, given it all up in the hope that Charles would regain the throne. Taking his young son, he had joined the small band of English, Irish and a smattering of Scottish royalists. They had allied themselves with the Spanish rulers of the Netherlands, in opposition to the French and the English Commonwealth. And most especially, Cromwell, the Lord Protector of that Commonwealth.

"So? Did we charge?"

His son shook his head. The sun caught the sides of

his wind-burned face; his cheeks flush with the vigour of youth, and wisps of a beard yet to fill out. Bright blues eyes were wide and excited. Auburn hair, just like his mother's, fell down around his shoulders. His broad-brimmed hat kept the hair away from his eyes, whilst its white topping feather hung limply.

"No, father. The Duke has met with the commander of the redcoats. They have agreed that both armies withdraw from the field. No Englishman will spill the blood of his countrymen today. We are to march away in good order."

John grunted, and was rewarded with another surge of pain.

"Ah, I cannot blame the Duke for that. We are outnumbered and outgunned. At least the redcoats have the good grace to let us retire."

"And it means we can live to fight another day."

"Yes, James, it does." John didn't have the heart to tell him that, in all likelihood, with their Spanish allies gone, the royalist cause had no supporter of note to shelter them. Cromwell's troops could afford to let them go. They were not considered a threat anymore.

"Father, I've sent for the surgeon. He will be along presently."

John shook his head.

"James, I've lived the life of a soldier long enough to know a mortal wound when I see one."

His son's face blurred between looks of confusion and despair.

"But, father. The surgeon can stitch you up and put a bandage on the wound."

"No, son. I'm hit in the belly. I'm as good as dead.'

Fitzwilliam's eyes misted up and he moved around and took his father in his arms.

"Steady, lad," John hissed.

"I'm sorry, father."

John managed a wry smile.

"I'm not dead yet. I want to you to listen to me. I had hoped that you and I would be there to see the monarchy restored and that we'd return home to Scotland together. That will not happen. So instead, I charge you with upholding the honour of the Fitzwilliam house, though I fear you may be the last to do so."

"I intend that not to be so, father," said James, with a determined edge to his voice.

John nodded.

"Good. Now, you are well thought of and you have those who will sponsor you in the days to come. I expect you to stay with the army and continue your service to your king. Mark me well. Remember your loyalties." John felt his lungs rattle. He coughed and the sound was harsh and ragged. Flecks of blood dotted his chest. His reached up and gripped his son's arm.

"Perhaps I have a shorter time than I imagined. I am sorry, my son. I ripped you away from your home for a cause that you were too young to understand."

"I understand it now, father. As long as our King is denied his rightful place, I will always have a purpose."

John looked at him with pride, managing another smile despite the agony in his belly. He was proud of his son. If only he had more time.

Behind them came the sound of a drum. It beat a slow, rhythmic pace, the cadence muffled by the slopes around them. At the crest of the slope, shapes appeared, the sun, appearing from behind a cloud, blinded them to nothing but the dark silhouettes of marching men. Pikes waved above them and the sharpened metal tips glinted. As the men started their descent, the watchers could discern the garb and faces of their comrades. A mixture of weariness and relief reflected in dozens of visages. Further columns of troops, struggling through the sand, moving northeastwardly away from the battle, joined the group of men. The solitary drum became many, marking out the time for their particular company, the beat becoming discordant and irregular.

Behind the first column, a band of horses arrived at the ridge and quickly made their way down, overtaking the last few lines of the infantry. One horse reined in beside John and James.

"Young Fitzwilliam. The battle is over – we are heading back to the baggage."

James looked up at his commanding officer, Colonel Sir Robert Harley.

"It's my father, sir. He's wounded. We're waiting for the surgeon."

The Colonel shifted his position, leathers creaking, and studied John with an appraising but not unkind eye.

"I fear your wait will prove fruitless."

James looked back at his father. John's eyes had rolled back in their sockets, only the whites were visible. No breathe escaped from his lungs.

"I'm sorry, Fitzwilliam. I'll send word for one of the carts to come along and collect his body. At least this engagement has allowed us to conduct the full civilities of war. Now, I suggest you say your farewells and rejoin the army." The Colonel moved off, leaving James by his father's side.

The last of the infantry passed by. A gentle breeze sprung up, carrying the smell of the sea. A tear rolled down James' cheek and fell into the sand, sinking away to nothing.

1September 1661
Dunkirk

The rain beat down heavily on the worn cobbled streets. The air was humid and made everything sticky; it clung to everything, clothes and structures alike. It was oppressive. The garrison town of King Charles II's final mainland holding was a wretched, dirty and unkempt place. Only a few folk were outside and they did not tarry. As one sodden individual moved past the entrance to one of the local taverns, he heard raised voices and the sound of tables and chairs falling to the ground. Shaking his head he moved quickly on. It was best not to be too close to one of the garrison drinking dens when it got heated.

As if to prove the point, the door behind him was thrown open and a figure was thrown in the air to land in a heap on the road. It let out an audible grunt before struggling onto all fours. Behind him, emerging from the doorway came three more men, all in their middle years and rough looking. All wore the long red coat of the King's army. One man, with a bloodied lip that was dripping onto his shirt, was rubbing his jaw, a pained expression on his face.

"Now why did you 'ave to go and do that, Sir?" he stood over the crouching figure, his two companions taking post on either side. "There was us having a decent game of cards and then you go and get all upset because of an offhand comment." He moved round to the side of the figure and squatted down companionably.

"Just because I made a friendly observation about how you cavaliers never did know how to pick a winner," he sighed theatrically. "It is common knowledge that your king only got back in because we said he could."

"Our King," said James Fitzwilliam as he raised his head, his bearded face obscured by a shaggy mane of hair that had worked free of its ties. Through this veil he looked left at the young lad with a poxy face to his left and the balding older fellow to his right. Neither looked like they could handle a fight by themselves.

"Ah yes, our King. The one that never pays us and doesn't give a damn about what happens to us."

"Best you lot are left here to rot than cause trouble back home," replied Fitzwilliam.

"Hah! You're probably right, Sir. But I just can't help taking offence. So why don't you just let us give you the beating you deserve and we'll call it quits?"

He reached over to grip Fitzwilliam's shoulder. As he did so the Scot pushed upwards and slammed a fist into his stomach. The bloodied man issued a grunt as he fell backwards, his two companions momentarily stunned by the turn of events. Fitzwilliam was up and barrelled headfirst in to the younger man stood to the left carrying both of them into the wall. As they impacted, Fitzwilliam clenched his two hands tightly together and brought them up to strike the chin of the other. The force of the blow drove the youngster's head back hard against the stone facing of the tavern and there was a loud crack and the lad slumped to the floor. Fitzwilliam turned to face the last of his attackers only to see a fist flying straight towards his face; he ducked to the left and allowed the arm to carry onwards, the attacker overextending as a result. Taking advantage of this, he threw a punch into the balding man's side, making contact with his kidney. The man cried out in pain and fell to his knees.

Fitzwilliam stood up and looked about him. The three were all down and did not appear to be showing any enthusiasm to continue the disagreement. He walked over to the prostate man who had done all the talking. Fitzwilliam tilted his head and put his hands to his hips.

"Now, I do believe that manhandling an officer is a punishable offence. But I think we can call this quits."

The first man looked up and spat.

"You ain't no officer of mine. I don't take orders from cavaliers."

Fitzwilliam stroked his beard. "I suppose we'll just have to-" Two arms reached through under his armpits and met behind his neck, putting him into a headlock. Fitzwilliam struggled to free himself, but to no avail.

The man on the ground spat and grinned, showing off the gap where his two front teeth used to be. He stood up and made a show of dusting his clothes down.

"As I was sayin', I take orders from proper roundhead officers."

He flexed his shoulders and neck. "Hold him good, Jed."

"I got him, Dick," growled Jed, the bald one.

The solider called Dick fired two punches into Fitzwilliam's stomach and followed this up by a roundhouse punch to the left side of his face. Fitzwilliam slumped in Jed's arms, breathing heavily and tasting blood in his mouth. He was hoisted up again to receive his next blow.

It never came.

"Stop that now!" bellowed a loud and savage voice.

Dick turned around and found himself face to face with the Provost Sergeant. Behind him stood his band of four provosts, all similarly attired and carrying stout wooden clubs. The sergeant, mutton-chopped and ramrod straight, eyeballed both men with a glare from under his tricorn hat.

"I expect you two know that Garrison orders forbids brawling' in the streets during daylight hours?"

Dick returned the glare.

"Aye, Sergeant, we bloody know the rules. And we'd have followed them to the letter if it wasn't for us getting provoked."

"Then you also know that attackin' an officer is a court-martial offence. In fact," the Provost Sergeant scratched his chin, "if I am not mistaken, it's an 'anging offence too," he finished with relish.

"Look, Sergeant, we-"started Jed, a hint of panic in his voice.

"We was just helping the young master," interjected Dick. "He'd had too much of the rough stuff. Found himself without his wits if you know what I mean. So we thought we'd just give him a helping hand. Get him on the right road as it were."

The Provost Sergeant tipped his head and looked up into the sky.

"And I suppose what I mistook for you smacking him in the mouth was actually you trying to slap him awake."

Dick nodded and spread his arms wide.

"That's the way of it, Sergeant. We know our duty."

The Provost Sergeant leaned forward.

"Do you indeed. Well I know mine. You can come with me and the boys back to the gaol. And we can see about making the officer here a mite more comfortable whilst we wait for him to wake up."

Fitzwilliam was more than awake, but he thought it best to let this one play out.

"We'd be happy to carry him along, Sergeant," said Dick quickly. "We'll just leave him at the gaol with you and then we'll be on our way."

The Provost Sergeant rocked back on his heels.

"Oh no, that won't do at all. I want you to be there just in case the officer recalls something of the story you haven't told me yet. I've got a lovely cell for you," he tilted his head to look at the young lad who was crumpled against the wall.

Dick looked crestfallen and glanced at Jed, who swallowed nervously.

"Come along, then. You help your mate carry the officer."

Dick took one of Fitzwilliam's arms and put it round his shoulders. Fitzwilliam let his body drain of energy and he slumped further. He might as well get this pair to do all the work; it would be a small victory.

"What about that one?" asked one of the provosts, indicating the soldier slumped against the tavern wall.

The Provost Sergeant looked at Dick.

"Dunno, just another drunk, unreliable soldier, Sergeant," the man replied with a shrug.

The Provost Sergeant scowled and spat.

"Aren't you all? Come on."

The group moved off down the street. The rain continued unabated. A gentle sheet of water ran down the tavern wall against which the comatose soldier rested.

As it gathered on the ground

Around him, the water mixed with blood. The two fluids, murky brown with red veins, flowed towards the nearest drain. No one would care to check the man until the following morning; at which point they would find a body. And no one would care overmuch. It was not an unusual thing to discover yet another casualty of a decaying garrison.

6 September 1661
Dunkirk

Colonel Harley entered the gaol via a side entrance. It was still raining, although the clouds were clearing up and patches of blue could be seen in the far distance. He removed his hat, shook it vaguely in the direction of the open portal then closed the door. A man in his late forties, blue-eyed and clean-shaven with thick black hair tied into a short ponytail in the back, he had weathered his own storms well. Brought up in wealth and privilege, he had given his life to the Royalist cause, and in so doing there had been many lean years since. He had grey hairs aplenty amidst the black, but hard living had kept the slow creep of corpulence at bay, and his frame was still lean and muscled. He looked around the room and frowned. It was sparsely furnished: a desk, a small wardrobe and, on one wall, a series of hooks where a number of chains and manacles were suspended. There was a small fire built into the wall on his left, struggling to hold onto life. Harley doubted the blackened pot above it absorbed any heat from the tiny flames below. The room was cold and lifeless. Most apt considering its purpose, he conceded. The Provost Marshall rose from his desk and hurried forward. Rake thin and sallow-skinned, his hair hung down in greasy strands.

"Good morning, Colonel. A fine day is it not?"

"Hmm, I rather think there's change in the air."

"Yes indeed, Colonel. A fair change, I warrant."

Harley eyed the man as he took off his long coat. The Provost was an obsequious sort with his superiors, and a stern, no-nonsense disciplinarian with the other ranks. A man who valued his rank and the social standing it granted him. Harley did not believe him to be a proper military man but he was loyal and he didn't cause trouble, and for Harley, that was a blessed relief. For the last two years he had had to contend with the gradual dissolution and dismemberment of a once highly effective fighting force. Garrison duty should not be the fate of veteran fighting men. They had to be kept busy, their minds focussed. Instead, sloth and debauchery had become the norm.

Ever since the restoration of His Majesty the year before, the garrison had witnessed a merging of both the remnants of Cromwell's New Model forces and the King's loyalist troops from the Netherlands. Thankfully both sides had been professional enough and equally tired of the fighting to take this new order relatively well. Harley had considered this garrison duty to be a chance to create a new standing army, mustered proudly under the King's banner. Instead, they had been forgotten. Pay was intermittent at best, what coin that did arrive was quickly spent on booze, barter and women. Parliament seemed not to care about its foot soldiers, the men that had brought them victory, and His Majesty's gratitude was mercurial. The King's attentions were elsewhere, towards the Indies and Portugal. Dunkirk was the home of the forgotten army. Well, perhaps no longer. Today would mark a sea change in their fortunes to be sure. He was just thankful there appeared to be a place in this future for him.

"So, Provost, how has your guest been?"

The Provost shrugged.

"Ah, you know young Fitzwilliam. He and I have often shared this roof together. Once he has dried out he tends to be a well-mannered and thankfully peaceful tenant. No trouble at all."

If only that were the case, thought Harley. "Indeed. The man suffers from our inactivity worst than most of my other officers. At least they choose to drink and gamble within their own social circles, away from the other ranks. Not Fitzwilliam. He enjoys his interactions with the ranks far too much."

"I hear that today brings us some interesting news, Colonel?"

"Indeed it does, Provost. Things will change. But that will come at the muster. Now, if you please, I would like to talk to Fitzwilliam."

"Yes, Colonel. Of course."

The Provost led him through a doorway to the left of his desk and into a long corridor. On the right hand side were a number of cells. Each door was shut and, as was his want, Harley took a moment to look into each one. They contained the usual mix of drunkards and brawlers. Men who would be flogged or pay docked for their crimes. He ensured each man was given a suitably withering examination before he passed on. At the final cell he stopped and studied the occupant, whose current disposition was to gently snooze upon the pile of straw that served as bedding. His feet were crossed one over the other, his arms propped behind the head and a hat covering the top part of his face. Harley put his hands behind his back, harrumphed, raised himself onto his tiptoes and said in a loud, commanding voice: "Provost. Open this door, if you please. I wish to speak to Ensign Fitzwilliam in private."

The cell's occupant swiftly stirred from his repose and pulled back his hat. Fitzwilliam blinked a couple of times and, as recognition dawned, leapt to his feet. After some hurried patting down and rearranging of his soiled garments, he adopted a semblance of standing to attention.

Harley stepped back to make room for the Provost, who in turn stepped forward, unlocked the door, swung it open and then stepped back.

Harley eyed the Provost.

"Ah yes. My apologies, Sir." The Provost gave a small bow and departed. Harley remained at his station, his face concentrating on some unseen object, whilst the steps of the provost faded away. At the sound of the far door closing, he looked up briskly towards Fitzwilliam and stepped through into the cell.

"Ensign Fitzwilliam," he began in a perfunctory fashion, "I am led to understand that you are aware of the articles by which this garrison are governed."

"Yes, Sir, I..."

"It wasn't a question, sir, it was a statement of the inalienable obvious. And those articles I am bound to uphold, am I not?"

Fitzwilliam remained silent. Harley looked at him expectantly, though in truth he knew there would be no satisfactory response. He tutted. "And in those articles, it is laid down that no officer will fraternise with his men whilst not in the pursuit of his duties. That is to say, no officer of mine will end up brawling with soldiers in the middle of the bloody street in the middle of the bloody day!" He paused, took a breath and continued. "Now, in most circumstances, I would at the very least have to demote you. But I've already done that. I could fine you but I know you have not a penny to your name. I could have you flogged, but that would be unseemly and would incur poor morale amongst the men. So what am I to do with you?" He stopped and waited a moment, just to give the lad a chance. It was a futile gesture. "That is a question, Fitzwilliam."

Fitzwilliam worked his mouth a few times then shrugged.

"I try and do my duty, Sir. I occasionally get carried away with my more passionate beliefs. But my loyalty is without question."

Harley nodded. "And that's part of the problem. Your loyalty to the King is unquestioned, but you have to get over the inescapable fact that the armies of the war no longer exist. Roundhead and cavalier, professional soldiers alike, march under the same banner. Now the drinking, gambling and squabbling I could almost ignore. Most of my officers do very little else with their time and your actions are no different. It's just that you seem to delight in finding the nearest group of Parliament men to go and taunt. That time is over, Fitzwilliam. And I will have no one in my command who does not understand that. So, I had decided to end this state of affairs and let you go."

Fitzwilliam rocked back as if stung; a look of genuine concern finally showed on his face. Good, thought Harley, the shot finds its mark.

"Colonel, I..." said Fitzwilliam, trying to find the words.

Harley put his hand up to silence him.

"I said had. Instead I will use the last scrap of goodwill I bore your father. It has transpired that today will see a changing in all our fortunes. And this may be the making of you. The garrison is disbanding, Fitzwilliam, many men will find themselves without employment. You on the other hand, are fortunate to be part of my regiment. I need officers who can handle themselves. And, in your case, have nothing to lose."

Fitzwilliam leaned back and blew out a sigh.

"Colonel, thank you. I am most fortunate to have you as my benefactor."

Harley snorted.

"You may not thank me when you hear what we are tasked with. Be warned, you have no more credit with me now, Fitzwilliam. What I do now, I do with military expedience in mind. Mark me well, lad. I grant you this one final chance to prove that you are worth your father's name."

Fitzwilliam stiffened at that remark, but nodded curtly.

"Now," Harley looked Fitzwilliam up and down. "I suggest you hurry off and see if you can find a change of clothing. Our new commander has arrived and he plans to address the entire garrison in one hour's time. Off you go, then."

Fitzwilliam bent down, retrieved his hat and hurried out of the cell. Harley watched him head off and wondered, not for the first time, if the young man was really worth all the effort.

*

Fitzwilliam leant forward, dipped his hands into the bowl of cold water and splashed his face. He rubbed his checks vigorously and sought to untangle his unkempt beard. It was increasingly fashionable to sport a long moustache or simply go clean-shaven but some of the older officers did still affect goatees. His father had had a beard and Fitzwilliam felt that it suited his Scottish heritage to have a wilder look about him. He examined himself in the small sliver of mirror that rested against the wall. His facial growth created the impression he was older than his twenty years and today his bloodshot eyes, a dark brown hue, rather served to aid that notion. He leaned back, ran a hand over his head, and thought about running a brush through his shoulder length hair but thought better of it. Instead he reached for a leather braid, gathered his longs and tied it back into a ponytail. He raised his right arm and sniffed under his pit. He winced in disgust. Well, that wouldn't do. He bent forward once more, picked up a wet cloth, and applied it to the offending region. After some vigorous scrubbing his repeated the motion on his left arm. He stood up again and nodded.

"Better," he pronounced.

He wandered across his room to a chest, resting at the end of his bed. He stretched - hearing an unpleasant click in his shoulders - then took to scratching various parts of his torso. Well muscled and boasting a generous amount of body hair, he was pleased that most of the bruises he had received from his slight altercation a few days earlier were starting to fade. They were a light yellow and green as opposed to the angry purples and reds he'd discover after waking up in the cell. He opened the chest and dug around in its contents, the sum of which represented almost all his worldly goods. He found a reasonably clean white shirt and put it on. He also found a grey and worn scarf lying on the bed and tied that round his neck. He then retrieved his red longcoat from the floor and beat it half-heartedly, in an attempt to get rid of the worst offending accumulations of dried mud and grime. He gave up after a few more slaps and struggled into it.

Dropping onto his haunches he reached under the bed and grasped hold of his sword and scabbard. Withdrawing the weapon from its resting place, he stood back up and buckled it on against his left hip. It was good to feel the reassuring weight by his side. He reached over with his right hand, withdrew the blade and held it before him. Well oiled, the metal gleamed, and there was not a bit of rust. It was a claymore, the weapon of choice for any self-respecting Scotsman. The sword had been his father's and his grandfather's before that. It was set within a wheel pommel, capped by a crescent-shaped nut and a guard with straight, down-sloping arms ending in quatrefoils and a shallow depression running down the centre of the blade from the guard. It was designed to be used two handed and did not lend itself to being carried on the hip. He much preferred having it strapped to his back, but English military etiquette did not approve of such a flagrant display of uncultured loutishness. Most of the other officers now relied on the lighter, thinner blades, which were useful for duelling. In his opinion, they weren't much good for anything else. Give him something hard and heavy to lay about with every time. Be that as it may, he would get far less looks of disapproval wearing it as he did now, and he did rather want to avoid any more unnecessary attention for the time being. He considered taking his two pistols but decided against it. He wasn't planning on going to war. As an afterthought he did pick up his dirk from a nearby table and slid it into his right boot. You couldn't be too careful. Especially as he did have a long list of people who wanted to inflict harm and discomfort about his person.

He took up his hat and walked out of his room, and the house that doubled up as a junior officer's billet. He had been able to procure a couple of apples from the mess kitchens and munched on one thoughtfully. He had been lucky this time. He'd been sure that the Colonel would have forgiven him as he always had, but Fitzwilliam had been decidedly disconcerted by the tone his commanding officer had taken. It did indeed seem that his credit had run out. He really did not understand why everyone got into such a bloody state about his attitude towards the Parliamentarian rabble. Had certain folk not noticed that for all their posturing and self-congratulation, it had been the Royalists that had had the last laugh? After enduring ten years of despotism by Cromwell, Parliament had recanted and acknowledged their mistake. The country needed its King, just as the King needed his country. As separates, neither was as good as the whole. His occasional scraps with the soldiers, were, he felt, just a way of reminding them of this fact.

He strolled down the street towards the main barracks and noticed the large number of men gathered; there was quite a crowd, most of them wearing their redcoats or leather jerkins. Many soldiers had taken up residence in houses within the town, often with a local lady. A lot of them now had families of screaming children and shouting wives. Fitzwilliam shuddered at the thought. It seemed to him nothing more than a curse, the worst of the dictates of Catholicism, that a man must burden himself with women and offspring. Well, not for him. Stay unfettered and free. That was the natural state of things, what King Henry VIII had rebelled against the

Papacy for. God bless his memory.

"James!"

The cry broke him out of his reverie. He looked about him and saw his friend, Lieutenant Rupert Drummond, pushing through the crowds towards him.

"Rupert. Good man. How are you?"

The other man joined him and clapped him on the back.

"Well and rested. Although I do hear that the Provost's cells are often more comfortable than the rooms that we are forced to endure."

Fitzwilliam laughed.

"Don't believe it. Even cockroaches have the sense to steer well clear of that place." He smiled at his friend. A year or two younger older than himself, Drummond was another child of the Royalist cause, although in his case, his father was alive and well, back in England. Drummond had connections and support, but being the third son meant he could not rely on any significant inheritance. So instead, like so many others, he had become an officer in the Kings' army. In that sense Drummond had been fortunate to find employment. There was no shortage of experienced officers who had been part of the great disbandment of the military at the end of Parliament's reign. Now there were a large number of English, Scottish and Irish gentlemen who plied their trade in the armies of Europe.

Drummond was taller than Fitzwilliam by a good couple of inches, but lacked the broadness of frame, being more spare and willowy in build. He did affect a long and lustrous moustache that Fitzwilliam had to admit was very impressive.

"I'm glad you could make it to muster," Drummond said.

"I wouldn't miss it. I hear we have a new general?"

"Indeed we do. It is the Earl of Peterborough, Sir Henry Mordant."

Fitzwilliam raised an eyebrow.

"A King's man."

The first Earl, Mordent's father, had commanded a troop of Parliament men at the start of the war. Upon his death the new earl had swiftly switched sides to the crown and had fought with distinction.

"Colonel Harley had said that we should be expecting some changes. Any idea what?"

Drummond shook his head.

"We've heard many things. It's become quite the topic of conversation over the last few days. The Earl has been appointed by the King for a special mission and it sounds like we'll be going along."

"Now that sounds interesting. It's not as if we've had a surfeit of excitement."

The two men walked under the barracks gate and onto the large parade ground. It was a little more than a patch of worn, dusty ground. Fitzwilliam had precious few recollections of any parades or gatherings happening on it. Gathered around the edges were various buildings, tents and supply dumps. It was as if the garrison had arrived but had decided to never fully put their roots down. Speaking of which, the regiments were forming up, and he had better show willing.

"Very well, Rupert. Best go and make a show."

He patted his friend on the back and hurried over to where Harley's regiment had gathered. Numbering a little under a thousand men, they were a mix of both cavalier and roundhead troops, although the majority of the officers were Royalist. His regiment was a mixture of English and Scottish soldiers, although other regiments of the garrison were made up entirely of Irish. Men who had resisted Cromwell's pacification of their country and who had sided with the Monarchy. Fitzwilliam located his own small command, the Quartermaster's troop, at the rear of the rest of the regiment, occupying the place they would normally do in any actual battle. Made up the sick, lame and indifferent, the men of the Quartermaster's troop would never be expected to fight, only to make sure the soldiers were supplied with food, water and shot. It was the only place left that the Colonel could find for him. He drew up next to Quartermaster Sergeant Smythe and nodded curtly. Smythe reacted by very slightly drawing back his shoulders. This attempt at springing to attention was the most Fitzwilliam could expect from the man. Dour and sour, he bore Fitzwilliam the barest respect due him as an officer, which was fine with Fitzwilliam as he barely spent much time with the soldiers anyway. Smythe took care of the day-to-day business and, as this was a garrison, there was precious little to do that wasn't routine anyway. All in all there was precious little that Fitzwilliam felt he had to be either concerned about or, indeed, physically present to witness.

He tried once more to arrange his uniform into some semblance of order but the weight of his sword belt meant his jacket was dragged to the left. He settled it more comfortably about his hips just as the call was given to bring the assembled garrison to attention. A small group of riders appeared at the head of the formation. He recognised Colonel Harley and the other senior officers but the man leading the group was unknown to him. That must be Peterborough. He couldn't tell for sure but the man looked middle-aged, in his forties perhaps. That would fit in with what he knew about the man. He did look very fine on his mount. Very clean and polished. It was an unusual sight around here.

The mounted party halted but Peterborough continued forward a few steps. He surveyed the gathered troops for a moment then revealed a sheet of paper that had been rolled up in his hands.

He commenced to read from it in a clear, cultured voice.

"By the grace of God, his Majesty, Charles II of England, has commissioned the Earl of Peterborough Captain-General of all the forces in Tangier. He is to proceed at his best pace, with forces deemed sufficient, to take possession of the colony as Governor, and to commence the construction of a sea port, the like of which will rival any in the Mediterranean and command the trade lines into the aforementioned sea."

He finished, rolled the paper up and leaned forward in his saddle.

"Gentlemen. I shall attempt to give this command a little more clarity. The colony of Tangier is a Portuguese possession. And, as perhaps some of you know, His Majesty's wife is from that fair country and that colony came as part of her dowry. The King desires that we seize this opportunity to further our influence in that region. The region, I might add for those of you unaware of such things, is the mouth of the sea known as the Mediterranean. That mother of antiquity and the greatest empires the world has known. Tangier commands the narrow gap of the Straits of Gibraltar and is to be found on the Barbary Coast, home to the Moors or, as they refer to themselves, Berbers. A most ignorant and savage foe. The colony faces Spain across the water to the north. If one controls such a site, then they can perhaps hope to control and command all shipping that enters those sea lanes. I have been appointed to lead this endeavour.

From henceforth, the garrison of Dunkirk is to be disbanded." That caused a stir as men shifted and whispered to their companions. Even Smythe shared a looked of surprise with Fitzwilliam. "Sir Robert Harley is to make his regiment ready to sail. With him will go the regiments of Colonels John Fitzgerald and Lewis Farrell. I will bring my own regiment of foot, a troop of horse and an artillery train, as well as the required number of staff officers." Peterborough paused and once more looked out across the assembled troops. "Men, this is a great honour. We lead the vanguard of England's revival. This is but the beginning of a new age as England, led by His Majesty, once more declares its right to be one of the great powers of Europe and the world." He ended with a flourish and quieted. Men looked at each other; there was the occasional cough and shuffling of feet. Fitzwilliam tried to suppress a smirk. No doubt the Earl had hoped for some kind of spontaneous, rousing cheer. Well he could sing for that with this crowd. While Fitzwilliam was quietly excited by the prospect of this adventure, he was also inured to the garrison life. He understood these men would be sceptics, even if the Earl had promised them they were to take charge of the lost cities of gold.

After a few more moments of awkward silence, Harley rode forward and whispered to the Earl, who nodded in response. Harley looked out at the assembled troops and sat forward in his saddle.

"Soldiers of His Majesty's army. You have heard our orders from the Captain General. Over the coming days we will start preparing for this new task. We will issue our own commands and furnish you with the correct directions to prosecute those orders. A fleet will be formed to transport us to the African continent and this will arrive within the next few months. I expect you all to behave in a proper manner and commence the settling of your affairs." He paused, nodded and sat back. "Parade. Dismissed."

"Alright, you lot. Back to your duties!" shouted a nearby sergeant. The gathering split up in a less than orderly fashion. It slowly fragmented into groups of thoughtful men, heads together, close in conversation. Fitzwilliam took their measure; some looked concerned, others angry and yet more just appeared somewhat bewildered. There were precious few who showed any excitement at the thought of the journey south. He was clearly in the minority.

As Smythe gathered up the troops he turned to Fitzwilliam.

"If nothing else, I'll get some work out of this lot. It takes effort and planning for this kind of thing. Done badly, we'll all end up dead of starvation or pox."

Fitzwilliam gave him a sidelong glance.

"You make it sound so romantic, Sergeant."

Smythe grunted.

"Might even get some work out of you, Sir."

Fitzwilliam ought to have reacted to that but Smythe had a point.

As the rest of the regiment moved off, Fitzwilliam waited for Drummond to wander past and joined him.

"Rupert?"

"Hmm?"

"Well, what do you think?"

"Of what?"

"Don't be an arse, man!"

Drummond smiled wanly.

"I'd say that we are entering interesting times."

"And what do you mean by that, then?"

"Well, for a start, the North African coast is wild

country. Untamed. Home to warlords, pirates and tribes of vicious hill men. Or so I'm led to understand. In fact," he stopped "it'll probably remind you of home".

"Oh aren't you the joker," said Fitzwilliam.

"Things are going to be different, James. For everyone."

"Ach, it'll do the lads good."

"Those that are coming."

"What?"

"Weren't you listening? They are disbanding the garrison. There are four thousand men here. Only half are going on this expedition."

"Oh."

"Indeed, James. The other half now find themselves without pay or employment. There'll be trouble over the next few weeks. Mark my words.

"Then I promise to stay out of trouble."

"Yes, James, do try and stay in the Colonel's good graces. We are fortunate to be part of his regiment."

"Rupert, I have no intention of rocking the boat. I for one am excited and have an abundance of enthusiasm for this undertaking. It's an adventure and I am young, fit and able-bodied. I'll face the perils of the south, for King and country!"

Drummond smiled with affection and twirled his moustache theatrically.

"Then I look forward to seeing your enthusiasm put to good use."

26 January 1662
Off the Northern Coast of Spain

"Oh my god. I'm dying." Fitzwilliam leaned his head forward into the slops bucket cradled tightly in his arms and let fly with another blast of hot bile.

"I must be dying. Rupert, my dearest friend. You must finish me off. I cannot go on like this."

"Finish yourself off, man."

Fitzwilliam groaned and leaned back against the bulkhead. He glared at Drummond who was sat on a barrel, smiling broadly.

"You really should come up top. You'll find it's a great deal easier."

"It's blowing up a storm out there."

"I have spoken to the captain. Apparently this is nothing more than a gentle squall. In no way an impediment to our journey."

"That's something at least," Fitzwilliam grunted. The less time at sea the better. He was glad his father had not made him join the Navy.

"We should reach our destination in the next few days.

34

Just think, James. Dry land beneath your feet."

The boat lurched to the left. Fitzwilliam felt another surge of vomit building.

"A few days? I'll never make it."

Drummond laughed.

"That's the spirit. I'm going back up to the Colonel's cabin. He's broken open another bottle of port to celebrate our passing of Portugal." Drummond stood up. "And he has some very fine cheese."

"Oohhh…" Fitzwilliam leaned forward and retched again.

He heard Drummond chuckling to himself as he made his way to the steps leading up from the hold. Fitzwilliam knew he was never going to live this down. Three days they had been on board, the first two of which had been quite pleasant. The regiments had boarded the waiting fleet in good order and settled down to watch the crews do all the work. The Navy had always been a mainstay of the country and they conducted themselves with a busy and bustling competence. Fitzwilliam had been very impressed. He would have felt embarrassed about the state of the soldiers, but all those embarking had spent the last two months training in a manner he had never seen before. The colonels had decided to remind the men just what exactly they were paid to do.

For hours, red-coated soldiers worked hard at their trade. Blocks of pike would march and manoeuvre around the parade square, sergeants and corporals barking out orders and admonishments in equal measure. The pikemen were deliberately fully equipped and wore pot helmets, back and breastplates over a buff coat, and armoured tassets to protect their upper legs. They carried their sixteen-foot pikes and a sword known as a hanger. Not particularly elegant, more of a bludgeoning weapon, but it gave them a chance in a melee if the push of the pike was unsuccessful.

Musketeers fired their weapons, using up and replacing their smouldering matchlocks many times over. They wore a bandolier from which were suspended twelve wooden containers each with a ball and measured charge of powder for their muskets. They deployed six ranks deep, the front rank firing a volley and then marching to the rear. Then the next rank would step forward and fire their volley. By the time the first musketeer had reached the front rank again, they should have reloaded and been prepared to fire. Fitzwilliam noted that wasn't always the case, as men fumbled with the ammunition or were just far too slow. For protection, most only carried long knives or poor quality swords. Some would have to resort to using their muskets as clubs. Carrying over the tactics developed in Europe and refined by Cromwell, the pike and muskets worked together on the battlefield, the muskets outnumbering pike two to one but lacking adequate protection against a determined cavalry charge. It was all quite a sight.

Inspired by this industry, he had even taken care to practise and clean his own brace of pistols, a pair of flintlocks that were becoming all the rage in the armies of Europe. He had acquired them from a French merchant who charged a tidy sum but promised it was worth the expense. The flint striking mechanism proved to be far more reliable and faster than the matchlocks. He was sure that the army would soon disregard the matchlocks in favour of the flint strikers.

At the end of this training, as the last muster was made before embarking, Harley had declared that he was quite satisfied. The force had then taken ship back to England and had mustered on Putney Heath. It had been bloody cold but his spirits had been high despite this. It was good to be back on home soil if only for a short time. What had made the occasion truly momentous was when the regiments were drawn up in parade formation, each man and officer attired in their finest accoutrements, polished and gleaming. A carriage had pulled up, flanked by a troop of horsemen. Exiting the carriage, wearing breastplate, sword and a fine hat with purple feathers, was the King himself. He proceeded to inspect the assembled force, marching along the front lines of each regiment. As he passed Fitzwilliam by, he noted that the King had put on weight, his jowls were pronounced, his moustache wider and less cultured and his skin had a light shine to it. When last he had seen the King, prior to the Restoration, the man had been leaner and fitter, a result of the hard years of constant campaigning. As it was he looked happy and contented, and it was a fine send off for the troops, his redcoats, knowing they had the support and affection of their lord and sovereign.

Fitzwilliam was no longer sure if the men would be quite as effective after such an arduous journey as they now found themselves on. He could scarcely stand. If he did indeed survive this voyage of the damned, he had every intention of finding the nearest tavern and cleansing his palate with as much ale as he could drink.

*

The captain of the Earl's flagship made his way down the sodden wooden steps leading from the aftcastle. Surefooted and confident, he moved with the sway of the ship and opened the door leading to the cabins off the main deck. He closed the door behind him, removed his hat, wrung it dry and stamped his feet a few times to shake off the worst of the drips. Back home, England was in the grips of winter, and even this far south the weather was little better; still cold, wet and miserable. Northerly winds brought the winter to them. Once he was finished, a small puddle of water between his feet, the captain proceeded down the short corridor to the Earl's quarters. Usually they were his but he was forced to vacate the spacious chamber whenever a person of note required it. With so many officers aboard, he had been forced to bunk up with his own under-officers in the hold, which were jammed to the gunnels with men and materiel. He knocked firmly on the door.

"Enter."

The captain entered the cabin, shut the door, and stood in a suitably subservient manner, waiting to be addressed.

At the far table, the Earl sat with a number of his staff officers clustered around him. There was a map rolled out before them. The Earl held a quill in one hand and a glass of wine in the other. He looked up.

"Ah, Captain, so it seems the weather remains suitably inclement."

The captain nodded. "Indeed so, my lord. But nothing to concern ourselves about. Normal for this time of year."

"Quite so."

Peterborough beckoned the captain over.

"If you would be so kind, perhaps you could show us our progress and tell us more of our destination?"

The captain stood at the head of the table and placed a finger upon the map.

"Sirs, we are here, almost at a point where Spain becomes Portugal. This time tomorrow we'll be sailing south following the coastline, and then turning east toward the Straits and the Mediterranean. Here," he pointed to the narrows that separated Europe and Africa, "is Cape Spartel. Tangier is a little ways east of that."

"And tell us, Captain, is the weather fine there?"

"Oh, quite temperate, my lord. The heat is less bothersome than Iberia."

"And what of pirates, sir? I hear they are rife in these parts."

"That is true, your lordship. Corsairs, Sir. Of Moorish belief but freebooters with it."

"And can we expect trouble?"

The captain shrugged.

"That I couldn't say, but I doubt they would wish to tangle with armed vessels if they didn't have to. And having the squadron ahead of us should clear the way."

"Yes, indeed. Lord Sandwich's squadron has been sent on to secure the waters about the port to ensure our arrival is unhindered." The Earl sat back, a smile on his face. "Gentlemen, I believe that all is set fair. When should we arrive?"

"If this weather blows northerly, then the next two days, I would warrant," said the captain.

"Good, then prepare yourselves for our arrival in an expedient fashion, gentlemen. I wish us to take possession of the colony in fine style, and to impress upon the inhabitants the true measure of our quality," announced Peterborough, taking a sip of his wine.

The captain tipped his forehead and took his leave. As he returned to the wet deck and shielded his eyes from the persistent rain, he grunted. He wasn't at all convinced the inhabitants would be impressed with their new colonial masters, but then what did he know? He'd only been sailing these seas for nigh on thirty years.

29 January 1662
Tangier

The skies were relatively clear when the expedition finally arrived off Tangier. It was with some surprise that the Earl discovered Lord Sandwich's squadron had already taken up residence in the harbour. The captain of the flagship watched from the forecastle and took note of how deflated the Earl looked as he boarded a skiff to take him to the sand and shingle shoreline. It was one of the problems with this town that there was no proper harbour or dockside. Having to transport everything onto the beach and up to the town was a significant barrier to its success as a trading hub. He noted, too, that there was a great deal of activity on land. It seemed the whole population was out to welcome the Governor's arrival. At a distance, the red-roofed, white-walled town had looked quite pretty, but the nearer the ships had drawn to the land, so the lack of upkeep and general wear and tear had become apparent. More than that, the coming and going on the shorefront was mostly conducted by English sailors, some milling about watching their arrival, whilst others were engaged in more nautical activities. A few of them were even armed.

As soon as the skiff had finished tying up, Peterborough climbed the steps to the Watergate and was met by Lord Sandwich.

"Ah, Henry, so glad you are here. I trust your journey was uneventful?"

Peterborough eyed the naval commander, Edward Montagu, First Earl of Sandwich. A man of similar years to his own but blessed with flowing locks, ruddy cheeks, a sparse moustache and a generous waistline. Peterborough did not like the man. He had served Parliament during the war, but he was currently in the King's favour and was the second to the Lord Admiral, the Duke of York. As such, Peterborough had to remain civil.

"Edward. I understood that you were to remain on station until my arrival? Why are your men ashore?"

Sandwich bowed his head, a slight smile playing on his lips.

"And I would so have done, had it not been for the entreaty of the colony's current governor." He indicated a man, grey haired and looking slightly peevish, who stood slightly behind the sailor.

"It would seem that the Portuguese are none too pleased with having English masters. In fact, so distressed are they, that they wish for nothing more than to return to their homeland."

Peterborough felt his cheeks flush and made to respond but Sandwich raised a consoling hand.

"Now, not to worry. I have landed most of my crews for some shore leave. The extra coin has done much to soothe our arrival."

Peterborough shook his head. This was not the arrival he had imagined for himself.

"More importantly," continued Sandwich "we have taken the responsibility of manning the walls. It seems that there are a number of Berber rebels that have been trying their luck."

"You've seen action?" asked Peterborough. He felt eagerness, a desire to do battle. That would be a far more auspicious arrival.

"No, actually, it's been very quiet. On further investigation, the local lord has been engaged in adventures further east and has not given too much thought to this place."

"No doubt he will when he learns of a large English garrison on his doorstep," said Peterborough, not to be dissuaded of his plans.

"And no doubt he'll get a sore lesson for trying to counter it," agreed Sandwich solemnly. "Henry, I think perhaps we should deal with the formalities?" he said, looking toward where the soon to be ex-governor waited impatiently.

Peterborough nodded. There were formalities that he had to attend to, no matter the situation. "Very well. Let's get this over with. My men will be landing momentarily. I want it to be on English soil."

Sandwich beckoned the Portuguese governor forward. The man straightened up and pulled down his ill-fitting white tunic that was brocaded with gold trim. He strode up to Peterborough, bowed stiffly and handed over a scroll. Peterborough took it and unrolled the paper. On it was a great deal of unintelligible scrawl, but it was plainly a certificate of ownership of some kind. He spotted the name of the colony in a number of places and what appeared to be the signature of the Portuguese monarch.

The old governor bowed his head again, turned stiffly, and marched away.

"I think that means you are now His Majesty's Governor of Tangier, Henry," said Sandwich, an amused tone to his voice. "Enjoy it. I hear it is lovely during the summer. Now, why don't I take you on a tour? You'll find your accommodation quite palatable. I've been using it myself. I am a little concerned things might get a little crammed with your garrison. I understand that you have brought along a number of wives? That is an unusual enterprise, is it not?"

Peterborough nodded.

"Yes, we have some two hundred or so wives and families on the ships. It was deemed that as we were undertaking a garrison duty a long way from home, it would be good for morale if the men had their families nearby. It would also help cement the town as an English colony."

Sandwich made a sour face. "Hmm, well, I suppose it has a modicum of sense to recommend it. Better that than a host of camp followers, eh? Now, come along and I'll get you settled, I'm sure your staff can deal with the landing." He turned and wandered casually towards the gate leading into the town. Peterborough sighed again. Not the start he had wished for by a long measure.

*

"This looks like a nice enough place. It even has a promenade of sorts," announced Fitzwilliam.

"You mean the path leading up to the wall from the beach, James?" asked Drummond.

"Well, yes. But it's dry land. And it has put me in a

rare fine mood,' replied Fitzwilliam.

Drummond smiled.

"Indeed it has. And to think, that not hours before you were willing to throw yourself off the tallest rigging with an anchor clutched to your chest."

The weather this day had been calm and Fitzwilliam had ventured, with no small measure of trepidation, onto the deck. He had breathed in the familiar smell of the sea and the scent of new horizons. Then he had sunk to his knees in blessed relief as he saw the North African coast go by.

The two men stood on the beach as all about them chaos reigned. There had been a general belief that there would be an ordered arrival, whereby the arriving troops would be welcomed and billeted by an advance party. There had even been some idle speculation that there would be some kind of welcome by the grateful locals. It seemed that neither was the case. The naval squadron had done little to facilitate their arrival. A number of Peterborough's staff officers were trying to direct the efforts of the arriving garrison although they seemed to have as little idea of the available accommodations as anyone else.

Fitzwilliam scratched an annoying itch under his armpit then followed it up by a rummage through his beard.

"So where are we supposed to go?"

"You could help your men in getting the stores unloaded," suggested Drummond.

"Oh, that wouldn't be a good idea," Fitzwilliam sniffed. "See? Smythe is doing quite well without me."

He pointed to where the Quartermaster Sergeant was busy berating a hapless soldier who had spilled a sack of grain. A flock of gulls and pigeons were gamely launching strikes at the pile as other equally hapless soldiers tried to shoo them away.

Drummond raised an eyebrow. "I think it best that we at least look like we're doing something. I suggest securing our own quarters. It seems to me that we have a wide range of premises to choose from." He frowned at the crowd watching their arrival with sullen faces. "Do you think they might like to put us up? Perhaps we can find a tavern?"

Fitzwilliam found that suggestion most agreeable. "Sounds like a good plan to me. Hang on."

He picked up a canvas sack, which contained his worldly belongings, then looped his sword belt over his head and shoulder. He clapped Drummond on the back and gestured him to lead on. The two men headed for the gate and the town proper. As they walked through the streets of their new home, Fitzwilliam was impressed that, in comparison to Dunkirk, it was a well-ordered and reasonably pretty one. You could see there was a great deal of neglect on the edges, even a little dereliction in parts, but by and large he felt quite content. It was a shame that the same could not be said about the locals themselves. They had already adopted an unfriendly look. Well, he supposed he couldn't blame them really, though he was sure that they'd come to like being under English patronage.

"Ah, James. I think this might a likely candidate," said Drummond.

Fitzwilliam looked at the building his friend had pointed out. Similar in most respects to the rest of the terraced streets, it had shuttered windows, whitewashed walls, three floors and the obligatory red tiled roof. A sign, affixed to a metal stanchion, hung from the wall slightly higher than the reach of a tall man. A painting of a red faced, moustachioed sailor clutching onto a tankard of foaming ale, made quite clear this particular building's function.

"Perfect!" Fitzwilliam felt himself smiling for the first time since he had taken ship.

Drummond walked up to the door and tried the handle. It turned and swung inwards. There was little light inside and they stood just inside the entrance, waiting for their eyes to adjust to the gloom. After a few moments they could see a number of tables scattered around a large room, a range of different chairs and stools gathered amongst them. The floor was wooden and stained but swept clean of dirt and dust. Facing them, up against them far wall, was a long counter top. Behind that, another counter held several barrels.

"Top of the morning to you two fine gentlemen," a voice with a familiar cadence spoke from the shadows.

Fitzwilliam looked to the sound of the voice and found a dark figure stood by a doorway to the side of the bar. The figure moved forward and they found a man of middle years with a shock of black hair, a sharply defined nose and a warm smile. He was running a rag over a pewter mug.

"I was wondering when my new clientele would arrive. Didn't think it would be officers. But," he shrugged, "it bodes well for the high reputation this establishment will have in this bright new age of English rule."

Fitzwilliam and Drummond looked at each other.

"Irish?" asked Fitzwilliam.

"Right you are. My name is Donahoe. Thomas Donahoe. Welcome to the Jolly Sailor Tavern," he said, in his broad, lilting brogue.

Another figure emerged from the doorway in a swish of long skirts and came to stand next to the Irishman. A pretty young woman in her late teens with thick, flowing black hair, a freckled nose and a mouth set stern and thin lipped. She slipped an arm through Donahoe's and glared at Fitzwilliam.

"And this is my daughter, Siobhan," he announced.

The friends shared another look. Fitzwilliam felt himself beaming. Things were definitely improving by the moment.

30 January 1662
The Jolly Sailor Tavern

Fitzwilliam woke with the dawn. He felt alive and revitalised. It was incredible what a real bed, soft sheets and an absence of constant rocking, interspersed with bouts of nausea, could do for a man. The previous evening he had spent only a little time getting acquainted with his new landlord, allowing Drummond the pleasure of negotiating a long term arrangement. Instead he had eagerly followed the young woman of the establishment, who had consented to show him to his room. Trailing behind her had been an adventure. She was quite the beauty, dressed in a plain orange skirt and a white, off the shoulder, blouse. Simple clothes yet they complemented her figure: not too thin, not too large. He knew then he was overcoming his seasickness. Siobhan had taken him through the kitchen to a rear courtyard, up some wooden steps to a landing and shown to one of three doors leading off it. He had been very gracious in his thanks to her, but the response had been icy at best. He was willing to put this down to her nervousness at having new colonial masters.

He leapt out of bed and swiftly dressed, anxious to see this new garrison. He thought it best to arm himself, so kept his sword, and pushed his two flintlocks into his belt. He descended the stairs, passed through the kitchen and stopped at the heavenly smell of freshly baked bread. He paused to help himself to a loaf, just out of the oven. Finding a knife he sliced off a generous piece. It was still very hot to the touch and he blew on the edges so he could keep a grip. Once done, it was into the tavern itself, which was deserted, and out onto the street. He looked left and right, noting that it ran in a roughly north/south direction. The cobbles on the street where well worn but most seemed robust enough, likewise the houses, which crowded on to each other, many three stories high. The street was empty of life but he could hear raised voices, speaking for too fast for him to follow. Somewhere, a baby cried.

He resolved to learn the lay of the land and set off south, attempting to retrace his steps. It wasn't difficult as there was a gentle downhill slope that assured him he was heading in the right direction. After no more than a couple of minutes of gentle walking and eating he found himself back at the Watergate. There were two guards, who reacted rather slowly to his appearance. Once they had braced into a salute, he bid them a good morning and looked out into the bay. The skies were leaden and the water lapped sluggishly upon the beach. A skiff was coming to shore from one of the naval squadron's ships that were moored a short way out. The beach was littered with supplies: crates, barrels, netting and rowboats were spread about in a haphazard fashion. He watched two men who were working their way through the mess. One would stop by a pile of stores, inspect them, and announce their contents to the other man who was carrying a sheaf of papers. He would consult them and then, in short order, give a curt nod. Wonderful job of work this time of the morning, thought Fitzwilliam. Thank God I have Sergeant Smythe to do that for me.

Having his fill of the scene, he retreated back through the gate and took himself on a tour of Tangier. He decided to start in the north-eastern quarter, having earlier spied an old keep facing onto the beach. From there he worked his way round the entire perimeter of the fortifications before zigzagging through the town, west then east, in a manner he felt was a systematic pattern. As he wandered the streets, lanes and alleyways, he recalled that Drummond had told him Tangier was an old, old town. Both the Romans and Byzantines had had a settlement here before the advance of Islam took it. It was then held for many years by various dynasties before falling into the hands of an expansionist Portugal. Fitzwilliam did wonder how Drummond knew so much, but the evidence of its past was clear to see. He passed by old stone structures that still bore delicate carvings, walked under high archways supported by long, thin brick pillars and buildings whose windows were elaborately topped off by long, rounded curves meeting in the middle to form a point. It certainly spoke to him of exotic cultures and histories far beyond his experience. Back in France and England, the style of construction he was used to seeing seemed so much fussier when compared to these smooth, sleek lines. They were beautiful in their simplicity.

On his travels, he examined the larger fort that formed the north-western tip of the walls. It was far more impressive than the one facing the sea, though it had been poorly maintained. It commanded fine views over the interior lands adjacent to Tangier, and had its own curtain walls separating it from the surrounding town. If the Governor had any sense, work would start on reviving its fortunes. He also discovered the market square, located in the south of the town. It was not large, little more than sixty or so yards wide in every direction, and remarkably empty. A few sacks stacked idly against a wall, a solitary empty cart sat by a well in the middle of the space. A dog idled by and Fitzwilliam observed its passage. It was lithe, shorthaired with a black muzzle and a decidedly disinterested attitude. It sniffed at the sacks then wondered off down an alley. Perhaps he was too early, perhaps it wasn't market day? A woman carrying a pail, Portuguese by the look of her, entered the square and made for the well. She glanced at him and he tipped his hat in greeting. Her response was to look away, as if he wasn't there. Oh good, he thought. It's nice to be wanted.

Fitzwilliam left the square and headed back to his lodgings, hoping his travels had given him a solid sense of direction. Sure enough, he soon found himself back on the street of the Jolly Sailor. He crossed the threshold and entered, keen to report back to Drummond regarding his expedition.

"Ah," said Donahoe from his position behind the bar counter. "My daughter wants a word with you. She is keen to find out who it was that stole the bread she'd just gotten out of the oven this morning."

"Ah," responded Fitzwilliam, putting on his best winning smile.

12 February 1662
York Castle

It was another grey, cold and miserable day. On the eastern side of the town sat the old decaying fort, which looked out onto the bay of Tangier, another remnant of Portugal's failed expansionist ambitions. The inner walls had fallen into disrepair and in the courtyard piles of rubbish and waste were left to decay in the sun. Various outbuildings had the look of being half finished, just empty shells, windowless and containing nothing more of value than the excrement of rodents and the occasional goat. The rear of the fort backed onto the curtain wall itself, and this was in a better state. Solid, if well weathered. The walls of Tangier had the enviable history of never having been breached, at least not in living memory.

The main building was habitable, but only just. No one had lived there for a number of years. Now it was being hastily fitted out for the Governor and his headquarters staff. In deference to its new owners, it had been given a new name: York Castle, a far grander name than it deserved. Work teams of grumbling soldiers cleaned and tidied rooms, repaired doors and patched up holes. The larger fort on the western side had been dubbed the Upper Castle. This was in a similar state but significantly roomier. Further bands of men were tasked with its renewal, the expectation being that it would become the proper future residence of the Governor. There was even a reasonably well-appointed house within its walls which would fit the bill of private residence and officers' repose. However, it was also located at the north-western edge of the city walls and was overlooked by higher ground. Peterborough did not as yet trust the protection it offered. It was far too visible to prying Moorish eyes.

In the main hall of York Castle, Peterborough sat behind a large wooden table that was worn, scratched and stained but had at least been scrubbed clean of the dirt and detritus that had covered it for an indeterminate time.

He removed his hat and ran a hand trough his thinning hair. Reaching for a nearby goblet, he took a long sip from it, enjoying the temporary respite from his waiting audience. The wine it contained was from Portugal, sweet and thick, but with a strong aftertaste of alcohol. He needed that right now. Before him stood the old Governor and a deputation of the leading citizens of Tangier. That in itself was rather laughable. Peterborough doubted that any man of quality or rank would install themselves as patricians of this miserable place. Beside the old Governor stood an interpreter from Sandwich's command, who shifted uncomfortably whilst he waited.

Peterborough sniffed loudly. "Very well, continue," he ordered.

"Senior Velasquez would also like it known that whilst the behaviour of the soldiers is unacceptable at the best of times, it is the public indiscretion and liberties that these men take with the wives and daughters of the men folk that is of greatest concern. He cannot vouch for the discretion and forbearance of the husbands and fathers for much longer. He fears that any more occasions may well tip the balance and violent retribution may ensue."

Peterborough waved a hand.

"Yes, I have heard this entreaty before. And I have responded with a counter proposal. What does he say about that?"

Peterborough was well aware of the situation. Having arrived with over three thousand souls, it had become apparent that the town did not have the capacity to house such an influx. The locals had been compelled to billet a number of troops. Some folk had had to be moved out of their homes to make way for English families, there being almost two hundred wives who had accompanied their husbands on the journey. He could well see the strain this was causing and already his men were starting to slip into bad habits. Lechery, drunkenness and ill discipline were threatening to overturn the thin veneer of military discipline that had been drilled into the troops.

Having thought long and hard about how to bring about an integration of the Portuguese and English, he had hit upon a fine idea. He had offered to every local man the opportunity to sign up and become a soldier for the Crown. Outside of fishing and subsistence agriculture, there was little industry. It would be an elegant way for the two sides to reach an understanding, and the Portuguese had local knowledge of the surrounding area that would be most useful.

In response to the question, he received a polite cough from his left. He turned and looked at Harley.

"Yes, Colonel?"

"I can report, Sir, that our offer has been met with a most disappointing silence."

"What, no one?"

"Indeed, Sir, it appears that not one soul wishes to be part of our engagement."

Peterborough slammed a fist onto the table, he felt his face reddening and his frustration could not be contained.

"Then we should sequester them, Sir!"

"I'm afraid that really isn't possible, Governor," said Sandwich, who was sat to his right, at the far end of the table. "These individuals are still citizens of Portugal until they declare otherwise."

Peterborough suppressed a glare at his fellow lord.

"Governor?" asked the interpreter

"Yes, what now?"

"The townsfolk have another matter they wish to address. One I fear you may find even less palatable. I am indeed embarrassed to even broach the subject with you. But I am compelled."

Peterborough sighed. He would need to lie down after this.

"Out with it then, man."

"His lordship," the interpreter nodded towards Lord Sandwich, "has hit upon an important matter of fact. The inhabitants of this colony are still Portuguese citizens. And as such, are entitled to certain, um, rights and privileges."

Peterborough huffed at that. Didn't they know who ruled them now?

The interpreter continued. "One of these rights, as is apparent - as we are not at war with Portugal - is that they have the right to be settled on Portuguese soil."

Peterborough tilted his head and sent a confused

glance Harley's way.

"What does he mean?"

"I believe he means that the Portuguese want to live in Portugal, Sir," responded Harley

"What? What on earth? I have never heard such nonsense. This is their home. This is where they live. And we are the legitimate government of this place!"

"Unfortunately, my lord Governor, their monarch is the King of Portugal. As such, Senior Velasquez requests that provision be made to ship he and his people back to the mainland," said the interpreter in a calm voice.

Peterborough sat back and waved his hands dismissively in the air.

"Quite impossible. We are far too busy and do not have the resources. The supply ships are not charged to ferry people. No, the best I can do is to submit a request to His Majesty. That will take time. Convey this to Senior Velasquez, if you please." He sat back feeling satisfied. The cheek of the man! The townsfolk were needed to ensure that the place ran smoothly. How on earth can we claim this as proper colony if we have no folk to live in it? He reached for his drink.

As the interpreter started to speak to the assembled group, Sandwich stood up.

"I believe I can assist with this matter."

Peterborough turned sharply towards him, his wine splashing slightly onto his breeches.

"I beg your pardon?"

Sandwich smiled sardonically.

"No begging required, my lord. I was intending to announce that my squadron and I would be setting sail back to England. I believe that we will be ready to leave the day after tomorrow. I should be happy to ferry these people back to their homeland."

Peterborough was stunned into silence for a moment. Damn it all but that man had trumped him. He quickly tried to think of another reason he could deny this request and failed miserably.

"So you have sufficient room for all these people?"

Sandwich shrugged.

"It will no doubt be a snug fit, but I have transferred a number of stores into the garrison here, at your request, Governor." He nodded at Peterborough, who in turn responded with his best scowl. "I believe, by taking just sufficient supply to reach our destination, we can manage it. It still might take us a couple of trips. No matter. It is not far after all."

There were a few tense moments of silence as Peterborough and Sandwich looked at each other.

Let him go and he can bloody take them all with him, I care not, thought Peterborough,

"Very well. I have had my fill of this constant malcontent. Perhaps it would be better for all concerned if the inhabitants did indeed evacuate. It will remove certain, ah, diversions from the men's minds. Yes, quite so."

He indicated to the interpreter to speak. Peterborough waited while Velasquez made several unintelligible remarks. Others in the group crowded round and asked their own questions. After a minute or two the interpreter nodded and turned back.

"They say that this is acceptable. Preparations will be made."

"Well, I am so pleased they find it acceptable to them," said Peterborough, who really wasn't pleased at all.

Senior Velasquez gave him a short bow then led the delegation out of the hall.

Once gone, Sandwich walked round to the head of the table.

"Governor. It seems that I must begin my on preparations. I have several hundred civilians to transport home."

"It appears that you do, Sir. Do not let me detain you any longer," said Peterborough.

Sandwich smiled, and swung his arms wide and gave an extravagant bow. He rose and turned in a swift movement, replacing his hat as he did so and marched purposefully towards the exit.

Peterborough looked around at the assembled staff officers and harrumphed.

"Gentlemen, that was a most unfortunate turn of events."

"Indeed, Governor. My first reaction is that it does rather relieve the pressure from our billeting quandary," said Colonel Farrell, a well-built man fast approaching his fiftieth year.

"I quite agree, Colonel," said Peterborough, glad of some support.

"There is a question," observed Harley, "regarding construction works."

"That is true. It was hoped that we could employ the population to assist in the endeavour," added Colonel Fitzgerald, an experienced officer with long sideburns, curly hair and a kindly face.

Peterborough sat back and chewed his inner lip. The construction works they referred to was the necessity to build a mole around the bay. At present, ships had to anchor with no protection from the elements. A proper harbour had to be constructed for passing trade fleets. It was crucial to the success of this whole enterprise. Without it, there could be no realisation of the King's vision of England as a Mediterranean power. And without it, Peterborough's tenure as governor would be seen as a failure.

"Gentlemen, the solution seems remarkably clear to me. We have a large number of soldiers without an enemy to fight. We shall put them to work. Such a force should make short shrift of this."

Harley and Farrell exchanged looks. Fitzgerald coughed. Peterborough ploughed on regardless.

"Where is our engineer?"

"Major Johnson is currently upon the shore conducting various observations and surveys of the site, Governor," said Fitzgerald.

"At least he is showing some industry. Ensure that he is sent word. In the meantime, gentlemen, we have much work to do. I expect you to start drawing up allocations for the billets. And send word to your officers that they can expect their men to be ready to commence work on the moles."

"What of our security, Sir?" asked Harley.

"I have received intelligence regarding the situation. It appears that the local warlord hereabouts goes by the name of...Gheelainn, or some such." Peterborough waved his hand dismissively. "I cannot pronounce it, though the use of the name Guyland is, I'm told, an adequate interpretation. An energetic and aggressive individual he has, by force of will, carved himself quite a powerbase."

"How many men does he command?" asked Farrell.

"It is difficult to say. The local Moors, or Berbers as they are more commonly known in this region, are a tribal people. They gather at the request of their ruler when needed and swiftly disperse when not. As such, campaigns tend to be short lived affairs."

"That would seem to be good news for us," remarked Fitzgerald.

Harley nodded.

"It certainly grants us some respite. It appears that Guyland is currently engaged against the Barbary pirates to the east of us."

"Good news indeed," pronounced Peterborough brightly. "It would seem to be the case that this local warlord is little more than a brigand. He certainly shouldn't be any more than an irritant to our purposes here."

Harley nodded gravely.

"Quite so, Governor. In response to the question, it is unknown how many men he can draw upon. But the tribes are numerous and the fighting men number in the thousands."

"But a militia at best," interrupted Peterborough. "We have enough experience to know how effective a properly trained army is against such a force, eh, gentlemen?" The local tribesmen had never faced a proper army and Peterborough had absolute confidence in the martial power he could array.

There were wry smiles around the table but Harley persisted.

"Guyland had no love of the Portuguese and only his other endeavours have so far kept him from turning his ire onto this place. What then, when he completes his business?"

"Then he'll rue the day when he faces English pike and shot, sir!" said Peterborough, emphatically. "Now, I've had enough for one morning. I suggest we all retire for a spot of refreshment."

14 February 1662
The Jolly Sailor Tavern

Fitzwilliam opened up his right eye and then squinted. It was far too bright; the white walls of his room gathered up the incoming sunlight from his wide-open window. They positively glowed. His head hurt. To give the place its due, the stuff it served was reasonably decent, but the wines particularly packed a punch. He had been led to believe that in the rarefied cultures of the Mediterranean, they were taken to watering down their wines so they could be consumed in greater quantities throughout the day. He had some support for this notion, but it was clear that master Donahoe had yet to adopt this approach. He retained the Irish and English manner of drinking whatever came out of the bottle. Another notion he also had some support for.

From what he could recall, it had been another wonderful evening at the Jolly Sailor. In the two weeks they had been stationed here, both he and Drummond had gained lodgings and set themselves up as the most valued regulars and confidants to the landlord. In return for late night drinking and regular meals, they ensured that only the finest and most upstanding of the officer class were allowed to frequent the establishment, the only one in the town English speakers were actually welcomed. Fitzwilliam dreaded to think what would happen if some of the rank and file had found the place first. He was sure it would have fallen to rack and ruin within days. And as for fair Siobhan, he shuddered to think how swiftly her dignity might have been compromised. She need not fear, she was under his, albeit undeclared, protection. Ah, but there was a woman to gladly go the gallows for, a mix of Irish wildness and Portuguese passion. That was a heady combination and dangerous to boot. He should have been on the receiving end of said passion already, had it not been for her studious and determined efforts to completely ignore his presence. Actually, that wasn't entirely true; he often caught her scowling at him when his back was turned. When confrontation was unavoidable he made every effort to appear gentlemanly, and in turn received icy indifference.

Clearly the gallant approach to making her acquaintance was not going to work. Drummond had commented that not every woman of lowly birth exercised their bedding choices by how well a man could bow before her. Fitzwilliam had responded that whilst that may be so, no woman could resist the promise of a gentleman's attentions and the future opportunities that may bring. The riposte was that whilst it may be so, since when had Fitzwilliam considered himself a gentleman? A point that he found himself, on diligent and long reflection, forced to agree with.

So he had changed tack. If he couldn't charm her with a frontal approach, then he would attempt a more subtle method. He made it his business to become firm friends with Donahoe and see if he could not build up a firm and favourable position from which to strike. In conversation with the man, he had learned this much. The unusual situation of having an Irish tavern in this far-flung place sprung from the old legacy of England's war with Spain. It would seem his family had some Iberian blood in them; this had led to a younger Donahoe travelling to discover his ancestry. Along the way he had found himself in Portugal and in the arms of a local lovely. One thing led to another and he found himself following the family to Tangier and inheriting a hostelry. His wife had died a few hours after childbirth, and instead of choosing a Portuguese name, Donahoe had continued the legacy of mixing cultures and christened the girl with a proper Irish moniker. So far he had found Donahoe an amiable and talkative host, although he often wore a scowl when dealing with both the locals and soldiers alike. His daughter was the source of much pride and consternation. She drew many potential customers into the Tavern then drove them away in equal measure when it became clear she neither wished to entertain their crude manners nor their cruder attempts at wooing.

"It is like the finest curse: a beautiful daughter, perfect for a businessman like myself, but a harder daughter you couldn't imagine. I feel there is no hope for this father to ever ensure she is married off and provided for," Donahoe had lamented to him one night.

"A tough nut to crack, is young Siobhan, I wager," Fitzwilliam had observed.

Donahoe had given him an appraising look.

"Oh, I wouldn't even try. Many have, and many have been cracked in return. She'll not suffer fools and barely tolerates wise men. Be thankful she condescends to clean your rooms." The Irish man had sighed, rocked back on his heels and folded his arms. "Times are hard, we must all earn what we can when we can," he pronounced with a serious tone, and pointed a finger at Fitzwilliam. "And that's why you have a residence in the bustling and overcrowded patch of land, young master Fitzwilliam."

"Indeed, master Donahoe, indeed." Clearly Donahoe had seen this game played before and was watching him carefully.

Fitzwilliam ended his comfortable reverie and rolled himself off the mattress. It was a big day today. Virtually the entire population of the town was taking ship back to Portugal and he wanted to see them off. It was rather a godsend that their departure had ensured finer billeting arrangements. He was certain that his excellent commandeering of the Jolly Sailor would have had come under scrutiny from Harley. Many of the garrison officers were holed up together in a most unbecoming manner in the outhouse of York Castle. He was quite sure that his room would have swiftly gone to a higher ranking - he was loath to use the word - gentleman. He dressed quickly, dropped his hat on his head at an angle he was sure was sufficiently rakish, and left his room, buckling his sword belt around his shoulders as he did so. He hurried along the short balcony that serviced the rooms and overlooked the rear courtyard of the Tavern. Then he was down the steps and into the kitchen. Siobhan was at the table kneading dough. A tray of bread rolls was resting upon the fireplace. He reached over and took one, blowing his fingers when he realised just how fresh and hot they were.

"Morning, Siobhan. And a grand one it is for seeing you!" he announced cheerfully.

She looked up and sneered.

"That'll teach you to take things that aren't yours."

"Is this not my breakfast? Do I not pay for bed and board?"

"Breakfast was two hours ago. Your friend had his. Those are for supper, for paying customers."

"Then I promise to have one less tonight than I would have."

She snorted and turned back to her dough.

He gave her his best bow – clearly wasted on her but it was the principle of the thing - and headed for the bar. Donahoe was inside cleaning tables.

"Good morning, Mister Donahoe."

"And good morning to you, Mister Fitzwilliam. Up slightly earlier today, I see."

"Ah, it's a momentous morning. Our Portuguese cousins are finally giving up the ghost and leaving this place to our tender English mercies."

"Is that so, Mister Fitzwilliam? I thought you were Scottish? Well, you enjoy it."

As Fitzwilliam hurried out the door, it occurred to him that it was an odd statement for the innkeeper to make but quickly dismissed it. As he bustled down the streets and passageways it did seem strangely quiet. In the far distance, he could hear the repeated, staccato cracks of musket practice. A resupply fleet had arrived with food and victuals for the garrison. They had also bought a consignment of flintlock muskets, a real boon. The men were practicing with their new weapons and no doubt finding how much more effective to fire they were. He'd have to pop along to watch after the squadron had left. He arrived at the beach and took a moment to survey the scene.

He shook his head at the sight.

"Oh, bloody hell."

In the distance he counted the masts of Sandwich's squadron as they headed west, out of the Mediterranean.

"Morning, James!" said Drummond, brightly.

"Rupert."

"Thought I'd hang around, see if you got here in time. At least you did get to see them off. A distant part of them, but a part nonetheless."

"You can wipe the smirk, Rupert. How come you made it here so early? You were drinking as much as I last night."

"I was drinking water for the most part, James. I'm not sure if you noticed when I actually left."

"Well, they should have bloody waited for me." Damn it but he'd gotten out of bed for this.

Drummond laughed and clapped his friend on the back. "Come on. Let's wander over to watch the shooting display."

They walked idly up the main road as Drummond shared the story of the morning's mass departure.

"Well, I was rather lucky to catch it myself. These people start early, I swear half of them were aboard before the sun was fully up. You should have seen it. I've never seen such a bunch of miserable wretches, all charging onto the boats with as much stuff as they could carry."

"All their worldly goods?" asked Fitzwilliam, concentrating on refastening his sword strap.

"Oh, a little more than that."

"Hmm?"

"James, have a look around you. Notice anything?"

Fitzwilliam sighed. "What are you talking about?" He stopped, placed his hands on his hips and looked about him. The streets were quiet; the buildings were virtually empty of life. A dog wandered by, barely giving them a glance. Doorways were wide open, window shutters thrown back, the hallways leading into the interiors dark and gloomy. He opened his mouth to demand more information from Drummond as the dog walked past him and sauntered into the house to his right. He thought it a bad policy to leave these houses open for the wildlife to move back in.

"What?" he blurted out. Fitzwilliam did a double take at the houses nearest to him. They looked exactly the same, all uniform in style and shape, each one open to the elements. "The doors. They took the bloody doors!"

Drummond laughed. "Realisation dawns!"

Fitzwilliam reached his fingers under his hat, scratched his head then readjusted his headgear back into its correct angle. He walked over to the same building the dog had entered and examined the doorframe. Some care had been given to remove the hinges. Inside the room was almost bare. The floor was dusty, there were some paw marks leading into a far chamber that had a pile of rags in one corner. He stepped on through and into the back room. A chimney and fireplace, blackened and sooty, to the left, on the floor a circular mark where a table must have sat. He grunted and went back outside to rejoin his friend.

"They didn't mess about, did they?" he said.

"Indeed not, and you'll find that every house occupied by a Portuguese family is the same."

"Why?"

Drummond shrugged. "It's the wood, I wager. There isn't much of it about. And I would presume it was a final show of ingratitude towards our benevolent rule."

"Hardly a significant one," replied Fitzwilliam, as the two men recommenced the journey. "I mean we are completely surrounded by wilderness, are we not?

Getting wood for doors should be easy!"

"James, have you actually been outside the walls yet?"

"Well, no, not really. Haven't quite gotten round to it."

"Ah, then this should be an education for you."

"You know, it's a good thing I like you, Rupert. Your tone can be most aggravating at times."

"That's true," agreed Drummond. "But I do it for your own good. You are smarter than you look, although you hide it well." Drummond smiled as Fitzwilliam sent a hard stare his way. "Besides, you should be grateful. Who else is going to keep you company?"

The gateway proved to be sturdy set of wooden doors, high enough to accommodate riders, or pikes for that matter. There was a large crossbeam resting against the left side of the gate and the iron brackets looked worn but well fixed. The right hand door of the gate was open and the men walked through and past two bored looking guards. A murderous look from Fitzwilliam made them adopt a more alert pose. He looked back at the gateway and along the walls. They were high, and looked impressive enough. But he did wonder how long they would stand up to a few well-aimed artillery salvos. Some bracing on that gateway wouldn't hurt either. Fitzwilliam dismissed it from his mind and directed his attention at the firing line just ahead of him.

A number of the garrison musketeers were taking pot shots at some hastily constructed targets. These ranged from empty barrels, to baskets and bales of hay. One wag had placed a hat on top of a pole and a number of the gunners were trying to dislodge it.

"So, these are the new flintlocks?" asked Drummond, hefting one of the weapons out of a crate.

Fitzwilliam nodded and held his hands out.

Drummond handed it over and Fitzwilliam inspected it. Still as heavy as the matchlocks but that wasn't the issue. It was the firing mechanism. The flint held in the cock was far more effective at igniting the powder in the pan; the old matchlocks were prone to failure. Cocking the hammer fully back he held it up to his shoulder, the weight of the barrel straining his arms a little. He sighted down the length and squeezed the trigger, a click denoting the successful action of the piece. He passed it back to Drummond.

"Is not technological advancement a truly wonderful thing?"

"I suppose it is. As long as we have it and the enemy does not," replied Drummond, as he replaced the musket back into the crate.

"I hear the Moors have muskets."

"Yes, but they are not proficient. They still rely on sword, shield and arrow."

"In which case they'll be at a disadvantage against my brace of pistols."

"There are rather more of them than us, I believe."

"And that," said Fitzwilliam, as he reached behind and pulled out his sword, "is why I have this."

He held it out in front of him and then gave a few theatrical swings. Drummond cocked an eyebrow.

"I do have a question. Have you actually ever used your weapons in anger?"

Fitzwilliam stopped and thought about it. "I've never used them sober."

Drummond frowned. "I think that is broadly the answer I was expecting."

Fitzwilliam laughed and sheathed his blade. He looked around. For the first time he took in the lay of the land. It was certainly very different to home. The immediate ground in front of the walls was covered in gently rolling grass. He did see some cultivation but it was restricted to a narrow band of fields close to the walls. The same with the cattle pen, which had been hastily built to house the beasts that had been brought with the garrison. He also took note of the high ground that encircled almost the entirety of the town. Apart from a flat and poorly maintained lane, some one hundred yards to the southeast, everything was a slope, and by the looks of it, some of those slopes would be particularly devilish to navigate.

"We are rather hemmed in here aren't we?"

"That is the precise reason Tangier has never expanded beyond these walls. The Moors overlook the position and report back to their leader, Guyland. Whenever the Portuguese have tried to claim further possession, they have been driven back. The ground may be fertile – 'black soil' it's called - but there are also plenty of places to hide. It is a speciality of the Berber tribesmen." He paused and looked about him. "For all we know they may be watching us now."

"Very dramatic!" barked Fitzwilliam. "So let them watch. They must realise that they aren't dealing with the Portuguese anymore?"

"Perhaps. I hear from Thomas that the Portuguese kept the Moors at bay, so any half decent command should be sufficient. I'm sure they must know that a large force of armed men has replaced the population. And all this firing is going to give them an inkling, no doubt."

"So, what did you call that man, their leader? Gayland?"

"Or Guyland. At least that is what we call him. His actual name is something unpronounceable. I hear that he is otherwise engaged at the moment. Consolidating his holdings."

"Good for him. As long as he leaves us alone, I'm sure we shall all get along famously.

3 March 1663
The walls of Tangier

The emissary appeared just before mid-morning tea was served. The Governor was summoned to the walls and was joined by a fair number of the garrison. Men pointed, laughed and joked about the new arrival. Some shouted out colourful suggestions and observations. Peterborough scowled at the wags but let it pass. This was the first time they had seen the locals. The Moors had started to take on mythical proportions. Peterborough had started to wonder if anyone was going to show up. Consequently it was rather good just to see one of them in the flesh. Sat on a white horse, only a hundred yards from the walls, the Moor carried a lance crowned with a white flag. He was robed completely in black, including a large piece of cloth that was wrapped around his head, in what the English had been briefed was the common style of the region. His face was at present unmasked, although in more inclement weather only the eyes would be visible. The rider stood quite still, content to wait. His horse, slighter in stature than

European breeds, cropped lazily at the grass, its tail swishing in half-hearted strokes. Peterborough called for his staff officers. The consensus was clear that someone should be sent to treaty. A staff officer, Major Allinson, was elected to ride out and meet with the Moor. As the best linguist and only Portuguese speaker, he seemed an appropriate choice. The Major also had some understanding of the culture, which should help to avoid any faux pas, although as he did state quite clearly, he didn't actually speak the local tongue. Peterborough dismissed this of little concern. It was then pointed out that there were no horses present for him to ride out on.

"For the love of bloody God! Get out there, Mister Allinson. I don't care if you walk, crawl like the penitent man or get some poor beggar to carry you out. We must answer, sir!" responded Peterborough.

He and his staff watched as Allinson, with a robust belly and rampant mutton chops, walked out flanked by an honour guard of two, very nervous-looking, gate guards. Their heads shifting right and left, they displayed some measure of control by keeping their muskets held to attention. The rider waited patiently for them. When the distance had been closed to a few yards, Allinson stepped forward and saluted. He quickly followed this up with a deep bow, eager as he was to ensure the proper etiquette was observed. There followed a very short exchange, where the men upon the wall strained to here the conversation. The few words that drifted towards them were unintelligible. Allinson bowed once more to the emissary, who in turn tilted his head before turning his horse and kicking it to a trot, heading for the gap in the high ground to the southeast. The crowd watched him return to ramparts, silent for once, eager to hear his news.

"Well, sir, what is the word?" asked Peterborough, impatient and a little discomfited at the number of men who were standing by, paying them such close attention.

Allinson pursed his lips.

"Unfortunately the gentleman had no command of the English language, nor of French. Fortunately, he had a passable knowledge of Portuguese and so we were able to make a decent fist of communication."

"And?"

"It would seem that the local lord is not overly pleased with our arrival. He is very keen that we do not display any attempts at usurpation of his territories."

"That is certainly not our intention!" Peterborough declared.

"However," continued Allinson gamely, "he has decided that the expansion of our farmland is an 'aggressive' attempt of usurpation."

"What? What nonsense is this? We are hardly going to allow ourselves to starve when there is perfectly good soil at our doorstep."

It had been ascertained that in more peaceful times the Berber tribes had openly traded with the Portuguese. Since the impending arrival of new colonials was made clear to the Berbers, the locals who had had cordial relations with the town had ceased their relations. It was the only source of locally grown produce that could be gained in light of the difficulties of creating their own plantations and crops. Apart from the sporadic catches of amateur fishermen, all supplies were coming, at great expense, from England.

Allinson shrugged. "That is all to report I'm afraid."

"Nothing else?" enquired Harley.

"Did the man not say anything else? Are we not to treat? And didn't you stop to remind him that we have a right to plant crops to feed ourselves?" added Peterborough.

"I did attempt to be reasonable but the Moor simply stated that we should withdraw within our walls. He said it would be best for us and would please his Lord, I believe I have this right, Abd Allah Ghailan."

"Who?"

"Ah, Guyland, my lord Governor."

"Oh. Well. And what did you say to that?"

"I informed him that such a proposal was unlikely to gain much purchase and that only His Majesty King Charles can order us not to hold this land."

There was a general murmur of approval from the assembled officers.

"Well done, Major. A most suitable answer!" the Governor looked out across the open ground. The rider had disappeared. "That is a shame. I have a message for this Guyland. No matter, I have no doubt that he will receive it soon enough." He looked around his party. "Where is my officer of engineering?"

"Here, m'lord." A well-proportioned man in his mid-twenties, with a mop of thick brown hair and a broad moustache stepped forward. His red coat was simply adorned and unbuttoned. Beneath it a white tunic was marked with dark stains. Peterborough looked him over with distain.

"I expect a rather better turnout, Major Johnson."

The Major blushed but held his ground.

"Just come from the mole, m'lord. The work requires I get involved and dispense with niceties on occasion."

The Governor sniffed. "Well, no doubt you'll enjoy the next task. I presume you have knowledge of military engineering."

Johnson nodded.

"Good. Then I wish you to undertake the construction of fortifications."

"Where, m'lord?"

"Why, out there," he waved beyond the walls. "We will expand our lands as we feel necessary and we will protect it as we see fit. We are well supplied with water and wells. The Portuguese did that right at least. But we must have land! These Moors do not possess artillery, do they?"

"Not from what we understand, Sir," said Allinson helpfully.

"Very good. Major Fairborne here," he indicated one of his staff officers, "came up with the idea. And a damned fine one it is too."

Major Fairborne stepped up to Johnson and clapped him companionably on the back. He was a bull of a man. His thick curled hair that spilled out from under his hat looked at odds with his broad mutton chops. He smiled broadly with genuine good humour. Fairborne was forty years of age, a seasoned campaigner, and expert in the art of stores and supply. A highly competent man amidst the mediocrity, if a tad too jolly for Peterborough's tastes.

"I'll talk you through the plan, Mister Johnson. Have no fear," said Fairborne in a broad West Country accent. It sounded to Peterborough quite out of place in this landscape.

"There you are. Now, Major Johnson," smiled Peterborough. "I suggest you focus your attentions on building some forts. That will give the local barbarians pause for thought, eh?"

"Yes, Sir," responded Johnson with a salute.

Peterborough nodded in return then withdrew from the walls along with most of the party.

Johnson remained and looked out across the ground.

He idly scratched his head. "Now where am I going to put these bloody things? And what am I going to bloody build them with?"

4 March 1663
Northern Fez

"Leave me now, I wish to rest."

Two young women, barely into their teenage years, arose from the bed, quickly collected discarded robes, and left silently from a side door to the chamber. Abd Allah Ghailan stretched out amidst the cushions and let out a contented sigh. He allowed himself a few brief moments of self satisfied relaxation. His body was still strong, very strong, for a man in his fourth decade of life. Allah had been kind to him. He had thought himself exhausted on returning from his campaign to the north against the man known as the Saint of Sallee. His adversary had been a wily and stubborn opponent, but he had finally succumbed to the greater numbers of Ghailan's Berbers. The Saint had agreed to a very impressive ransom and, in return for a significant portion of his loot, would be allowed to continue to use the ports of the Barbary Coast to ply his piratical trade. Ghailan had returned exceedingly happy with this arrangement. It would have been near impossible to capture the Saint, he would have taken off in his ships and sailed away, no doubt further to the east, and would have made arrangements with other local rulers. On reflection, his exhaustion had been tinged with elation. It certainly showed in the vigour of his lovemaking with two of his wives. He blew out a big gust of air and rubbed his face, trying to break himself out of the post coital slumber that threatened to overtake him. He spun himself round, pushed himself off of the bed and dipped his hands into the wash bowl resting on a side table. He scrubbed his face and neck, feeling the thickening lines of skin to either side of his eyes, then he rubbed a finger of his right hand across his front teeth, taking a moment to dislodge a piece of goat flesh from in between two of his molars.

Once done he retrieved his own white robe from the floor and wrapped it around him. He walked towards the doors that lead on to the balcony. He pulled them back and stepped outside. The balcony overlooked the courtyard of his mountain hillside fortress. Ancient whitewashed walls and crenelated battlements snuggled tightly against the backdrop of the mountainside. Modest by comparison to some of the fastnesses in the region, he had immediately chosen this as his home when he claimed his right to rule over the local tribes. It was hard to access, overlooking a long winding valley and its tallest tower commanded a fine view of the wider area. A small, winding track lead up to the gates; a route that was designed to be vulnerable to attack from above. There were caves within the mountain to the rear of the fortress and they ensured that the defenders would be well supplied with stored food and water. No force would willingly undertake a siege of this fastness if they had any wisdom. He had thought in the past to wall off the many towns and villages that lay under his sway but had quickly dismissed the notion. It was not their way. The dwelling places and markets of his people should always be open.

The tribes he ruled were true Berbers, brave riders and vicious, determined swordsmen. Fiercely independent, they would not bow to any man unless he had proven himself worthy. A nomadic people by nature, droving their cattle far and wide in pursuit of good pasture, still they recognized the need for some permanent places of settlement, where they could meet and conduct trade for goods. Haggling was in their blood as much as war. It was a source of entertainment as much as good business sense. It was these settlements that Ghailan had first brought under his control. Though he had been a son of a tribal leader, he had always had greater ambitions and had understood that to achieve them he needed fame, needed his name to be known, feared and respected. By ensuring safe and fair conduct for all who travelled to his towns, his influence had spread amongst the tribes. And now, after years of consolidation and victory, he need but call and they would gather to him.

His kingdom was expanding and now that he could finally see an end to the endless squabbles with the pirates he could at last look to show his support to Mohammed, the ruler of Barbary. His lord, who ruled in Marrakesh, was under pressure from his own brother, Er Rasheed II, who claimed the throne for himself. That would not do. If Er Rasheed made a bid for power, Ghailan would gather his forces and march to support Mohammed, thus gaining favour with his lord. Er Rasheed would not forgive him for his deeds but no matter. Abd Allah Ghailan was, by his own hand, a force to be reckoned with and not easily cowed.

There was a knock on the door.

"My lord?"

Ghailan turned and looked upon the emissary he had sent to the settlement to the north. It would seem that his affairs with the pirates had allowed a movement of populations from the town of Tangier. The Portuguese had returned to their lands across the straits, and new faces, even whiter and more outlandish than their predecessors, had arrived. The English Christians from far to the north. He knew little about these people, yet his scouts had told him they were a military force. Perhaps they sought to challenge him for the right to rule? It was best they learned the folly of such ambition.

He summoned the man to come forward. The emissary knelt and placed his hands out before him, his head bowed in supplication. Satisfied with the proper gesture of respect, Ghailan bid the man speak.

"Did you meet with them?"

"I did, my lord."

"And what did you liken them to?"

"They seem like children. They hooted and pointed at me, showing much excitement and foolishness. They wear red topcoats, it makes them stand out, easy to see."

"Then they would seem little better than the last band of robbers," mused Ghailan. The emissary knew well not to respond. "And what of my demands? Rest assured I will not harm you for your answer, for I believe I already know what you will say."

The emissary looked upon his lord and then lowered his head once more in gratitude.

"It is as you say. I spoke to their man in the tongue of the Portuguese. I made it clear that they were not welcome and that it was not wise to test your power. The English man indicated that they would do no such thing, that they only wished to plant crops."

Ghailan regarded the prostrate man for a moment. He

knew this game, and he knew how foreigners loved to play it. They liked to take small bites, forever tempting fortune, to see if the lion bit back. He nodded. "Then they wish to test me. Very well." His mind was already thinking upon his strategy but the emissary coughed.

"My lord?"

"Yes?" he replied, irritation creeping into his voice.

"I remained out of sight and continued to watch the walls. Soon after there was much activity and a group of men came out of the gate. They spent much time walking the ground. Pointing and waving their arms. They placed sticks in the ground and marked out lines with shovels."

"What do you believe they were doing?"

"It seemed to me, my lord, that they were making preparations to build defensive works."

"Indeed." They do not waste time in responding to my challenge, Ghailan thought. Then I must not either. He placed a hand upon the head of the emissary.

"You have done well and earned favour. Go now."

"Thank you, my lord."

The emissary stood up and placed his right hand upon his left breast and bowed. He paced backwards away from Ghailan until he had reached the door and departed.

Ghailan returned to the balcony and gazed once more upon his holdings. This was an unfortunate turn of events. He had hoped to avoid having to commit to a military venture. His warriors could not be relied upon to fight long campaigns. Already they had returned to their homes across the mountains, back to their flocks and families. It would take some time to gather them again. But he would not let this insult go unanswered; it was time to summon his captains.

31 March 1663
Outside the walls

"By God, but this is thirsty work!" declared a young, lean-looking soldier of twenty years, stood to his waist in a thin trench. His chest was bare and his trousers covered in dirt. "Who'd have thought it would get so warm so bloody quickly? Here give us some of that." He beckoned over a young lad, who was walking down the line bearing a bucket. He picked out a ladle and took a long drink of the water it held. He replaced the ladle and nodded to the lad. He wiped his face and ran his hands over his head, pulling at the knots in his thick brown hair. He then picked at a piece of dirt from his eye and looked up along the line. To either side of him a large number of men were labouring with picks and shovels. They were constructing an uninterrupted series of earthworks stretching from one fort to another. If you could call them forts. They were barely more substantial than the trench they were digging, but that's what the officer of engineers was calling them. In truth they were little more than blockhouses; square constructions of earth and timber that could hold perhaps a dozen men.

"Hey, Jacob?" he called to the man next to him.

Private Jacob Blair looked up, sweat beading his bald pate. He was perhaps forty years of age, but a hard life in the wars had made it difficult to tell.

"What'd you want, Simon? Can't you see I'm busy?" he hefted a shovel load of dirt onto the topsoil.

"Was just taking a break. Doing some thinking," replied Private Simon Swallow.

"Don't let the Sergeant see you doing either of those things."

Simon snorted and spat. "He's not even here. Got a case of the mucky arse. Saw him running to them boulders way over yonder."

"He ain't the only one. Half the company is down with it leaving the rest of us to do their share," replied Blair, resting his hands on his shovel.

"Not much of a change really, is it? But I was thinking, as I said. Do you reckon they are watching us right now? The savages?"

Blair undid the scarf from around his neck and used it to rub of the sweat from his head. He looked at Simon with piercing blue eyes. They looked sharp and bright, at odds with the craggy, weathered face.

"I've heard it said. Look at this ground. Plenty of places for 'em to hide. There's the high ground all around us and plenty a gulley and draw down here. Why I daresay they could creep up to us within a hair's breadth and we'd not notice."

Swallow scratched his ear as his face adopted a serious look.

"Do you think?"

"I do that. And before you know it they'll be running us through with those scimitars of theirs."

Swallow started to feel a little fearful. "Then we should maybe get ourselves back to the walls?"

Blair gave a phlegmy, amused cough.

"I shouldn't worry yerself. We got it easy. We got flat ground to dig and a straight run back to the walls not two hundred yards from here. And there's men on the walls armed and ready with musket and cannon. I'd feel sorry for the poor bastards up on the highline yonder." He indicated the higher ground to the south, where men struggled to take the line up steep slope to join it to another blockhouse upon the top. "Plenty more places for the savages to hide up there. No, we're alright. We ain't lost anyone, have we?" He smiled, revealing a mouth with no more than a handful of remaining teeth, and dug his spade back into the earth.

Swallow watched him for a moment longer before staring at the high ground.

"Not yet we haven't." He shook his head and got back to work. There was another two hours of daylight and they were supposed to be down to chest height. Not much chance of that.

*

To the south, stood on the crude rampart of a new fort, Johnson pulled a scroll of paper from inside his jacket and placed it upon a small, field table.

"Lord Governor, sir. I have here a sketch map showing the line of fortifications that we are constructing."

Peterborough moved next to the engineer and squinted at the sheet.

Johnson placed his finger on the map. "This is where we stand right now. I have called this place Bridges Fort.

It is at the right angle of our lines." He traced his finger along several black lines on the map. "These lines are essentially communication trenches that will allow each fort to stay in contact with its neighbours and the town. To the east, we have a small blockhouse and at the end, Cambridge Fort. That final fort is overlooked by the Old Gate and the Eastern tower and would act as the link between the town and the line. From Bridges Fort we strike out northwest taking in Pole Fort, this will be a major construction, and will overlook the lower ground filtering through the gap between the hills into the immediate arc of ground that surrounds Tangier itself. This fort will mutually support another that will be built directly facing the gap, called Whitehall. This will cover our main gate, Catherina Port. Then the line will run on a straight course climbing up to the far corner of the high ground where it meets the sea. A major emplacement known as Whitby will occupy this space. It in turn will be supported by the Upper Castle, in particular the bastion, which I have taken the liberty of calling Peterborough Tower."

Peterborough glanced at Johnson, a smile playing on his lips.

"A liberty I will allow, Major Johnson."

"Thank you, Sir," the Major coughed. He was glad to see that his decision to name that place had gained some currency. All works on the Mole had been halted to accommodate this endeavour and when the Governor's attentions turned back to that, he wanted to have some way of softening the ire that would no doubt be generated by the delay. "So, as you see. These lines and forts will encompass the lands we have annexed for agriculture."

"What of our artillery?" asked Peterborough.

Farrell, who had been standing silently by, spoke up.

"As you are aware we have limited numbers. We have placed guns overlooking the main approaches to the town. I believe a request for more has been sent to England. Two on the Old Gate, two upon the Upper Castle and four more along the walls just south of Catherina Port."

Peterborough grunted in surprise. "Named after our King's new wife? It seems today is a day for declaring names."

Farrell and the rest of the party smiled or laughed indulgently.

"We thought it only right to honour His Majesty's wife. After all, she is the reason for our tenure," he replied.

"Good. Very Good. All is progressing well."

"It is Governor," agreed Johnson. "But I would make a request to you."

"Hmm?"

"We have precious little good building materials. There is no spare wood to speak of and more importantly we need strong stone to bolster the larger forts."

"Yes, Major Johnson. I am well aware of this. But as you know, such things are in short supply, as are many other essentials. We have had to tear down a number of dwellings just to provide us with firewood. We should at least be thankful the winter months are coming to an end."

"There is, I believe, a possibility of finding such materials further inland. Perhaps we could organise parties to investigate?" offered Johnson.

Peterborough thought for a moment.

"Yes, yes. I believe that is a good idea. Make it so, Major. Form up your party tomorrow morning to foray out into the hinterlands. I believe finding a useful store of building materials will benefit all of us."

"Thank you, Governor, this will enhance our fortifications no end." Johnson said with a measure of relief. Clearly his buttering up of the Governor had worked.

"Quite so." Peterborough looked about him and took a breath. His chest expanding, he slapped his thigh. "Let the Moors come," he announced. "They will find us more than equal to the task."

*

"I was under the impression that the nights would start to warm up here," grumbled Fitzwilliam. He drew his cloak tightly about him and stamped his feet.

"It's not the season yet," replied Drummond. "We have been fortunate with the weather, in a manner of speaking. Although the ground has dried up somewhat and made the soil firmer. That means it is harder for the men to dig. Hopefully the rain will return soon."

"You want it back? Bah, there must be something in the beer. It's addling your brain. A bit of warmth won't go amiss. I've had enough of the miserable cold. No better than France!"

"Oh, I think you'll be pleasantly surprised soon enough. And before you know it you'll be complaining to me about the weather again."

"I look forward to that moment."

"Still, it's nice of you to come down from the walls to share the night air with me."

"It's my pleasure. Just making sure we keep communications up."

Fitzwilliam had been given the task of duty watch

officer upon the defensive works, while Drummond had secured the responsibility of the walls. It had finally come to Harley's attention that the two officers had a good thing going at their Tavern and had decided that they clearly needed their share of the deprivations others were experiencing. So night watch it was. At least the Colonel had a measure of appreciation for their enterprise and had not ordered them out of their accommodations. Fitzwilliam had questioned the need for men to man 'the Lines' as the meagre fortifications were becoming known as. In reply, the Colonel had patiently explained that now the Moors' danders were up, they might take a fancy to not only occupying the forts but quite possibly tearing them down.

Fitzwilliam jumped up and down and looked out across the broken ground. He, Drummond, a corporal and a private stood inside the defensive works known as Bridges fort. In truth the fort was little more than an excavation in the ground, at a depth no greater than a short man. Earth had been piled up to the front of the fort to supply extra cover and a firing step placed in the fort to allow men to climb up and look out. There was no roof and no protection to their rear. At best it offered a small salient, where a number of musketeers could bring their arms to bear whilst sheltering against any incoming fire.

The night was cloudless and the moon waxing. Fitzwilliam blew out a gush of air that turned to mist. He watched it curl up for a few moments then fixed his attention to his front. He could see a little better now and the ground directly in front of him was quite well defined. But there were still far too many shadows and shapes that he could make neither hide nor hair of.

"We need some torches. Like what they have on the

walls," he declared.

"Better to see by, I presume?" asked Drummond.

"Aye and there would be no harm in warming one's hands on them either!"

"I hate to disappoint you, James, I really do. But you'll just have to rely on your hardy Scottish blood to keep you warm. I on the other hand, being an effete English weakling, will return to my post and gain the benefit of the meagre warm our few torches have to offer."

"Off you go, then," said Fitzwilliam. "At least make sure there is some mulled wine waiting for me when I get back to the Jolly Sailor. Oh, and make sure Siobhan is the one serving it. She'd warm the cockles no end."

"And tan your hide in the process." Drummond turned, walked over to the rear of the fort and hauled himself out, back onto ground level. He stopped and slapped his hands together to rid them of the dirt. "I'll see you in the morning. Enjoy the rest of your night."

"Aye, thanks," grumbled Fitzwilliam, waving his friend goodbye.

He returned his gaze out across the interior. It all seemed quiet enough. Every now and then some small shape would be seen moving stealthily across the ground. At first the guards had reacted with some alarm. One had even fired his musket. That had caused a bit of excitement and had threatened to rouse the whole garrison, though any panic was quickly scotched when Fitzwilliam had pointed out that it was likely one of the large number of rodents that lived in the area. A quick cuff round the head of the offending shooter had helped to ease the situation and given the men an unwilling target to relieve their tension on. Since then the night had settled into one of boredom and unsuccessful attempts to keep warm. A condition that Fitzwilliam could easily have remedied by excusing himself back to the Tavern. Unfortunately that was not a sensible option. Harley would have his guts for garters if he was found to be derelict in his duty. Having already been caught out with his billeting arrangements, he was keen to avoid any more reasons to provoke the Colonel's ire. Fitzwilliam was well aware of his own occasional shortcomings and enthusiasms but he was not a complete fool. He needed to keep his head low and his disposition steady. That way he and Drummond might just get to stay put. He also considered his friendship with Drummond something of a boon. He suspected the Colonel was glad he consorted with someone who had a clear sense of how things were supposed to be conducted. No doubt he expected some of Drummond's disposition to rub off on Fitzwilliam. Though, if one were keeping a tally, the opposite, it could be argued, was true. Drummond's life would have been so much duller if it wasn't for his association with Fitzwilliam.

He clapped his hands together, made a fist, then opened a small hole and blew hot air into it. He'd had enough of standing around. Time for a walk. He looked at the soldier stood next to him.

"Corporal?"

"Sir?"

"Off to do my rounds."

"Right you are, Sir."

Fitzwilliam looked about him and decided whether to go left or right along the communication trenches, now called by all, the Lines. He chose the right and walked along the sloping trench that would take him towards Pole Fort. Within a minute or so he reached the open depression that was the foundation of the earthworks. It was little more than a pit. A collection of stones had been piled up against its front edge as a crude firing step. A soldier rested against the earthen wall, his musket propped up next to him.

"Everything alright?"

The soldier started a little.

"Oh. Yes, Sir. Cold night, quiet night. Didn't hear you come along, Sir"

"Well, buck up there. The Moors are wily bastards from what I hear. Can creep up at you from any angle and you wouldn't know it."

"Yes, Sir. I'll listen harder."

"Good man. Just don't go shooting off your musket unless you've got a clear target. We don't want another panic, do we?

Fitzwilliam left the fort and picked his way down the trench which led onto lower ground. As he did so, he noted that the night seemed to have gotten darker. Which was a shame because he could no longer make out the next blockhouse along the route. The trench, uneven and sharply sloping, proved devilish and he lost his footing. He threw his hands out to the sides to steady himself, but the resultant noise of tumbling loose soil and stones seemed magnified tenfold in the night. Fitzwilliam held himself still and concentrated his senses. He looked about. There was no movement and the land was silent. He waited a few moments then took the last few steps down before the trench levelled out once more. He regained his composure and entered the blockhouse, situated some fifty yards from the slope. The blockhouse was in a better state of construction than the fort on the higher ground. The earth walls were shaped and flattened, stonework was placed all around its edge and had already been built to a foot in height. What was odd, though, was the total absence of occupants. There should have been a guard present, although, it was entirely possible that the man had simply wandered off momentarily to empty his bladder.

Fitzwilliam turned and squinted to the rear. Nothing. No noise or movement. He turned once more and made his way over to the firing position. Fitzwilliam placed his right hand on the soil and harrumphed. As he did so, he felt a warm, moist sensation against his middle finger. Intrigued he moved his hand across the ground and then brought his fingers up to his face. He couldn't see much, just dark smears; he sniffed and reared back. It was a smell he knew only too well, coppery and acrid. He stepped back from the edge, his eyes narrowing, his gaze sweeping his vision left and right, looking for a hint of movement in his peripheral vision. He couldn't know for certain, but there was blood upon the ground and a man was missing and that was enough for him. Fitzwilliam turned and ran back along the trench, his heart pounding in his chest, his breathing quickening. Most of all he felt a surge of excitement. As grim as the situation was, finally something was happening. He hadn't realised how bored he had become. Lost in his thoughts it took him a moment to realise that a dark shape had dropped down into the trench just a few yards ahead of him. The shape rapidly turned into the outline of a figure, one that appeared to be holding a blade. It was not one of his soldiers. Realising that there was no way to bring weapons to bear, Fitzwilliam charged forward and, leading with his right shoulder, slammed into the man, who let out a grunt as the air was knocked out of him and fell back. Fitzwilliam did not check his momentum but continued on, reasoning that where there was one, there were likely more. He was proved right as another shape emerged out of the gloom. This one was in the act of turning towards him. Fitzwilliam pulled back his fist and let fly, connecting with a face as it completed its turn. A satisfying crunch meant he had connected with his nose. The man raised both his hands to his face, dropping the weapons he had been carrying.

Once again Fitzwilliam pushed past, continuing onwards, reaching the slope and scrambling frantically upwards, using the sides of the trench to gain purchase. He wasn't sure if he was pursued. There was an almighty racket being created by his passage, surely someone must be following. He certainly did not wait to find out. He reached the top and ran the short distance to the fort. He stumbled inside as the soldier on guard turned, his musket rising.

"Who goes there?" the soldier demanded in a querulous voice.

Fitzwilliam flung his hands up.

"Whoa, stop pointing that bloody thing at me!"

The weapon was quickly lowered.

"Sorry, Sir. There's all sorts of commotion. I swear I keep seeing something out there."

"You are not wrong. Our lines are being probed. Now follow me to Bridges Fort. Quickly now." He looked behind him to for signs of pursuit and was relieved to see none. The two men he had encountered were no longer visible in the dark.

The soldier nodded and fell in behind Fitzwilliam, as he led the way onwards to the next emplacement. He looked to the west, scanning the ground for movement. It was next to useless, the darkness, the speed of his passage and the unevenness of the terrain made it impossible to discern anything. They slowed as they reached the entrance to Bridges Fort.

"Corporal, you there?"

"Sir?"

"Ah." He nodded to his companion. "In you go." He ushered the soldier in and turned to look back, checking the route they had taken. Still nothing.

"Sir, what's going on?" asked the corporal.

"We have enemy troops out there. They have already penetrated through the Lines. And we have at least one sentry dead."

"Dear Lord," responded the corporal. "What should we do, Sir?"

Fitzwilliam made to speak then stopped himself. It was only then that it occurred to him that he had never been in this situation before. He had never needed to do this, never in all his adult life.

Now, for the first time, men were looking to him for leadership. And their lives might depend on the decisions he made.

"Sir?"

"We hold our ground for the moment. See what happens. You." He pointed at the soldier who had accompanied him. "Keep a watch a watch here. See if we are followed."

The soldier moved swiftly to cover the fort exit.

"You," he pointed towards the corporals' companion. "Keep a sharp eye to your front."

"Yes, Sir!"

The corporal moved towards Fitzwilliam.

"Sir, Should we send a runner? Inform the other forts?"

Fitzwilliam shook his head. "No telling whether they are still manned. It's possible they have already been conquered. Better we send word to the walls. We can be assured of support that way."

"I'll go, Sir."

"Good man, tell-"

His words were cut short by the loud crack of igniting gunpowder. Ears ringing, he turned towards the direction of the report. It was the soldier guarding the entrance; he was on one knee, his smoking musket held out before him.

"I saw something, Sir. A figure. He was running along the trench."

"Did you get him?"

"Don't know. He's disappeared. He might have fallen."

Another loud report echoed from the front of the fort.

"What do you see?" Fitzwilliam shouted to the man on station, who was already in the process of reloading.

"At least three men. They were coming right at us!"

"Then bloody well reload faster, both of you," ordered the corporal. He had drawn his hanger and held it ready before him.

Within moments a dark form appeared upon the earthen rampart and the soldier on the firing step was down, killed by a swift slice to his neck. A dark spray fountained from the wound. And then two more shapes leapt down into the fort itself. Moors. One came at Fitzwilliam, sword raised to the side, shaping to repeat the killing blow that had felled the soldier. Instinctively Fitzwilliam ducked, and heard the whine of the blade as it carved into the air above him. He responded by thrusting his blade straight forwards. He leant into the move ensuring the point penetrated and entered the stomach of his assailant. There was a hard grunt from the man as he staggered back. Fitzwilliam kept up the pressure, pushing himself upward and onwards, driving the man further back and the sword deeper. His opponent had dropped his own weapon, his life already draining away. Fitzwilliam turned to check on the others. The corporal was down. The other soldier used his musket to block a downward cut and stepped forward to club the Moor in the face and knock him to the ground. A good move, but the remaining Moor, sword already dripping with the corporal's blood was readying to engage and the soldier was off balance.

"Hey!" Fitzwilliam roared. The Moor responded to the diversion and checked his advance to look behind him. That was the opening Fitzwilliam needed. Employing what was becoming a habit that night, he charged head first into the man, winding him and driving him to the floor. He followed it up with a hard kick to the groin. The Moor doubled up in pain but had scant time to suffer it as the musket-wielding soldier drove the butt of his weapon hard into the dark face with a sharp crack.

Both men were breathing heavily. Fitzwilliam shook his head, trying to make sense of what had just occurred. Damn but it had all happened so fast.

"Good work, soldier," said Fitzwilliam. He looked around. "Do you see any more?"

"No, Sir."

"Me neither."

Further gunfire to the south told him that they were not out of the woods.

"They are attacking all along the line. Not in numbers though. Seems more like they are probing. Testing our mettle."

"And making a decent fist of it too," responded the soldier.

"Aye."

"What do we do? Hold?" The soldier asked as he went

about reloading his weapon. This one knew his business, thought Fitzwilliam, which was probably why he was still alive.

Fitzwilliam moved across to check on the corporal. He knelt down to examine the man. There was no movement, no breathing that he could hear. He reached to the neck, to feel for a pulse, like his father had taught him to. He felt nothing. Nothing but the sticky warmth of spilt blood upon the skin. He reached across and gathered up the hanger.

"Here. You best take this."

"Thank you, Sir." The soldier took the weapon, tucking it through his belt. "I take it we plan to stay here, then?"

Fitzwilliam stood and turned to look towards the town. He could see lights moving upon the walls.

"Aye. We stay. Backs together and keep low. We each watch an entrance to the fort and keep half an eye to the front. We wait for relief."

"As you say, Sir."

He moved across to the first Moor he had engaged and withdrew his blade, from where it still lay embedded in the body. It took a bit of a tug to get it free and he had to place his boot on the torso for extra leverage. Then the two men took up position and commenced their watch. If it had been any other man in command of the walls this night he would have suggested a retreat. But he knew his old friend wouldn't leave him out to dry.

"What's your name, soldier?"

"Simon, Sir. Ah, Swallow, I mean. Simon Swallow, Sir."

"Smartly done, Mister Swallow."

"Thank you, Sir."

As they waited, the night began to close in. They could

hear sounds, scrabbling and scraping against rocks, the brush of something heavy against the bushes. And sometimes, what almost seemed to be the faintest whisper of a voice. But it was hard to tell. Fitzwilliam wasn't sure if the noises were real or simply phantoms born of fear.

"Hello, the fort?" a crisp, concerned voice called out from a short distance away, coming from the direction of the town.

"About bloody time!" responded Fitzwilliam as he stood up. A few dozen yards away was a knot of soldiers, with muskets pointed and torches held high. At their head was Drummond.

"You could have sent a runner back, you know?" he said.

"Was a tad busy. Holding off the hordes," replied Fitzwilliam.

"Yes. Well…" Drummond sent his men forward. They dropped into the fort and spread out.

"We have two of our own dead. Three of the locals," advised Fitzwilliam.

Drummond detailed men to remove the bodies and others to take up post upon the firing step. He turned towards his friend.

"There are more men heading toward the rest of the forts. I stripped most of the wall guard, excepting those at the gates. The garrison is awake and will soon fill the space I have left. From what I can tell, this wasn't a major assault else we'd already be overrun."

Fitzwilliam nodded.

"My thoughts too. They were coming at us in small groups. Testing our vigilance."

"And how did you think we did?"

"I'd say about evens in the fighting bit of it."

"Speaking of which, it looks like you got yourself involved in the mischief. You alright?"

"Me?" Fitzwilliam hadn't stopped to think about that. "Well, yes, I think so. Did a lot of smashing and battering." He recounted his brief engagement of the evening. "Had to use my bloody shoulder more than my sword."

Drummond pursed his lips then pointed at his friend's waist.

"Did you not think those might have been useful in a tight spot?"

"What? Oh."

Fitzwilliam realised what his friend had pointed at. His brace of pistols, sat primed and snug within his waistband.

"I didn't think."

Drummond laughed.

"That's often your problem. But you're a brawler. And it has served you well this night."

He clapped his friend on the back. "Now, I suggest you hold things here whilst I head back. Someone will need to make a report. Sergeant?"

A soldier upon the firing step turned round.

"Yes, Sir?"

"Ensign Fitzwilliam is in charge of the Lines. You will take your orders from him now."

"Very good, Sir." Fitzwilliam noted the sergeant had an Irish accent.

"James, I'll see you later. No doubt in the morning. Try not to get into any more trouble." He hauled himself out of the fort and dusted his red jacket down. "Oh, and get your story right. You'll be up in front of the Governor. He'll want to hear first-hand what happened and whether to apportion any blame."

"Grand. Just grand," muttered Fitzwilliam.

Drummond waved and hurried off into the night.

Fitzwilliam sighed, he suddenly felt very tired.

"Sergeant?"

"Yes, Sir?"

"Detail two men. Send one in each direction of the Lines. Get them to gather information and casualty figures. Tell them to be quick about it."

"Right away."

The sergeant tipped his head in salute them began to bark out orders.

Fitzwilliam drew a cloth from his pocket and ran it along the length of his blade vigorously. He wanted to get the worst of the dry blood off. Once satisfied he sheathed it, resolving to give it a good clean and oil on his return to the tavern in the morning. He might also award himself a good drink, although probably best to wait until after he had reported to the Governor.

As the hours passed and dawn approached, the daylight flowed from the east, across the fort and onwards. Fitzwilliam felt his thirst build. Maybe just a wee nip wouldn't hurt, just to give him some courage before seeing the Governor. That thought quickly died as he looked out into the hinterlands.

"Oh, by all the saints," muttered Swallow, from his position on the wall.

"And the sweet mother herself," whispered the Irish sergeant

"Now I *really* need a drink," declared Fitzwilliam.

In the distance, arrayed upon the higher elevations to the west, a mass of men waited. The sun's rays glinted off a thousand blades and spear points. No, more than a thousand. Many more. It was hard to say, their position made it impossible to guess.

"What numbers, do you think?" asked the sergeant.

Fitzwilliam shook his head.

"More than enough to trouble us, I'd hazard."

"Then we'll be pulled back, will we not?" asked Swallow.

Fitzwilliam turned and looked back at Tangier. There was a fair deal of excitement upon the walls. He could make out cannon being pushed into position, their black muzzles poking out from the embrasures.

"Don't count on it," he muttered.

*

"How many you say?"

"I'd say several thousand, Governor. But it is hard to say, our view is obscured."

"And do they encircle us?"

"The forts to the north and south have seen nothing."

"Then they are confident. And foolish. Let them have a taste of our cannon."

Harley shook his head; he had been waiting for this moment in his report.

"Regretfully they have positioned themselves outside the range of our guns."

"More's the pity," grumbled Fitzgerald.

Harley watched Peterborough stalk the length of his table. They were gathered in the Governor's new residence within Upper Castle. After two months of diligent labour Peterborough had deemed the place fit to decamp to. Harley agreed that it was a far better arrangement. They now had a proper headquarters for the military staff and a proper home for the governor of a colony. It was a pity that the Governor's good humour and sense of progress was now hampered by the arrival of yet another annoyance.

"They leave their flanks open and hold a position in front of us," Peterborough mused.

"A taunt, Sir," said Harley.

"A taunt?"

"Absolutely," continued Harley. "They have not deployed themselves for battle."

"They have no siege materiel to speak of," added Fitzgerald.

"It is a show of strength," finished Harley, a sidelong glance of irritation at his counterpart.

"Do they think they can intimidate us?" laughed Peterborough. "They must be ignorant of our ways and experience. We are all military men here."

"Yes, Governor," said Harley. He moved forward. "So what should be our position? They probed us last night and proved themselves able enough to slip men into our lines. They know the ground."

Peterborough stopped his pacing and regarded the gathering of officers.

"I would like nothing more than to send them a show of strength back. Teach them a very swift and stern lesson."

"We have many men who have the flux, Governor. I would be cautious about committing them to a fight," warned Harley. It was of no surprise to him that many had succumbed to a wasting sickness that affected the bowels most virulently. It was the Achilles Heel of any army that it could be brought to its knees by one of many maladies. Such numbers gathered in one place always guaranteed a swift transmission.

"We could send out the cavalry, out round the southern flank?" suggested one staff officer.

"Quite so. But I do not think they wish to give battle

today. No. Let them sit there. Let them watch and let them grow tired and restless."

"And what shall we do in the meantime?" asked Harley.

"We continue as planned. We allow the sickness within the troops to run its course and we plant crops on the land we have annexed. Major Johnson?"

"Sir?" The engineer stepped forward from his place at the rear of the gathering.

"Continue your work," commanded Peterborough. "Indeed, double your efforts. The longer they wait, the stronger our hand becomes."

"Yes, Sir. If you consent, I will requisition more men, those that are able, at any rate," replied Johnson.

"Very good. Divert all efforts from the mole, let us deal with this immediate issue first," said Peterborough with an authoritative wag of his finger.

Harley nodded. He was pleased with the Governor's decision. It was a cautious yet prudent course. Whilst he did not doubt the mettle of the troops under his command, he also knew that the sickness afflicting many limited the fighting effectiveness of the garrison. Of more concern to him was the nature of the enemy they faced. Brutes and savages though they were, the incursions of the previous night suggested the Berber tribes had knowledge of stealth and preparation that did not bode well for the English. Yes, the Governor was right. Wait them out; grow stronger whilst they grow weary. A very sound course of action indeed.

*

"You look like hell itself. And you stink of blood," announced Drummond.

"Thank you," replied Fitzwilliam.

"Like a true savage."

"Yes, yes."

"Been fighting the locals have you?" asked Donahoe as his dug into the depths of a tankard with his cloth.

"A wee scrap, you might say." Drummond took the tankard and filled it from one of the barrels. He waited until it foamed and placed it before Fitzwilliam, who acknowledged the gesture with a weary nod of his head.

"And what have you to say for the local lads? Find them to your liking?"

"I like them well enough when they are dead," muttered Fitzwilliam.

Donahoe raised an eyebrow.

"Oh they aren't so bad. I know a few of them. Decent enough fellows."

"They ever stuck a sword in your face?" asked Fitzwilliam.

Donahoe held his hands out.

"My apologies, young master. I can see you are sore on this matter," he said.

"Oh, don't worry about him, Thomas," interjected Drummond. "He's always grumpy when he hasn't had enough sleep."

"A day and half was the last time I slept. Can you credit it? They sent no bloody relief for another twelve hours! What did they expect us to do? Frighten off the savages with the sound of our snoring?" said Fitzwilliam. He found venting his frustrations had lent him fresh energy.

"Our commanders were taken aback by the arrival, to be true. Things like relief do tend to leave their minds when weighty matters of military planning are required," surmised Drummond.

"Good for them," responded Fitzwilliam. He picked up the mug and drank deep, When he returned it to the bar, the vessel was empty. Donahoe took it, refilled it and had it back in Fitzwilliam' hands within moments. Hands that began to shake, the liquid inside spilling over the edge and slapping onto the counter top. Fitzwilliam placed the mug down and balled his hands into fists, squeezing hard, willing them to stillness. What was going on with him?

"Things got messy out there then," stated Donahoe.

Fitzwilliam felt Drummond put a hand on his shoulder.

"Easy, James. You had a busy night."

"I don't know what this is all about," said Fitzwilliam, his voice breaking slightly.

"Drink up, lad, and then get you to bed," Donahoe kindly. "There's no one around but us three. No need to mention it again."

"Aye," responded Fitzwilliam. He took another long drink then replaced the mug. He nodded to both men. "Must be more tired than I thought." He left the bar and headed for his room. He could still hear the two men talking, and he stopped in the kitchen to listen.

"Killed a man, did he?" asked Donohoe.

"Yes," Drummond replied. "He won't thank me for saying it, but that was his first time. Before this he's only ever laid men out cold. Not dead."

"Then it's only natural. A bigger thing than most men realise, to take a life."

"I wouldn't know. But judging by my friend's reaction. I'm not looking forward to my first time."

"No. No man ever should."

Fitzwilliam chewed his lip and took a moment to look at his hands. They were steady once more.

2 May 1663
Upper Castle

"This is intolerable, gentlemen. Intolerable!" Peterborough slammed his hand onto the table top and stood up, casting an angry and accusing glare over his assembled commanders. "How many men have we lost now?"

"Twenty," responded Fitzgerald.

"Twenty!" Peterborough started pacing. "Twenty men we can ill afford to lose. Twenty since that rabble arrived outside our walls. Six men lost last night. I thought I had ordered the guard doubled."

"You did, Governor. And it was duly done," replied Fitzgerald. "But it is difficult to cover the entire ground. The Moor is a slippery foe, this is his land and he knows it well. They are proving adept at night fighting."

"Not just night fighting," Peterborough grunted. This very morning, two men had been ambushed when they had left the protection of the town to tend the plantations just beyond the walls. Out of nowhere a half dozen Moors had appeared, dispatched the unarmed men and were been away before guns could be brought to bear. It was…intolerable.

"And you say that they have encamped but a few hundred yards away from the Lines?"

"Yes, Sir. Some hundreds of them," replied Fitzgerald.

"Gentlemen. I will not abide this a moment longer. It seems that beyond the walls the Moors can move with impunity whilst the best efforts of our defences and sentries avail us of nothing. I thought that we could wait them out, let them return to their homes disheartened and us unbowed. I had hoped this Guyland would have understood that his belligerence was pointless and counterproductive. I see that he will not learn. I see that he means to bleed us with a thousand cuts. But I will not allow him this! Colonel Harley?"

"Governor?"

"It is time that we engaged the Moors and gave them a stern lesson in proper military exercise."

"You wish to engage him?"

"I do indeed."

"About time," announced a staff officer with some glee.

"And in what manner are we to pursue this?" asked Harley.

"With as much vigour as is necessary sir," responded Peterborough. "I have seen for myself that there is an encampment of the enemy not a few hundred yards away from the Lines. Two hundred or so of these slippery savages sleeping right under our noses. How many men do we have to send against them?"

The regimental commanders looked at each other.

"Many of my men have only just begun to recover from the dysentery that has been rife of late," said Fitzgerald.

"And many of mine also," added Harley. "But I believe I can field a force of five hundred or so effectives."

"Good," stated Peterborough. "And that will leave us with a sufficient guard force upon the walls?"

"Indeed it should, Sir."

"Very well, then. Return to your regiments and ready the men. I intend to give battle at dawn's first light. They have taken command of the night. We shall take it back from them during the day."

His staff and officers bowed their heads in salute and dispersed to commence preparations.

*

As they exited the Governor's residence Fitzgerald leaned in close to Harley.

"Is it just my old Scottish caution speaking here or are we taking a gamble with this enterprise?"

Harley, staring resolutely ahead as he walked, smiled.

"All war is a gamble, sir. You know that as well as I. But the men have been well drilled and prepared. They need to be blooded. This insidious war of assassination and attrition needs to be brought to an end."

"Aye. And who is to lead this mission of retribution?"

"I have few men I would entrust. And fewer still are healthy and standing."

"Nor me. Though I note that Major Fiennes is hale and hearty. Competent too, though inexperienced in these larger scale actions."

Harley nodded. Major Fiennes was his chief of staff. A useful enough officer whilst prosecuting day-to-day administration. It was about time his mettle was tested.

"Very well. I will ensure the task falls to him. I will

send with him as many of my officers that are able," he said.

"I will at least try to give you a company of useful and disciplined soldiers," answered Fitzwilliam.

"I thank you for that."

The two men parted to their respective headquarters.

*

That night, Peterborough formally invited all the garrison officers to drinks and supper in his new residence. A great deal of work had been done to make the place fit for habitation by men of quality. The Governor had ensured he shipped enough furniture to populate the house to an acceptable standard of civilised comfort. As they arrived, the officers were shown through a door off the main hallway into a large drawing room, appointed with tables, chairs, and comfortable chaise longues. Servants moved about the gathering crowd distributing fine ports and wines from crystal decanters. Fitzwilliam and Drummond entered with other members of Harley's regiment and were suitably impressed.

"He hasn't done a bad job, has he?" said Fitzwilliam.

"Never underestimate what can be achieved when the right pressure is applied," observed Drummond. "More effort has gone into this place, in such a short space of time, than you'll see on any other endeavour we are required to undertake. The proper provision of gentlemanly repose is always foremost in our master's minds."

"That's quite cynical of you. Eloquent but cynical," said Fitzwilliam, impressed by the wit of Drummond's speech.

Drummond shrugged.

"It is just the way of things. I'll say this for Cromwell, the man never put on airs and graces. He put his objectives first and had no consideration to where he had to sleep that night."

Fitzwilliam sniffed.

"I suppose even Old Ironsides had to have some good points. He was a decent soldier. I'll give you that much."

"Well done for your equanimity, James."

A loud clapping drew their attention to the far side of the room. The chatter died down as the gathering gave their attention to the instigator of the noise, Peterborough himself. He stood before them, looking assured and self-satisfied.

"My fellow officers. Tomorrow morning we will engage the local tribes in what will be our first military action. I have no doubt whatsoever the outcome will be favourable. It will send a sure and certain message to the people of this land that a new power has arrived. We will be firm, sure and swift. I expect all of you involved in tomorrow's action to discharge your duties to the highest standards. Now, some further news. I declare this room to be set aside for the entertainment and repose of all officers of the garrison."

A delighted murmur went through the crowd. Fitzwilliam nudged Drummond. "Repose. Just like you said."

Drummond winked.

Peterborough smiled indulgently.

"Gentlemen. A toast." He raised his glass high. "To victory, to Tangier and to His Majesty, the King!"

Glasses were raised and loud voices cried out.

"The King!"

Peterborough smiled once more then stepped back

into the crowd. The conversation struck up again as the officers enthused about tomorrow's foray against the Moors, and just as excitedly about their new room.

Fitzwilliam emptied his glass and swiftly replaced it for a new one from a passing tray. Out of the corner of his eye he spied two men walking up to him.

"Is it true? I hear you were involved in fisticuffs with the local barbarians, Fitzwilliam?" asked Lieutenant Oates. A tall and slight figure, with black hair and an evil looking scar that ran down the edge of his right eye. The puckered skin dragged his eyelid down, giving him a permanent squint. Gained not through battle but through duelling, a pastime Fitzwilliam had always felt was a poor excuse for a fight.

"I heard he was actually charging into the enemy single handed!" exclaimed his companion, Lieutenant Green, blond, youthful and stocky.

They were two classic examples of arrogance, pride and privilege and either had possession of a jot of martial talent. Both reasons why Fitzwilliam had never got on with most of his fellow officers.

"Really, Fitzwilliam. Do you not realise that the place of an officer is by the side of his men giving them clear direction? Inspiring them to do the fighting?" asked Oates with a sneer.

"Yes, thank you, Oates. I will bear that in mind next time I find myself in a chaotic mess of barbarians and bastards," replied Fitzwilliam trying to contain his anger. He could feel his face flush with heat.

"Honestly, Fitzwilliam, you do the officer class no good," said Green sternly.

"Indeed, Green. I thank you both for your guidance in these matters."

"Quite so," said Oates with a sarcastic smile. "I'm glad

to hear you are starting to listen to your betters."

With that Oates and Green swaggered back into the crowd. Fitzwilliam watched them go and clutching his wine class tightly, threw its contents into his mouth and swallowed hard.

"I wasn't listening to you, you young shites. I was working out which one of you I was going to pummel to pieces first. You'll help, won't you, Rupert?"

"Gladly. I'll stand stolidly by your side and hold your coat."

"Bastard."

3 May 1663
The Main Gate

Fitzwilliam stretched his back then adjusted his headgear. It was, he was led to understand, important to look ones best before going into battle. It inspired the men and filled them with confidence, all in the observance of their betters swaggering into combat looking assured and cocky. Fitzwilliam felt that he would rather look mean, sourly disposed and armed to the teeth. It should, if nothing else, inspire second thoughts in any man that sought to face him. To that end he adjusted the pistols in his belt sash and tested the blade at his back for the ease of withdrawal. It slid smoothly from the scabbard and he replaced it once it was halfway out.

"Looking forward to seeing that in action again, Sir!" called a familiar voice.

He looked over at a company of muskets marching towards a marshalling area to the right of him. He spied a grinning Swallow at the near end of the third rank.

"Best you don't waste your time watching my heroics and look to the proper dispensation of your own business, private," he advised.

Swallow's face took on a serious, more deferential tone.

"Have no fear of that, Sir."

Fitzwilliam nodded. "Good. I see you still have the sword I loaned you. Make good use of it."

"If God so wills it, Sir," Swallow called back.

"Shut your insolent mouth!" cried a sergeant who marched the formation at the rear. His long pike held stiffly against his shoulder. The sergeant then shot Fitzwilliam a venomous glance before continuing his marching call.

Ah, clearly a New Model man, thought Fitzwilliam. He studied the pike the man carried. He had never liked the things. They were used to block the backward steps of men losing their nerve and to shove them back into the battle line. It just didn't seem right to him. "If a man does not have the stomach for a fight, they'll be no use for the scrap anyway," he mused aloud.

"Then you miss the point, James. For surely it is the fear of one's own sergeant that keeps a soldier in the line. There is nothing a howling devil can do to when compared to the wrath of a sergeant," said Drummond, joining him.

Fitzwilliam shrugged and looked over his friend. His uniform looked fine, his red coat clean and the brocades smartly sewn. Ribbons adorned his arms and legs, as was the emerging style of the gentlemen of Europe. "Why, you should just look upon my own sergeant, Fletcher," continued Drummond. "He is a terror to the men. They wince at his every bark and tremble at every rebuke, and more than half have borne the physical discipline of his craft."

"You look lovely. Going anywhere nice?"

"Ever the flatterer, James."

"But honestly. Surely a man is better served by the example of an officer in command of his senses and his blade. Men fighting willingly ensure a better outcome than men forced to fight grudgingly."

Drummond tilted his head. "I am in complete agreement with you on this, James. But that kind of inspiration is severely lacking these days. The men have not seen a successful action in years and have many officers who have never drawn blood beyond the duels of gentlemen."

"Do you think my charges will follow me?" Fitzwilliam asked, in all seriousness. "I have been assigned to a scratch company of pike, a mix of headquarter soldiers and those whose own bands are too depleted by the flux. They are all trained but have never drilled together. And I don't have any muskets. Where is the sense of that?"

Drummond shrugged.

"Use your head and employ your best judgement. Don't make that face! There are other companies, including mine, who are in better condition. Look to them. If we hold to our training, yours will follow suit."

"Well, I'll look to you for my inspiration, oh Barbarossa of Tangiers."

"Have you been reading history books again?" laughed Drummond. "Don't let Siobhan know, she might mistake you for a man of manners and breeding."

Fitzwilliam snorted. "No fear there. I deliberately went to her last night and wished her my heartfelt goodbyes in anticipation of a fate most eagerly unwanted. You know what she did? She raised an eyebrow and carried on gutting the fish I had caught her preparing! I fear that our relationship is not long for this world."

"Ah, at last understanding breaks like dawn across your craggy face."

"Shut up and go kill some Moors."

Drummond tipped his hat, winked then hurried off.

Fitzwilliam glanced at the sky above. It was a mottled grey in colour. A murky dawn. A depressing day. He looked about him. He had to admit, there was a fair degree of excitement amongst the men. Clearly they were eager to pick a fight. He wondered if that was a good thing.

*

Major Nathaniel Fiennes, a proud looking man in his late twenties, tapped his blackthorn against his leg and looked around impatiently. He was most anxious at the time it was taking the men to get ready. They seemed eager enough but this showed itself in a worrying inattention to their business. They needed to proceed in an orderly fashion and dispose of themselves in a proper military deployment. He was keen that this foray be seen to be a well-handled business. Truth be told, he was also keen to get it underway. He had waited a long time for such an opportunity and wanted to prove himself as a man to whom regimental command should be considered swiftly. Whilst experience in warfare was not necessary in attaining rank, it did no harm in favouring him with those who made such judgements. The time for them to commence the sally was almost upon them. He glanced towards the north, looking along the wall to where it disappeared into the gloom. He expected the Governor and the regimental colonels to be on hand, watching the deployment and the prosecution of the foray. As men were marshalled into position, finally it seemed that the troops were getting into some semblance of order. As soon as the gates opened, skirmishers would head out first, followed by the companies of pike and muskets bringing up the rear. They would shake into a battle line and then advance. The enemy, likely emboldened by the recent inactivity of the English soldiers, no doubt thought themselves secure. They would be in for a surprise.

An aide appeared by his side.

"Yes?"

"Sir, all commanders have reported their readiness."

"Good." He looked up into the sky. It was well into the first hour of dawn, even if it was but a dull blanket of dark grey above them. It would help them in their egress from the gate, hiding their numbers and no doubt lighten sufficiently for the advance itself.

"Then order the gate opened. We shall commence."

The aide bowed his head and took the message to the gates. They swung open and along the Lines of waiting troops, the order was given to deploy. There was a great deal of urgency and speed to the manoeuvre. Men jostled with each other, those in behind pressing those in front forward, as the formations pushed their way through the opening. On the far side of the gate, men spilled out and started to lose their coherence as columns became fragmented. Sergeants barked and officers exhorted their troops to better discipline. Fiennes was out at the front of the mass and quickly took in the situation. He could see ahead of him the incomplete earthworks of the Lines. Already the sentries were putting in place short planks, which the men would use to cross the trenches. He was disturbed by the noise the soldiers were making. He had hoped for a somewhat stealthier deployment. Clearly, that would not be so.

He dispatched a runner. The men must double to

cross the Lines, speed was of the essence to maintain their surprise and unbalance the enemy. He led off at a brisk trot, feeling rather proud of how he was heading the charge.

As the word was passed back, urgent orders were given to increase the pace. This had the effect of causing even more disruption to the companies, as the clear ranks of troops started to dissipate into a swaying knot of men. This knot began to form itself into a wave, as soldiers reached the Lines at a run and started to stream across.

Fiennes halted a hundred or so paces short of the enemy encampment. Even from here he could, with some satisfaction, see a great deal of toing and froing. Men were charging hitherto and herefore, pointing at his approach and exclaiming wildly. Perfect. The speedy advance of the English had caused disarray and doubt. Excitement welled in his chest and he felt a surge of energy within him. He turned to the mass of men behind him, at least those who had made it across the trenches. Pike blocks were forming and the muskets were placing themselves in support, but there was no time for that.

"Come on, men. We have them. They run!" He drew his sword and waved it into the air above him. "To me, men. To me. We shall chase these dogs down and give 'em a taste of their own medicine!"

Along the ranks of men, the cry was taken up and ragged cheers and challenges were called out. The front of the wave surged on once more, leaving the rear in its wake, struggling to catch up. The Moorish force was in full flight; they left campfires burning and blankets strewn on the ground. All of it was kicked up and covered in the dust and dirt of a half thousand English soldiers. The fleeing force headed for the southwest, skirting the high ground directly in front and funnelling into the lower ground that rounded it. Here the land was even more rugged and uneven than the approaches to the Lines. Draws and small canyons dotted the floor amidst the scrub and bushes. The Moors started to disperse into smaller groups, each taking differing routes through the maze.

In response, the English redcoats found themselves having to judge which force to pursue. Fiennes, much winded, did not mean to give up so easily. He called to those nearest him to stay close and ordered that others should chase down whatever enemy they saw fit. Better to blood them than let all get away unharmed. In so doing all semblance of organisation was lost from the English ranks, bands of men were fragmented and companies splintered into groups of tiring but eager hunters. Officers and sergeants did what they could to maintain control and gathered to them as many of their commands as they were able, but most men were too full of the chase. As the English forces penetrated deeper, it seemed that many of the fleeing enemy had stopped their headlong flight. Now bands of them were turning and were actually engaging their pursuers. More seemed to emerge from positions to the left and right, climbing up from the many depressions, cuts and defiles. Musket shots could be heard; puffs of smoke appearing from the slopes to either side of the lower ground. Fiennes saw a man go down to one such shot. It drew him up short. This was unexpected. He had not thought he enemy had time to stand and shoot. They were in flight. And yet, he could see a number of Moors stood too just ahead of him. Then to the left several of them emerged from hiding, shouting in their obscene tongue and charging into his men, their swords held high, slashing down and across. He saw men cry out and fall, whilst others tried to engage. But they couldn't bring their pikes to bear quick enough. After a few moments more, as his mind tried to make sense of the mayhem occurring about him, it occurred that what he was witnessing was a perfectly executed ambush. One which his men were completely unable to counter. He opened his mouth to order a general retreat but instead a gentle cough emerged from his lips, as he felt a hard pressure against his back, followed by a sharp pain coming from his stomach. He looked down at a spear point that had erupted from his belly. He felt a rivulet of warm blood running down his chin from his mouth, before he felt his legs go cold and he collapsed to the floor.

*

Elsewhere, the redcoats were desperately trying to regroup. Many of the smaller bands had already been eliminated once they had scattered out amongst the uneven ground. Survivors and larger bands were forming into tight defensive knots. Musketeers were sending out ragged volleys but finding themselves cut down by swift swordsmen. The pikes were unable to create the wall of steel that was their strength. The terrain just did not allow for it.

Finding himself to the rear of the press, Fitzwilliam was not in a position to understand what was unfolding. But he knew enough to realise things were not going as expected. There was far too much confusion and a spreading sense of fear. As he cast about he could see a number of Moors emerging from a draw to his left. They charged into a group of gunners who had been firing to the front. The surprise was complete and they quickly fell to the sharp blades of their attackers. Witnessing this filled Fitzwilliam with anger. He Looked about him and grabbed a sergeant.

"Where's the company commander?"

The sergeant shook his head. "I don't know. I haven't seen Captain Witham since we started the charge."

"It doesn't matter. Grab as many men as you can and follow me."

Not waiting to see if he had been heard, he turned and drew his blade. Clutching it with both hands he held it high and with a wild yell, charged at the Moors. In the short seconds it took for him to close the distance, not one of the tribesmen had reacted to his challenge. This proved to be more useful to him than if the reverse had been true. He took the first tribesman from behind with a swinging arc to the side of the neck, even as he swept the blade away, he was moving forwards again, pushing the falling Moor to the ground. The second one he slashed a wild uppercut that succeeded in connecting with the jaw. The head snapped back and the man fell away. Fitzwilliam was off balance but allowed his momentum to carry him into a third man. He used his elbow and drove it into a nose with a solid crack. The owner of said nose grabbed Fitzwilliam' arms as he careened in and the pair of them fell into a tangled heap. Fitzwilliam rolled away as a blade pierced the ground from where his midriff had been. He finished his roll upon his back. He looked up to see the Moor, lifting his blade and coming straight for him. Fitzwilliam reached down ad withdrew his two flintlocks. Holding them out before him, he squeezed both triggers. The Moor charged towards him, one arm held high with the blade and another, his shield arm, held wide to his left, presented his body as an open target. With a flash from the pans and twin cracks of sound, both sets of charges ignited, two balls were propelled directly into the chest as a range of no more than a yard. The force of the impact was not enough to check the Moor as he fell forwards onto Fitzwilliam who let out a grunt of pain and annoyance. The Moor was a dead weight, no sign of struggle. He tried to heave the body off but his hands were pinned firmly against his chest, making the effort twice as hard.

"Bloody hell, someone get this heap off of me!" he cried to the world in general.

Almost in deference to his request, the weight was at first lessened then removed completely as two red-coated men pulled the body away. The sergeant, whom he had bid join him, proffered a hand and hauled Fitzwilliam up.

"Sorry, Sir, you were too quick for me to get the lads together."

Fitzwilliam replaced his pistols and bent down to retrieve his sword.

"No matter, Sergeant. Let's deal with the others." He looked across at half dozen pikemen holding position in front of the draw from which the Moors had emerged.

"No need, Sir," declared the sergeant.

"What?"

"Look around you. You fair did for them all. Knocked 'em all down. We just had to skewer the one you copped in the face."

"Oh, right."

The sergeant gave him an appreciative grin.

"Never seen such a mad sight, Sir. Fair filled me with pride to see an English officer brawl so well."

Fitzwilliam was taken aback. It was the last thing he'd ever expected to hear from one of the men.

"Yes, well. Good work anyway, Sergeant. Now, let's see what's going on shall we?"

"Easy enough, Sir. Look about you, we been plum

suckered in."

Fitzwilliam could see exactly. There were a half dozen engagements going on amidst the scattered groups of redcoats. Those who were alone or in small numbers were quickly despatched. This winnowing was happening at an alarming rate.

"There." He pointed to where a larger body of men had formed up, at least fifty strong. They were had made a battle line and had yet to receive any determined charges.

"Quickly to them!" he ordered to the soldiers beside him and they broke into a run.

"James!"

Fitzwilliam saw Drummond waving at him from the centre. With a burgeoning relief at the sight of a friendly face on the battlefield, he led his men to the relative safety of the line.

"Rupert, what the hell is going on?"

His friend, smiled grimly.

"We are ambushed on three sides. Sergeant, put your men onto the left flank. Act as the link between that flank and this centre."

"Yes, Sir. Come on lads."

Fitzwilliam watched the soldiers run off. "This is a pretty mess," he declared.

Drummond gave him an appraising look. "Indeed so, looks like you've already seen some action."

"What? Yes," Fitzwilliam wiped at his face, his hands coming back with a stain of blood. "Not mine."

"Never thought it would be," said Drummond. "Now I think we need to get a grip."

"Good plan. Forward or back?"

"No point going forward. I think we need to conduct a fighting withdrawal. I have about forty pike here. The

Moor isn't so interested in charging us head on yet."

"Got any gunners?" asked Fitzwilliam, now engaged with reloading his own weapons.

"A few. I have them on the flanks. I think we should start pulling back. Keep our faces to the enemy."

"Alright. You start, Rupert. I'm going to try and gather as many of our lads as I can. If this turns into a rout, we'll lose most of the force. These bastards are too fast and too clever by half."

Drummond nodded and then shouted out across the line.

"Pike, begin withdrawal. Slow steps. Watch your footing. Keep your weapons to the front. Don't give them an opening. NCO's keep the line in good order. Muskets, protect the pikes. Make your shots count. Don't let any of those bastards through!" Sergeants and corporals took up the order and the line began the difficult manoeuvre of withdrawing while maintaining a frontal formation.

Fitzwilliam worked his way down the line; he held his pistols in front of him and kept one worried eye to the rear. As yet, no force had come to seal off their retreat. A blessed relief. He ran past a half dozen musketeers who stood just to the rear of the last pikeman and shouted.

"Look after the line, lads. It goes, we all go."

He ran past the pike wall and back into the interior. He started to cry out to fleeing redcoats. He could see large numbers already scrambling back towards the town, heading across the higher ground. Many were being run down by pursuing tribesmen or by others waiting for them amidst the undergrowth.

"To me," he cried, "King's men to me!"

Most did not heed him but some of those nearest to him ran towards the rally cry and he in turn sent them towards Drummond's withdrawing force.

"Get into the line. Hold it. It is your best chance."

He saw a redcoat dragged to the floor and he hurried over and fired a pistol point blank into the back of a Moor. He helped up the soldier and put an arm around the man. He was already injured and bore a bloody red wound on his left leg.

"Thank you, Sir. Bastard almost had me."

"Not at all. Here." He passed over his loaded pistol. "Any one come near us, let him have it."

"Gladly, Sir."

"You there!" A voice from further ahead caused Fitzwilliam to look up. Another group of redcoats, a score or so, stood fast in the chaos. Most were musketeers, keeping up a steady rate of fire, although it was rather indiscriminate. He recognised Captain Witham, a grizzled looking soldier who had fought for the King in twenty years of campaigning. His sword was drawn and he looked like he had seen some close quarters combat, his front was drench in blood.

"Sir, it's Ensign Fitzwilliam," he called over.

"Well, come over here man. You'll be cut down if you stay out here."

"Sir, the main body is withdrawing. You must pull back before the noose is closed about us."

Witham was silent for a moment.

"I am inclined to agree. Men, break ranks and follow me."

As the group reached Fitzwilliam, Witham ordered a soldier to take care of his wounded charge. The soldier handed back the pistol with a nod of thanks.

"Can't have an officer carrying wounded," he remarked. "Where is the main body?"

Fitzwilliam pointed at Drummond's troops. "Just

ahead, not far, they are pulling back."

Witham nodded. "Then we best be at it."

Fitzwilliam tipped his hat then made to head further inland.

"Hang fire, Ensign, where are you going?"

"Trying to save as many as I can."

Witham put a restraining hand on his right arm.

"I'd leave it. The ground gets worse ahead. These men are the only ones that made it out."

Fitzwilliam pursed his lips. Witham was probably right. But he didn't have to like it. "Bastard!" he shouted into the air.

"Quite unseemly," remarked Witham. "Now, come along."

The cohort of soldiers moved at a steady pace, as fast as the wounded, of which there were several, would allow. Around them, many of the skirmishes had ended and the Moors were banding together and making threatening moves towards them.

Up ahead, Fitzwilliam could see the battle line, still at least two hundred yards away. He looked about at the tribesmen. A few carried muskets and they were concentrating on his group. Most rounds missed their targets but one man went down screaming, clutching his face.

"Keep going!" ordered Witham. No one stopped to help the fallen soldier. No doubt everyone, Fitzwilliam included, felt the pull of self-preservation. Individual tribesmen charged the group, intent at breaking their cohesion. Scuffles broke out as soldiers sought to keep the enemy back without becoming separated. The group discharged their weapons and Fitzwilliam fired into the face of a charging Moor. He saw a soldier stumble and fall. Three Moors fell upon him, their swords rising and falling to the shrieking cadence of his screams. Fitzwilliam cursed but held his place as Witham exhorted the dwindling force on. His pistols now empty, Fitzwilliam drew his blade once more. They were but fifty metres away and more importantly the line itself had checked their progress, voices from it beckoned them to join them.

"Captain Witham, Sir. Time to break and run," he shouted.

The Captain turned and nodded.

"Men, run for our fellows! Follow me!"

"I'll cover the retreat," shouted Fitzwilliam.

He held his blade out in front of him and swung it in a lazy arc, smiling grimly at the Moors who pressed on the heels of the surviving soldiers, no more than a dozen left. He continued to pace back, never keeping his eyes from his foe. He gambled on keeping his feet and that his comrades would keep his back covered. He was gratified to see something akin to caution in the eyes of the tribesmen, many feinted forward but none committed to engaging him. He continued swinging his blade in a figure of eight; his arms ached but the years of drilling meant that his strength would last some time yet. Time enough at least.

"James!" Drummond's shouted from behind him. "Duck!"

Relying on the good sense of his friend he dropped to the ground in an ungainly fashion with a loud grunt. He felt the gust of disturbed air as several musket rounds flew past his head a moment before he heard the report of the guns themselves. He looked up and saw two Moors drop to the ground and a number of the others pull back. Not waiting a moment longer, he heaved himself up, gathered his weapon, and turned for the

English line. He sprinted the last twenty yards, angling towards its left flank and the musketeers, commanded by Drummond. He passed the hastily reloading shooters, while Captain Witham gave the order to continue to withdraw.

"You are getting to be quite the hero these days, James," shouted Drummond over the cries of tribesmen, musket fire and bellowing sergeants.

"It's dreadful work!" Fitzwilliam shouted back.

The battle line recommenced its slow, painful withdrawal, gathering the last few soldiers still standing. The Moors were now gathering their strength against the small band who had gained the open ground ahead of the Lines, not two hundred yards away. Fitzwilliam knew they would soon be within the protective arc of the cannon placed on the walls.

"Come on lads, almost home!" he shouted. He felt his heart lighten. It was obvious the Moors would not dare follow them too far forward. At least, he hoped so. This hope was swiftly dashed as he heard the dreadful cry from the right flank.

"Cavalry!"

Charging from the north, from a bend in the low ground, a group of Moorish horse were galloping at full tilt towards the English line.

"Pikes brace!" shouted Witham.

"Muskets, hold the flanks!" cried Drummond now positioned on the threatened flank.

Howling battle cries and curses, the cavalry charge hit the line at an angle. The bulk of it went straight for the pikes and met an immovable wall of death. A terrible slaughter ensued as the horses to the front tried to shy away from the line of sharp points and ended up being rammed into them by the horses behind them. The pikes pressed forward, driving their weapons into both human and horse alike. The creatures reared up in pain and their riders were thrown clear, only to be trampled by their fellows. The English line were well trained and drilled in holding against such charges. No European cavalry force would have attempted such a manoeuvre but clearly the experience was being rapidly brought home to the overconfident Moors. Perhaps they had expected the English force to collapse and break, but decades of hard fighting both at home and abroad had bred sterner stuff; they were still professional men and fighting for their lives. The part of the cavalry that had tried to turn the flank lacked the numbers to achieve their aim and was itself scattered by a volley blast from the dozen or so musketeers locked tight and at a slanting angle to the frontal pike line. The remaining enemy horse fled back the way it had came, its tails between its collective legs.

It was the first time during the engagement where English training and experience had proven its worth. The rest of the Moorish horde elected not to pursue the retreating force any further. The redcoats covered the remaining distance to the Lines in good order. Once there, the formation had to break its close ranks so that men could jump over the trench, those more injured being helped over by fitter men. The musketeers were brought into the collapsing centre to cover their retreat. The main gate of Tangier opened up and the troop of the Tangier Horse cantered out to cover the infantry. Fitzwilliam and Drummond, given the task of marshalling the rearguard, waited for the slower pikes to clear until only muskets were left. They sent half across to give them covering fire then commanded the remaining to heft their weapons and jump.

Drummond looked at his friend and jerked his head.

"Time we affected our egress from this most unwelcome party."

With that he took two long steps then leapt the short distance across the trench. Fitzwilliam was right on his heels. The musket line formed up again, firing a volley at a line of Moors where were once again pressing forward.

"Can we egress a bit faster?" asked Fitzwilliam, hoping the guns upon the walls were, in fact, loaded."

Drummond nodded.

"Muskets! Back to the walls. We've done enough."

Not waiting to be told twice, the gaggle of soldiers ran at speed to the safety of the gates and the small square beyond it. The Tangier Horse closed about them and marshalled them through. Once all were in, the gates began to close. Above, a ragged volley of cannons fired. No one spoke as the echoes thundered around the space and along its connecting streets. Then a great deal of cheering erupted from the walls above.

Fitzwilliam glanced upwards and saw the waving of hats and the occasional two-fingered gesture so beloved of the army. I assume that means they aren't coming any closer, he thought. And a good thing to, I'm too bloody tired to fight them just now.

He collapsed in a heap onto the cobbled surface and removed his hat. A shadow fell over him.

"Move over. You're taking up the best bit of floor, you know."

"Get your own bit," he grumped but shifted slightly to his left. The shadow moved and Drummond fell onto the floor next to him.

"That was not a bad egress," he announced as he looked about. Men lay sprawled on the floor, coughing, hawking and spitting and generally cursing their lives, their lot and the Moors in equal measure. Fitzwilliam did nothing more than a cursory count, but he reckoned on not half the original force had made it back to Tangier. The way the Moors had been advancing, he doubted any more men would be coming back.

"You look a mess," said Drummond.

Fitzwilliam sighed, shifted his position and in turn inspected his companion.

"No, I just look untidy. But that is not a new state of affairs, or so many who seem knowledgeable in such things have told me. You, on the other hand, do look a mess. My goodness Rupert, if the Colonel was to see you now. I dare say he would have you cashiered for letting the entire officer corps down."

Fitzwilliam did a quick personal inspection. His coat was covered in dirt and his white britches were now darkened with patches of blood and other things he dared not consider. He doubted that the Colonel would be so harsh on either of them. Though it did occur to him, now that the immediate concerns of the day had passed, that there would be a great deal of explanation required of the surviving officers. He was glad that Captain Witham had survived. In this situation it was good that there was someone with more seniority who would be the immediate target for such questions. Drummond poked him in the ribs.

"Come along, then. You've had your rest, now we need to start behaving like officers again."

"Why?"

"Because that is our job and we have a number of men looking to us for guidance. Let's stand up and get these men into some kind of order. Then no doubt roll calls will have to be taken to establish just who survived our first great battle for Tangier."

*

Night had fallen some hours before but a great many lights were still bathing the walls. Men prowled along the parapet, gazing often and pointedly into the hinterland. Earlier there had been the occasional crack of musket-fire as a nervous sentry spied a shadow moving with purpose near to the walls. These had lessened as Sergeants enforced the order that no such alarmist action should be undertaken, it was disturbing the thoughts of the Governor. And it was true, for he was greatly vexed. He returned from his vigil by the window and sat behind the table. Once more he gathered up the reports given to him by his staff on the day's events. Out of five hundred men, no more than one hundred and sixty had returned, many of them bearing wounds that might not survive the surgeon's knife. A full two thirds had been lost to the enemy in the very first action that they had fought. Now it was clear that this Guyland had the upper hand. Peterborough did not have the men to risk such another immediate expedition beyond the walls. It was a disaster. The enemy had outthought them, Peterborough was enough of a soldier to recognise that. Their troops had been drawn into a trap, one that had been prepared well in advance of his decision to send the sortie. Guyland had known exactly what to do. He had tested Peterborough's patience and won out. The English force had been disrupted and spread out when its strength lay in tight concentration, cohesion and discipline. Now the soldiery themselves would doubt the efficacy of their leaders. He recalled reading a similar fate had befallen the Roman commander Varrus, when his legions had been ambushed and massacred in the forests of Germanica. Fortunately, Peterborough had not lost all of his men and he still held the prize. Tangier was not so easily taken. The cannon had driven back the Moors and they had little to counter it with. So be it then. Let Guyland have the hinterland and welcome to it. They would remain safe behind the walls and continue with the construction of the mole. The state of Barbary would have to accept English strength when Tangier became the great maritime hub that the King wished it to be. Peterborough sat back and sipped at a goblet of wine. He felt old and tired. The day had been far too long.

11 May 1663
The Mediterranean

Sir Andrew Rutherford, the Earl of Teviot, climbed the stairs leading to the fo'csle. The weather was set fair and since they had sailed past the southern tip of Portugal, a gentle breeze had ensured a steady passage past the Barbary Coast and Gibraltar. The sky was blue and the sun hot, although not as hot as one might encounter during the height of summer back home in England. He was still wearing just his white shirt so for the moment the breeze continued to cool him and he enjoyed its force against his back. Soon he would have to put on his heavy redcoat and wide brimmed hat, all necessary to ensure he marched off on the right foot. He watched the crew hard at work, preparing themselves for an imminent arrival at their destination, admiring the swift purpose with which the men moved. The *Lady of Cornwall* was the next supply brig to be making the run into Tangier. Within its holds was grain, fruit, wine, preserved meats, cattle and tools for building, farming and war. It had been made clear to the King that the colony could not support itself, with neither the land nor the expertise to work it. So it was necessary to import virtually all the necessary materiel required. It was King Charles' earnest hope that this situation would change once Tangier become the trading hub that he so desired it to be. Until that moment, he was willing to subsidise the venture.

As well as the goods within its bowels, upon the deck was a small reinforcement contingent of a dozen men and one Governor in waiting. Teviot breathed in the salty air and reflected on his mission. It was with some urgency that his appointment had been decided. The frequent messages from Tangier had painted a decidedly poor picture of conditions. What had truly vexed Parliament was the absolute lack of positive progress made by the garrison. Constant requests for assistance, complaints about manpower, etcetera. This was not what they had wanted to hear. As it was, that august body was not entirely behind the King in the matter of Tangier. It was the swift action and heartfelt agreement by Charles himself had led to his recall to serve the Crown. Heaven forbid that His Majesty should feel any of his decisions to be wrong, but perhaps, he felt that he himself had wronged Teviot. After years of commanding the Scottish regiments of the Army of France, Charles himself had promised him the rule of Dunkirk, only to renege on the deal and sell it back to the French. At least, in part, the funding of that sale went towards the upkeep of Tangier, so it seemed only fitting that Teviot himself should be a part, even belatedly, of that upkeep. His orders, such as they were, could not have been simpler. *Make Tangier a power to be respected and observed.* Teviot could easily read between the lines on this, and he was pleased to have been given the authority to do so. To make Tangier the power, it needed to show power. And in this world, military might was the absolute power, not, as many devout countrymen would believe, the inalienable divine right of kings to rule. He was a loyal soldier to his King and country but Cromwell had proved that all power was winnable if one had an army at one's back. So, he would renew the garrison of Tangier, give it back its pride, and in so doing he may yet make a decent fist of taking his own place in the world. And, as he watched the walls of Tangier come into view, he guessed there was no time like the present to get started.

*

Peterborough slumped in his chair and looked aghast at the man before him. Of middle years, lithe, a sparkle in his eye, and a confident poise. "So this is the moment of usurpation? Always the old are cast out by the young," he said.

Teviot shook his head.

"Hardly, my lord Governor. I am just undertaking the King's wishes."

Peterborough grunted and reached for his wine.

"I suppose Dunkirk was a blow to you."

"Aye, it was."

"And I suppose you decided that you deserved another command?"

"I will not lie to you that I did not." Teviot folded his hands behind his back. "But I am a soldier first. I'll leave the political skulduggery to those who are better at it. I follow orders to the best of my ability."

Peterborough raised an eyebrow.

"Well, if it's soldiering you want, good luck to you. I pass you a garrison that is on its knees through pestilence and the devil's own barbarians. They beat at the very walls of this place and watch our every move."

"Well, that is something we'll have to set right."

Peterborough remembered being that confident not so long ago. "And when do I depart?"

"The ship I sailed in on has orders to bring back you, your goods and any staff officers that see fit to join you."

Peterborough sighed and placed his hands on the table.

"Then best I start packing."

"If I may impose on you a moment? I would much appreciate it if you were to summon the senior officers and your staff. I think I have much to learn and little time to do so."

13 May 1663
The Jolly Sailor Tavern

"Colonel Harley?" spluttered Fitzwilliam, in surprise.

"At ease, Fitzwilliam," commanded Harley.

He stood at the door his back framed in sunlight. He gazed about him with a disapproving stare and entered. He walked up to the bar and removed his hat.

Fitzwilliam, his hand still clutching his mug, shot Donahoe a confused and slightly panicked look. Donahoe did as he always did and shrugged.

"Get you a drink, Sir?" he asked.

Harley looked at him as if for the first time noticing his presence.

"Hmm? Oh, yes, why not. Might as well try out the potion that has so entranced two of my officers."

"As you wish, Sir." Donahoe furnished him with another mug and then made his excuses.

Fitzwilliam watched, in uncomfortable silence, as his commanding officer took a long draft and then wiped his mouth with the back of his hand.

"So tell me, for it has just occurred to me at this late

stage, how is it that this tavern even exists? How does it get its supplies? I notice it is stocked with wine as well as ale. The first could surely not come from any officer's private stocks, for I would know it. And the latter, well, we do not have the hops."

Fitzwilliam hoped this wasn't a misleading question, but felt he could at least show willing by giving a full and honest answer.

"Quite so, Colonel. But where's there a will, there's a way. The supply ships bring in a few sacks and the occasional barrel."

"The Portuguese did the same," added Donahoe.

"I was lead to believe that all stores were accounted for," said the Colonel.

"As the de facto Quartermaster of the regiment, I can assure every store is accounted for. These are goods transported on a purely independent arrangement," added Fitzwilliam, trying to be helpful.

"Indeed, Mister Fitzwilliam. I have no doubt." Harley studied his mug, swirled it around and took another drink. "If I was staying I might have more energy to look into this. But…"

That caught Fitzwilliam by surprise. *If he was staying?*

"Sir, you are leaving?"

"That I am. Time to go home. Time for a change. We have a new Governor, Fitzwilliam, so there are new ideas, new thoughts at how best to manage things here. You'll no doubt be informed in due course, but I am stepping down from command of the regiment." A wry smile played across his lips. "Such that it is."

"You are back to England?"

"Yes," said Harley brightly. "Back to England. Something I am earnestly looking forward to. Now then, Mister Fitzwilliam…James. With my departure I know full well that I am discharging any sense of responsibility towards you. So it will be in your best interest to establish yourself as a man of use within the new regime. You have already helped yourself in that regard. You have proven to be a brave fighter with a concern for the men. It has earned you some credit. Do not squander it."

"No, Colonel." Fitzwilliam felt a small degree of uncertainty. Whilst his patronage was minimal, it had been useful to know Harley. Now he had no one to call an ally.

"When do you leave?" he asked.

"In the morning. My staff are packing as we speak, as are Colonel Farrell's. He and a number of other officers are leaving alongside Peterborough. Orders and dispositions have already been passed from the Governor. You will no doubt receive them at the morning muster. Do try to make it."

"Yes, Sir. I will make every effort."

Harley placed his mug on the countertop.

"Well."

He looked up and smiled at Fitzwilliam.

"Good luck to you."

"And you," replied Fitzwilliam.

The Colonel nodded and walked out of the Tavern and Fitzwilliam's life. He felt quite sad, if the truth be known. There were few, if any, left with this army who had any fond remembrance of his father. It felt like it was becoming something new, a different beast from the one he had grown up with, one in which he had yet to establish his place. He had been pleased with his performance in the disastrous engagement with the Moors. He had certainly established himself as a fair fighter. That would hold him in good stead with the men, he was sure. It would get him some respect where it truly mattered. He hoped Siobhan recognised that, he did not wish her to think of him as some kind of…well, some effete Englishman. God knew there were enough of them around here.

*

Drummond smiled and sipped from his glass, gazing benevolently across the gathered garrison officers as they waited in the mess. The new Governor, Lord Teviot, had called them all to dine with him on the first night of his tenure. He watched as the Governor made his rounds of the various groups and cliques. He was dressed smartly, as etiquette demanded, but his garb was in no way overly extravagant or expressive. His clothes sat well on him and he had retained a lean frame that bespoke his reputation as a professional soldier. He smiled easily and joked with those he spoke to as he mingled.

"What do you think of him?" asked Fitzwilliam.

"Hmm. He is younger than the old Governor."

"Which means?"

"It means he has not grown soft or forgotten what it is to fight."

"Ah, I see what you mean."

"You know he was the new Governor of Dunkirk? Right before the King sold it to France? I would imagine he intends to seize this opportunity."

"And that would be what?"

"James, we have just lost a sizeable portion of our able-bodied men. For all intents and purposes, we cower behind our walls."

"You paint a fine picture of us," grumbled Fitzwilliam.

"Tell me that I am mistaken then," Drummond smiled. "No? I take your scowl as consent."

"He's coming," warned Fitzwilliam.

"Gentlemen, I see you two skulking in the corner. Is there a reason for that?" asked Teviot, an easy smile on his face as he joined them.

"Ah, we don't get to come to this sort of gathering too often, my lord," replied Fitzwilliam.

"Speak for yourself. I get invited to these all the time," sniffed Drummond.

"Gentlemen, please. I imagine I am talking to Lieutenant Drummond and Ensign Fitzwilliam?"

"We have that honour, my lord," said Drummond, bowing slightly.

"Captain Witham has recounted the events of our engagement with the Moors. There was precious little that was good to take from that. However, you both distinguished yourselves. Lieutenant Drummond, you showed presence of mind and held your men together. When an officer keeps a cool head under fire, their men are more likely to stand their ground. And that turns the fight in your favour." Teviot, his face now sterner, turned to Fitzwilliam. "And you, Mister Fitzwilliam. It seems that you do not lack for bravery. I imagine you are the man to lead a charge and spit in the face of the enemy, eh? Just remember, you are no good to your men dead. Courage is a necessity but leadership requires you to know when and who to sacrifice. That includes yourself."

Fitzwilliam looked decidedly uncomfortable. Drummond could have sworn his friend was actually embarrassed.

"Yes, Sir. I will bear that in mind."

"Good," Teviot's face softened. "Now I also hear you two have set yourselves up as freelance innkeepers."

"Hardly, Sir, we just happened to have secured ourselves very favourable lodgings," replied Drummond.

"Indeed. Normally I would question the matter. However, when on campaign it is often the case that the headquarters are housed in a hostelry. They can be found in every locale and have the necessary accoutrements to ensure a comfortable stay. So, in this instance, I say well done. Do not be surprised if I pay you a visit. It amuses me somewhat that one of the few drinking dens in this town is kept under your watchful eyes."

"We do our best to avoid trouble, Sir," said Fitzwilliam, trying to sound as sincere as he could.

Teviot gave him an appraising look.

"Quite. Now gentlemen, please enjoy my hospitality. But not too much. I will be explaining to you all my dispositions early tomorrow morning and it would not be wise to miss it with a sore head."

They nodded and bowed as Teviot moved on towards another batch of officers.

Fitzwilliam played with his tunic collar.

"What do you think?"

"He seems to know what he his is about. Very sure of himself," replied Drummond. In truth, he was far more impressed than he expected to be. This new Governor knew his business in a way that Peterborough never had.

"Did you not think he was a tad disapproving?"

"Of what?"

"Of me, Drummond! Gods, man. Do you deliberately set out to confound me?"

"I'm sorry, James," said Drummond with a grin. "You are far too easy sometimes. I know what you mean but I wouldn't worry about it. You've got recognition. That is no bad thing. Peterborough was friendly enough, though a little aloof. Our new Governor will take more of an interest, I believe."

"I wonder if that is a good thing," Fitzwilliam mused.

*

Captain Cobb stood off to one side, sipping idly at the glass of port he held in his left hand. His right rested on the pommel of his sword. Many of the officers had eschewed weapons for the evening, but he would brook no such consideration. A soldier should never be unarmed. He had learned that lesson the hard way. As a young lad of sixteen he had been bivouacking with other Parliamentarian troops when the cavalry of Prince Rupert had struck. It was the night before Naseby and they had all been convinced that the land surrounding them was clear of Royalists. He'd been sat round the fire with the other lads, sipping ale and joking about the day ahead, convinced of the victory they would earn with God's favour and Cromwell's endless training. Young and cocky the lot them. When the riders came crashing into their camp, most of their weapons were stacked a few feet away, or left under canvas. They lost dozens of men before the cavalry was driven off. Cobb had been lucky. He had his life and a permanent reminder of his foolishness. He ran a finger down the jagged scar on his cheek. Where had the sentries been that night? As drunk as the rest of them. Another lesson. Never trust anyone to your defence but yourself. He had taken those lessons with him through ten years of service under Cromwell, the Lord Protector, fighting in the New Model Army. He had fought against the Irish when they had risen against Parliament after Charles' execution, then he had gone with Cromwell and his Protectorate army to Scotland and chased Charles II and his army of northern renegades into the heart of England until finally defeating him at Worcester. And still they couldn't put the bastard down. And in the end Cromwell had died, the Protectorate failed and the Monarchy had lived. After every battle they had won, after every engagement they had been victorious, they had lain waste to Britain and fought beyond its shores to end the tyranny of the monarchy. And still it had come back. It had driven Cobb away to fight as a mercenary in France, serving under Teviot for a time. Now look where he was. In a backwater on a dark continent, doing the bidding of the very monarchy he had sworn to destroy.

"You look thoughtful," said Teviot.

Cobb shook his head; he hadn't noticed the man walk up to him.

"Oh, I am sorry, your lordship. I was deep in thought."

"Permit me a guess as to the subject. I would imagine you are thinking about the old days and how the officer class is not worthy of command?" said the Governor, smiling.

Cobb grunted.

"Sir, the officer class has never been up to much consideration. Unless you count the New Model. And of course those like you, Sir. Professional men who know their business."

"I shall take that compliment gracefully, Captain." Teviot took a sip from his glass then moved his hand to take in the gathering. "And yet here you are. A self-made man, risen through the ranks and now standing as an officer in the King's army. Are you not now one of these very men who you so despise?"

"Nothing like them, Sir," said Cobb, a harsh, bitter tone to his voice. "You and me, we learnt our trade, earned our rank. Fighting in the civil war and fighting on the mainland against all comers."

"And that is why I am pleased that you have joined

this enterprise, Captain," said Teviot. "But you must try and reach an accommodation with our new fellows. They are not all bad."

Cobb huffed.

"I will do my best, of course. I know my duty," he flicked his head. "Who is that young fool dressed like a rake? He stands out like a Frenchman in a field of Spanish."

Teviot raised an eyebrow but did not turn.

"You no doubt refer to young Fitzwilliam. You two should get on famously. I fear he has little love for the proper comportment of one's duty and a lively disrespect for the articles of good conduct. Also a real scrapper by all accounts."

"I'll have no patience with any man who cannot follow orders or display good discipline. They are liable to get men killed."

"Then perhaps you should take him under your wing instead?"

"He a Royalist?"

"His father fought in Europe for Charles, yes."

"Then he had best stay out of my way."

Teviot looked at him sternly.

"Cobb. Do you regret your decision to come to Tangier? To take up your commission in the King's army?"

Cobb shrugged.

"What else could I do?"

Teviot nodded.

"I understand. I need you. I need your experience, if we are to take the initiative."

"You have it, my lord."

Teviot nodded again, although doubt remained clear in his eyes.

"Then I shall see you tomorrow at the briefing. Goodnight, Cobb."

Cobb stood to attention and bowed.

Teviot clapped him on the back and moved off.

He had not lied to the Governor. He did not regret his decision. He had wanted to return to the fold of the Army. It was not the one he had grown up in, but there were still those who remembered Cromwell and what he did for them. Cobb was getting old. He didn't have too many years of fighting left in him, so he may as well live them out in the only home he had ever known. And he'd be damned if he'd let the Army become a haven for Royalist lackeys who knew nothing about proper soldiering. He looked the young fool in the corner up and down. Fitzwilliam was it? Bearded, hair tied back and shirt open at the neck. He would expect that from a country yokel or a German mercenary. Not from an officer. Soldiers had to look up to their leaders not think them a joke. Yes, he would have to put that one in his place.

12 May 1663
Upper Castle

"Good morning to you all!"

Teviot strode into the main hall of the castle briskly and stood post by the large briefing table. He was dressed in military garb, his redcoat looking slightly worn around the edges, a sword belted to his side.

"Forgive me for being a little late but I have been out surveying the land." To prove the point, Johnson, looking slightly harassed, followed him in and placed himself at the back of the hall.

Teviot looked around at the gathered throng. All of the officers had been gathered together, leaving Sergeants to manage the security of the town. There was insufficient seating for everyone so instead he stepped behind a table, hopped onto a chair and then the tabletop.

"You'll no doubt note that our numbers are somewhat thinned. I will be frank with you. The garrison is neither what it was nor indeed what it should to be. We have lost men to sickness and strife. The regiments are woefully under strength and we have too many officers to command them. As we speak, a number of your colleagues have elected to return home." Mainly thanks to Teviot's own design. He needed to remove the old guard, those who had failed.

"I have therefore decided that the garrison will reorganise. There will now be only two regiments. I shall take direct command of the first and largest, while Colonel Fitzgerald will command a second regiment, smaller in number, charged with the internal security and infrastructure of the garrison. This will take effect immediately. My staff will commence the work of reinforcing and reallocating manpower and materiel where necessary." He halted once more and took note of reactions. Some surprise, a little dismay and a fair deal of shifting in place and sidelong glances at one another. Good, they were starting to understand.

"I hereby issue a proclamation. There will be no more inappropriate behaviour from my officers. Gambling and drinking will be moderated. Any officer who is impoverished, in debt or in no fit state to conduct their duties, is of no use to me or the army. There will be no duelling, no quarrels over inconsequential matters. Spread the word. I will suffer no foolishness. We save our energy for the enemy. From now on we will be far more aggressive in our dealings with the Moors. Our action has been timid and ill conceived. Our foe has the lie of the land, room to manoeuvre and most importantly his morale has grown. We have allowed ourselves to become besieged. And all of you should know that no siege can be sustained. There is no relief force coming. Either they root us out or we dissuade them from even trying," he paused for effect and smiled. "I favour the latter option!" This brought a few chuckles.

"Men, from today we take the fight to the enemy. This Guyland and his Moors will learn to respect and fear us. We will show them that English iron, forged and tempered in the white heat of battle, will not bend or break. This place is now part of His Majesty's realm, and will be so for as long as we have breath to hold it. Long live the King!"

A gleeful roar went up as the gathered officers bellowed out the declaration. Teviot nodded. This was the easy part. Now he had to turn enthusiasm into action.

*

"Ah, the heroes of the great sortie!" declared Fairborne. "I see you gentlemen have elected to stay here for the great endeavour?"

"We wouldn't miss it for the world, Sir," replied Drummond.

"Aye, besides I haven't finished with the Moor yet," added Fitzwilliam.

Fairborne shook his head. "Lad, you remind me of me. All piss and vinegar. But you've got a fair right hook and bravery to match. Good man. We'll need men to scrap it up a bit with the local lads. Our boys have been far too worried about those scimitars. Let's get the Moors worried about that bloody great hammer on your back."

Fitzwilliam grinned. It was nice to meet someone who actually recognised his talents.

"Now, to business." He looked down upon a ledger running a finger along a list of names. Fitzwilliam tried to tilt his head to catch what was written. Against each name appeared to be an assignment but the writing was so spidery he could make little sense of it. "Right then, Lieutenant Drummond?"

"Sir."

"No, incorrect. Captain Drummond. You have the honour to be the Governor's new adjutant."

Fitzwilliam watched his friend's face drop in open-mouthed confusion.

"Um, what?" he replied, in an unusual display of ineloquence.

"Close your mouth, lad. You heard me. You made a good impression in the fight. Cool head, kept your men under control. Colonel Harley recommended you. Well done." He looked at the list once more, "Fitzwilliam, where are you?"

Fitzwilliam's mind raced with anticipation. He had acquitted himself well in the fight as well. The Major had said so himself. Perhaps command of a proper company?

"Ah, here you are. Officer in charge of the Lines."

"What does that mean?" asked Fitzwilliam, a cloud already starting to form across his previous sunny countenance.

"Just that. You'll be in charge of the security of the Lines. Under Fitzgerald. Make sure that none of the Moor gets in. Perfect for a scrapper like you."

"It's the damned night watch again, isn't it?" Fitzwilliam said with anger in his voice. He couldn't believe it. He had already done his turn in the Lines and damn near been killed for his trouble.

Fairborne's face hardened. "That is your charge and your responsibility. Better men than you have deemed it an appropriate role. It would behove you well to not question that." He glared at the ensign for a moment before giving a conciliatory half-smile. "Now, Fitzwilliam, I know what you want, you want command of a fighting force. Well, you will get that when we see some restraint in your actions. We need a cool head in large actions.

They aren't the same as brawls. Command, control and discipline will always win out even against larger forces," he tapped his forehead. "Think about the Romans. Top notch and vicious bastards when they needed to be. Your face is known, young man. That helps. People will be watching to see what you do with your charge. Do it well and things will come good for you. Right, that's it, be off with you. I have a great deal more to do today to get this army ready to fight!"

As the two men walked away from the castle, Fitzwilliam kicked a small stone and watched it bounce off a wall, knocking chips off of it as it did so.

"Bloody sentry duty. That's what I get. Where's the justice?"

"In charge of sentry duty," corrected Drummond.

"Oh, thank you, thank you very much, Adjutant. Forgive my misunderstanding."

"I'm just saying. You are not just one officer of many. You are now responsible for holding our first defensive line."

"Oh, you mean the one that the Moors just happen to have unfettered access to right now?"

Drummond tapped a finger to his nose.

"And just what do you think Teviot is planning on doing right now? The first thing will be to claim back the Lines. And he will be mightily displeased if it's lost again."

Fitzwilliam shook his head. "I just can't help but feel this is will be a dead end at best or a fool's errand at worst. I could lose what little of a name I have left."

Drummond gave him a surprised look.

"My goodness, things are changing. I've never known you be quite so concerned about your reputation. At least not in this regard."

Fitzwilliam sniffed and drew himself up.

"This is the first time that I have had an opportunity to show what I can do. I'm not a fool, Rupert. I know full well that I've little credit with most of the officers here. There's scant little I can do about that, and that's little more than I care to either. But perhaps I can still garner some respect from those who matter."

His friend smiled indulgently.

"Whilst some might argue with me, I think you will find that hope has already begun to take form. I've heard it said that some of the men have talked well of you in the last two adventures you've been on. They like the fact you're a fighter. You can use that. It will do nothing for most of the officers here, but if you can get your men to love you, it would go better for you in any engagement. And there are some out there, myself and perhaps our new Governor, who would believe that to be no bad thing."

Fitzwilliam looked thoughtfully at his friend for a moment and let loose a bark of laughter. He was right, perhaps that was the way to go. It certainly played to his strengths.

"Very well, Rupert. I heartily accept your viewpoint. Now, if you'll excuse me, I have to report to regimental headquarters, if I am to command the Lines, I want some say in how to go about it."

13 May 1663
Upper Castle

"Gentlemen, I do not doubt the training of our men and I acknowledge the drilling into them of discipline under fire. But what is apparent is that our foe does not conduct war under those terms." Teviot spoke from the end of the long table in the dining hall.

Seated along either side were his staff and senior commanders, summoned to attend a council of war. "The enemy does not fight battles like those we have become accustomed to in Europe. This is Africa, a dark land with mysteries and marvels. And war is conducted very much like it was for our ancestors, when King Henry led his men to victory at Agincourt. There men fought with the volley of arrows, and with cold steel, sword and shield." He lifted his hands up. "Do not worry my friends, I don't intend to issue out longbows and bucklers to our men!" This brought some gentle laughter from the gathered officers. Drummond sat to the left and rear of the Governor, observing the goings on with a detached eye. Yes, he was a part of proceedings but had little to do with the policy of matters.

Before him lay a large sketch map of Tangier and its surrounding hinterlands.

"There are three stages to the plan I am proposing. The first requires us to recapture the land lost to us. It is high time we brought about an increase of morale. God knows the men need it. Establishing our rule over the terrain before the walls will begin that process. The second is the continuation of building the outer works. These fortifications will be the lynchpin. Major Johnson? I have further work for you. The third and final part is to engage the enemy. Fight him and beat him." He paused, noticing the shift in the air, the silent thoughts of his officers were as clear as day to him, he expected as much. "I know, what you are all saying to yourselves, how can that be so? We have a depleted force, sapped of manpower and spirit. We cannot engage the enemy. We need more men. We need more time!" Teviot grinned and slammed his palm down upon the map. "I tell you, gentlemen, there is no better cure for such ill than a victory. Nothing short of that will do. We can huddle behind defences, safe and sound, assured that no Moorish weapon can breach the wall. And all the while our foe will surround us, and point and laugh and be satisfied that we are caught in a cage. Rats in a trap. Prisoners by choice and they are our jailers."

He pointed at the men nearest to him, those that stood highest in the chain of command. He looked at each man in turn, holding their gaze, making sure they understood.

"Gentlemen, it will not do. We will fight them. The men will have their victory, their pride and their morale. And the moor will know that they no longer dictate terms. That this is English territory, the King's land. The redcoat will walk where he will on this soil and no Berber will be in any doubt. To test us is to invite a bloody and bitter response. My dear colleagues. We shall fight." He set his face, a deliberate, grim smile playing on his lips and paused once more. There were nods of agreement, shoulders were pulled back, and men met his look with sparks of determination flashing in their eyes. He was pleased. Now for the next step.

"So, men, to business. I will show you on this map how my plan will unfold."

As men clustered around him, Drummond stood back and watched over the gathering. In his new position he had been fortunate to have heard much of the new governor's plans already. They were, if not audacious, at the very least considered and clever enough that he drew confidence from them. That was in and of itself an unusual and rare thing. Perhaps they would turn their fortunes around with this man leading them. But it would come at a price. They were truly going to war.

1 June 1663
St Catherine's Fort

Johnson stood above the rampart and nodded in satisfaction. After the disaster of the last engagement he had been uncertain whether his services would not be better served in an undertaking closer to home. Perhaps in England? Or even in the colonies of the Indies. Jamaica sounded intriguing. Granted, these places were further away from home but they lacked the immediacy of impending attack and the constant battle for supply. Nothing more than a few pirates and the Spanish to worry about.

As it was, the Earl had been quick to press him back into service. Once more the mole was forgotten, as his energies were directed with great vigour into the construction of this new redoubt. Its foundation was the blockhouse known as Whitehall, but Teviot wished it be a far grander affair. This work was but one of five new forts under his charge to create. Though in its prime position, some three hundred yards in front of the main gate, it was the prize, the keystone. And it was to be renamed St Catherine's Fort, acknowledging its close relationship to Catherina Port. It was with no small measure of urgency that he ordered those around him to spare no expense in the solidity of its structure or indeed the energy of their labour. It would be of no surprise to him if the Berbers had not taken the measure of this new enterprise and were not now planning an attack on the works. It would be a sore loss to the garrison if it failed. He had remarked as much to the night commander of the Lines. The jovial and ill-mannered man had laughed heartily at this, claiming that the Moor had already learnt to steer clear of the Lines at night for fear of the 'Scottish Wildman'. That last portion was at least true. The young officer had gained a reputation amongst his men of being aggressive and motivated in equal measure. He positively relished the chance to hunt down any nocturnal interlopers amongst the English trenches and positions. And it was certainly true that the Berbers had seemed to curtail their activities of late. Johnson sighed and put a hand up to his eyes, scanning the high ground into the distance. Yes, there it was. A flash, a gleam of metal reflected by the sun's rays. They were still out there and they were indeed watching. While he was pleased by the progress the fort was making, he just wished that the damn thing could go up quicker.

*

On the crest of a hill, facing onto the uneven ground leading to Tangier, Ghailan lowered his viewing scope. A fine piece, engraved with legendary beasts of the sea and other mystical symbols, it had come to him as booty from the corsairs. He handed it back to his servant and pushed himself off the ground. He was annoyed that it was required of him to return to this place. He had hoped that the Englishmen would have learnt their lesson. It would appear not. He lacked the naval strength to blockade them so he must keep them contained by land. Once more the English had resumed their attempts at extending and consolidating their territory. The new fortifications were taking shape swiftly and he could see that these new ones were far more substantial. By the size of them they would become true blockhouses, designed to withstand direct assaults. It was clear that to allow this to go unchallenged would be folly. The strength and confidence of the English would grow, and with it their arrogance. It would cost much if he were required to deal with a newly complete defensive line as well as the walls themselves. He muttered a short beseechment to Allah that he would be permitted to end this affront. Once done, he beckoned one of his waiting officers forward.

"They have had three weeks working on this, have they not?"

The officer dipped his head.

"Yes my lord, they have moved quickly and recovered well."

"Yes. There seems a new energy within them."

"Our scouts witnessed an exchange of men shortly before their industry commenced. Perhaps they have a new leader now?"

Ghailan chewed the inside of his lip.

"Yes, it is possible. And if so, then we must move quickly as well. We must test this new commander," he raised his hand and pointed towards the redoubt taking shape in front of the main gate. "There is where we must apply our force. We take that position and we command their lines."

"But master, will they not just pound us with their

cannon?"

Ghailan smiled.

"Quite so. And why would we stop them? Let them take destroy their own handiwork. It will do their spirit much ill to see it."

The officer nodded, "A good plan. We should attack soon then?"

Ghailan shook his head.

"Not yet. We do not have enough men here to be sure of it. There are only three hundred swords to call upon. We must wait for more to come. I have already sent word. A further three hundred will arrive soon. It is no bad thing. I would prefer they waste more of their time on this. Let them continue to build it so that it is sturdy and strong. Let them build until it is almost complete. It will make the taking of it sweeter. When we have the fort they must send men to retake it or destroy it. Either option will lend the advantage to us."

He took one more lingering look at Tangier then turned away. He had other matters to attend to. He needed to cement the rule of his chosen patron and in so doing gain favour and ascendancy. He had no desire to return to this place again. He would stay until the job was done and the English were finished.

"We wait. I am tired and thirsty from my ride. Come with me and let us refresh ourselves."

"As you say, my lord," said the officer, bowing deeply.

8 June 1663
Catherina Port

Fitzwilliam yawned as he approached the main gate. His duty as commander of the night watch had begun three weeks ago but he had yet to find his daily routine. That wasn't strictly true of course. His routine was there, just a little uneven. It depended on what time he started his early evening drinks downstairs. He tried to match the times when Drummond was likely to finish with the Governor. That was not a precise science as Drummond's role as Adjutant meant he was often required to work late into the night as their leaders plotted and planned. So in the true spirit of friendship, Fitzwilliam would stay as long as he would dare before he was required to inspect and mount the guard. That inevitably meant having to take a drink or two, but he prided himself on never being incoherent. Although he was not sure if it could be said of his men. When they had first started out, his force of twenty had been a rum lot indeed, yet there was a small core that seemed solid and trustworthy. That lad Simon Swallow and his older partner, Jacob Blair, were a pair in point. Occasionally Swallow was far too smart mouthed for his own good but Blair seemed to keep him in line. As for the others, a couple of swift punches to the gut had cured two of the worst drunkards of their lack of professionalism. It wasn't done for officers to have to administer their own field discipline, but the sergeant of the guard had courteously looked the other way and Blair and Swallow had quickly thrown their support behind the action. His reputation, it appeared, had been given another boost, which was all to the good.

He emerged into the square that served the gate to find his band of men gathered in two rows, muskets slung and each man issued with a hanger, of better quality than they were used to wielding, courtesy of Drummond. As Adjutant he was keen to not show any favouritism, but he couldn't argue with Fitzwilliam's assessment that the night guard did not have the luxury of daylight to see their enemies coming. His adventures had already more than adequately proven the point. The lads needed an edge when it came down to fighting in the Lines themselves. And if the Berbers could wield their blades with aplomb and infamy, it was about time they felt some English steel. Drummond had sardonically added a comment about Scottish spunk that Fitzwilliam had chosen to take in good grace. He straightened his shoulders, adjusted his weapon belt and picked up his pace, walking smartly towards his men.

He saw that another group of soldiers shared the space, at least three times the size of his command. They were arrayed in good order and appeared to be undergoing an inspection.

"Evening, Sir," said Fitzwilliam's sergeant, the man he had first encountered during Peterborough's failed sortie across the Lines.

"And to you, Sergeant White."

"Lads are ready when you are."

Fitzwilliam nodded but his gaze followed the small group conducting the inspection opposite.

"Who are they, Sergeant?"

"Them? Not sure, Sir. Marched in about fifteen minutes ago. Started their inspection soon as they were at rest. I got the men in position, thought it best to show willing, whilst we were waiting for you, Sir."

It did occur to Fitzwilliam that there was a thinly veiled comment regarding his tardiness. He ought to take affront but, as he directed most of his attention towards the inspection, he couldn't find it in him to disagree with White.

"Hmm, yes. Good thinking, Sergeant." The inspection group, consisting of three men, had now reached the end of the rearmost line; two of them were clearly officers, their manner and disposition obvious, even in the deepening gloom.

"They are our men, Sir, but I don't recognise the officer in charge, must be one of those what come in with the Governor," added White, helpfully.

"Right. Well, they're not here for the sake of it, but I'm not sure why I wasn't briefed about them. Look to the men, Sergeant, I'm just going to be a moment." He wanted to know who these fellows were and what they were about.

"Right you are, Sir."

The inspection was ending as Fitzwilliam drew near. He could spy a captain's rank upon the jacket of the middle man. To his left the second officer was a lieutenant and the third man was a sergeant. The group stood quietly and watched his approach.

Fitzwilliam doffed his hat and bowed slightly.

"Good evening, sirs. I thought it best to introduce myself."

He leaned back up and smiled at the trio.

The captain, a man well into his middle age, frowned and turned to the subaltern.

"Lieutenant, if you please, lead the men out. I shall be along momentarily."

"As you please, Sir," replied the lieutenant with a slight tilt to his head. The sergeant saluted and joined the officer in chivvying the troops out of the gate. The captain watched them go then turned to regard Fitzwilliam. As no more words were forthcoming and feeling slightly at a loss he began to introduce himself.

"I am Ensign-"

"Fitzwilliam," finished the captain. "Yes, I know."

"Ah right, then you know I'm commander of the night watch."

"Tonight you are not," replied the older man tersely.

"I have no orders to the contrary."

"No, I'm sure you do not. The Governor gave this order two hours ago. If you had been present at the briefing you might now have a greater awareness of the situation," the captain sneered. "And your place it in."

Fitzwilliam felt his face redden and his heart begin to race. Who was this fellow and why did he have such an ill-disposed manner? He studied the man closely. A man surely in his forties, he had a hard face, and a solid looking body. A scar ran down his left cheek tapering into his upper lip, the end hidden behind a thick moustache, the man also sported a thin goatee, as was the fashion. There was a palpable sense of competence and no nonsense about the man. Fitzwilliam felt with a keen prescience there would be little common ground between the two of them.

"Well, I found myself otherwise engaged," he tried another, hopeful smile. "Perhaps you will do me the honour of apprising me of my orders?"

The captain shrugged. "There is little honour to be had in that. But, so that you are clear, tonight I will take charge of the Lines. The Governor has deemed it necessary to reinforce our strongpoints, in the expectation of enemy action against them. He believes the Moors will be looking to counter our expansion once again."

"Then I am to be under your command, Captain, ah...?"

"Cobb. Yes. However, your dispositions remain unhindered. You men will conduct their normal business and routine, you will monitor that. Your force will continue to guard the Lines and keep a sharp watch. My men will in place purely as a reaction force. As such they will only maintain a sentry in their specific positions."

"And their positions?"

"My headquarters will be in St Catherine's. The bulk of the men will also be stationed there. Smaller parties will be situated in the other forts and blockhouses. "

Fitzwilliam nodded. "Then that is clear. It would seem that we are predicting a strike at your location then, Sir."

"That is what his lordship believes."

"So in the event of an attack, you wish my men to reinforce you?"

"No, I do not wish that at all, Ensign. You will tell your men to hold their ground. The enemy may strike at more than one location, or seek to circle round our positions. If they see their route is contested, they may well reconsider."

"That may go hard on my men, Sir. They are too few

to hold off a concerted effort."

Cobb grunted. He smiled at Fitzwilliam but there was no warmth in his eyes.

"I understand you are a brawler, Sir. You enjoy a challenge, like taking the enemy on one on one, yes?"

Fitzwilliam tilted his head to one side and shrugged.

"Call it my Scottish blood."

Cobb laughed. Its timbre was like a bark; short and mean.

"No doubt. Your ill discipline has earned you some infamy. You have far too much passion. An officer's role is to lead his men by example, to show a steady hand, a mastery of his emotion. Cromwell always claimed such men were the backbone of the New Model, men who understood what duty meant."

Fitzwilliam could not help but start at the mention of Cromwell. The events of the last few months had caused most men to move on from their past allegiances.

"You fought for Parliament?" he asked, realising as he did so that no good was likely to come from the question.

"Yes, Ensign. I was in the pikes before you were naught but a twinkle in your father's eye. I was there when Charles was finally defeated at Naseby. By God, that was a good day."

"And yet you find yourself serving his son. That must grate." That got a reaction all right. Cobb's face turned ugly. He seemed to swell up in front of Fitzwilliam, violence radiating from him.

"Look to your men, Ensign. Try not to fuck it up. Understood?" he growled softly through clenched teeth.

"Yes, Sir." Fitzwilliam saluted and turned about as smartly as he could. That hit home, he thought. He walked stiffly back to his men, feeling the captain's eyes burning a hole into the back of his skull.

"Ready for inspection now, Sir?" asked Sergeant White, casting a sidelong glance behind Fitzwilliam.

"Yes, Sergeant. I believe I am."

As he made his way to the first line and begun casting his eye over the man before him, he was acutely aware that he really wasn't in the mood. He had a feeling he might well be in for a long night.

*

At the fourth bell after midnight, mist had come rolling in across the Lines. It was an unusual sight; no one had seen its like since the garrison's arrival. Men began to predict the worst, looking out with dry lips and straining eyes into the surrounding scrub. Fitzwilliam and Sergeant White made constant sweeps of the trenches, ensuring the men stayed alert but not so highly strung that they shot at the first shadow they caught sight of. He could really do without Cobb finding a reason to question his ability to command the watch. Since beginning the shift, he had reported into the man at every bell, the very model of efficiency. He had apprised him of the disposition of the men and anything he felt worthy of note, not that there was much. Cobb had nodded perfunctorily then turned his back on him each time. Their audience at an abrupt end, Fitzwilliam took the time to check over the Cobb's men. Each man carried a full load of ammunition and more to spare. They lay low behind the parapets of the fort, most of them dozing, their muskets close but out of sight. Only one or two sentries were visible to the front, and, as Fitzwilliam had done in previous nights, they were positioned behind specially constructed wooden firing ports. Their vision was slightly restricted but it meant their presence would be harder to spot from any observers, hidden as they were within the shadows.

Now, as the mist started to fall into the trenches, its ghostly tendrils reaching down to the earthen lips of the Lines, Fitzwilliam made his way back to St Catherine's Fort. While he hoped he didn't show it, his own nerves were on tenterhooks. The place was damned spooky. He knew there was a whole continent out there, but he felt claustrophobic, like he was in some sort of enclosed space, its edges just beyond his vision. As he sucked in air through his nose, he looked up into the night sky. Dawn was near. The colour of night was shifting, pink tinges forming at its edges to the east. He looked into the mist, daring himself to find dark shadows flitting with purpose amongst the heaps of rock and scrub. It was so quiet. How could it be so damned quiet? He held himself still. His eyes moving rapidly left to right, then back again, his ears straining. Then, far off to his left, the mist flashed brightly, a ball of light that radiated unevenly as it travelled outwards from its source, then several more appeared, springing into life as quickly as the first flash vanished. Then the sound of wood snapping reached him. But it wasn't wood making that noise. It was just the gunpowder in a score of muskets going off. They were accompanied by the shouts of men and the cries of unseen attackers, hidden somewhere ahead of them.

"Bastards!" he muttered under his breath. The fort was under attack! He ploughed ahead, all attempts at stealth forgotten. He took a sharp bend in the trench before the short run to the entrance of the redoubt. He almost didn't make it. A musket round embedded itself in the earth to the side of him.

"Cease bloody firing!" he cried. "English bloody officer." He continued his forward momentum. Two soldiers jumped out of his way as he crashed past them into the fort proper, ducking as he did so under the lintel that marked the continuation of the fort wall across the trench. All about him was a rage of sound and motion. Men crowded onto the firing steps, shooting then ducking down low to reload as sergeants exhorted their men to load faster, to pick their targets and wait for a clean shot. Others had the benefit of shooting ports, small firing holes cut out of the wooden walls. He saw Cobb's lieutenant straining to see out of one. In his hand he clutched a pistol that he waved around the place with not a care to where it was pointing. He quickly ducked back as a spear embedded itself in the wood next to his position.

"They've got spears!" he shouted in report, not that anyone appeared to be listening. Fitzwilliam spied Cobb standing a little way back from the front of the firing line. His left hand rested on the hilt of his blade, still sheathed, against his left thigh. His right hand was tucked casually into his belt. Fitzwilliam moved quickly to his side.

"Captain?"

Cobb glanced at him before returning his attention to the firefight.

"Yes, Ensign. What is it?"

"Sir. We appear to be under attack."

"Really? Well then get out of my sight and hold the Lines. I am sealing off this fort. No doubt they will try and flank us. So you must stop them. Understood?"

"Yes, Sir," said Fitzwilliam. Oh yes, no nonsense from Cobb.

He turned and ran back towards the rear of the fort. A rude door was already being pushed into place by the two guards he had passed moments before.

"Hold up, coming through!" he cried. They turned to

look at him, their faces strained. "Thank you, gents," he responded as he ducked back under the lintel. He turned and knocked the door. "Close her up." Waiting until he heard the wooden bar fall into place, Fitzwilliam drew his pistols and kept a watch. On hearing the dull clunk of wood hitting the brackets, he kept his head low and retreated at speed back along the trench.

The firing behind him intensified as a ragged cry went up. He turned to look back and through the mist he saw a multitude of shadows rise up from the ground and charge headlong towards the fort. Ye gods, there must be hundreds of them, he thought to himself, struggling to make sense of the picture. New figures kept emerging from the gloom and joining the others in their attack. The Moors really were serious about this. He debated going back to help the defence as the black tide started to edge around the side of the fort. Individual fighters were briefly illuminated as igniting muskets flared and light flashed off raised blades. The fort had been designed with all round defence in mind and more muskets emerged from the ports built into the sidewalls. A volley swept away the encroaching tide, but only momentarily. Those lads were outnumbered, by an order of magnitude. He swiftly rejected his initial impulse to foolhardy bravery and instead proceeded along the trench towards the next fortified position another fifty yards away. Inside he found two of his own guard force, backs to one another, one looking to the front, one to the rear, their muskets raised in the high port position.

"At ease, men!" he ordered briskly as the man nearest him gave a small yelp on seeing his hasty arrival.

"Sorry, Sir. Thought you might be one of them. We're trying to keep a watch every which way. No telling where the buggers might come from," said the soldier.

"That's true, but have you seen anything? Any probes, shapes, shadows?"

The second soldier shook his head. "Nothing, Sir. Just the fight yonder. We've seen nowt but you."

Fitzwilliam nodded. "Then they seem to be concentrating their efforts there. That won't last. If they can't get in from the front, they'll try the back. Right, you," he pointed towards the first soldier. "Head on up the way. Gather in all of the lads and send them back here. And ask the garrison of Pole to join us as well. Seems to me like St Catherine's is the one they are after, not much point them missing out on the fun."

"Yes, Sir!"

"And try not to shoot anyone by accident!" he shouted as the soldier doubled away.

"So what are we going to do in the meantime, Sir?" asked the remaining soldier.

"We are going to wait here and see what happens."

"Fair enough, Sir."

As the minutes passed, Fitzwilliam continued to monitor the fight. The sky was continuing to lighten and the mist, whilst clinging gamely to the ground, was not becoming any thicker. The initial charge he had witnessed had been repulsed. This he could divine from the simple fact that the fort continued to keep up a healthy rate of fire. The Moors had started their assault at the perfect moment; when true dawn was still some time away and the fort's defenders were at a low ebb of alertness. It was now a matter of whether the English were able to avoid casualties. If they started losing men, the balance would shift in favour of the tribesmen. Behind him his guard force had trickled in. He took a quick count. Eight men, no nine, including his runner, who arrived breathless from his mission. That was everyone.

"Private, where are the rest of the bloody men?"

The soldier shook his head as he gulped in air.

"Sorry, Sir. They refused to move. Said their orders were to hold and defend. They'd only listen to the captain."

Fitzwilliam grimaced but forwent the litany of curses he wished to utter.

"Very well. Now, who do we have?" He scanned about the faces. Sergeant White was on the far side of the fort so whom could he rely on? That left..."Corporal Longshore?"

"Sir?" A slightly built man with greying blond hair that hung like string from beneath his hat stepped forward.

"You are my second in command."

"Right you are, Sir."

"Good. Now listen all of you. The Moors don't like the fact that we're building our forts. In fact they'd quite like to get their hands on one. And St Catherine's is it."

"Good for us then, Sir. Means they won't be coming round this way," said Corporal Longshore.

"No, hardly good at all, I'm afraid. Because even if they aren't coming this way yet they are going to start thinking about it soon enough. They want to get into that fort and the easiest way is from the rear. The fort is not fully complete yet. It has little cover to the top, and the back wall is but half built. They'll make a try for it, swing wide of the muskets and then dart back in."

"Right into the sites of the cannon, Sir," said another soldier.

"You expect our cannon to let fly a volley, in the gloom, to pound away at an enemy that is sitting right on top of our own position? And what do you think would happen in those circumstances?"

The soldier shrugged.

"We'd end up blowing our own men to Kingdom come, Sir," stated Longshore.

"Quite right, Corporal. The Moors know we'll destroy the fort if they take it anyway. So there is no choice but to fight it out for possession. Now lads, there is only one way to ensure they don't get their hands on it. We are going to double back from the Lines and work our way round to the rear. When they pass us by and make their charge to engage our boys, we charge them."

"Just us, Sir?" asked Longshore, the doubt plain on his face.

Fitzwilliam grinned. "I'd lay any odds you care to that they'll up and run when they see us coming. They won't like it up 'em. Especially with the Scottish Wildman leading the way."

*

It was another hour before the Moors made their move. Two more frontal assaults had been repulsed and only desultory musket fire suggested there was still a fight going on. From Fitzwilliam's position, some fifty yards back and to the right of the fort, he could not tell what sort of casualties had been taken inside. He did not wish to try and contact them for fear of giving away his position or indeed being shot at by one of the defenders. Dawn was but a short time away now and he did not doubt that this was the last moment for one more throw of the die. He had expected probes to be conducted further out from the range of the fort and so had got a message round to Sergeant White to concentrate the men on his side. If they caught sight of anyone they were to deliver a controlled volley and make as much noise as possible. That way the enemy would think they faced a determined and numerous foe. It would also make Fitzwilliam's previously retired flank far more attractive. He knew it would be the only way to save his command. Neither side would have been strong enough to hold off a hundred screaming Berbers. Whatever flank was hit would have been decimated. At least this way, he hoped to draw them into coming round the unprotected route. Draw them in and spring the trap.

He lay behind a slight fold in the ground, his men scattered around him, their heads kept low. The earth was cool and moist with dew, which he found quite refreshing. He was also growing thirsty. He reached down into his coat pocket and withdrew a small canteen. He pulled the stopper out and took a healthy sized swig of beer. It was cool, almost cold. It put him in mind of Donahoe's cellar. He squinted into the distance whilst absently trying to force the stopper back in.

There had been no volley fire from the right of his position, just the continued uneven series of barks coming from the fort as the defenders kept up a steady rate of fire to discourage the enemy. In the gloom he could see the glow of gunpowder as their enemy returned the favour. It had been, what, almost two hours since the attack had begun? The mist would very soon burn off. Perhaps they wouldn't try for it after all. He couldn't work out whether he was disappointed or not, he had gotten into the mindset for a fight and felt rather let down.

"Sir?" whispered Longshore.

"Hmm?"

"Over there." Longshore pointed to the far left of their position, some thirty yards ahead. A large group of figures were moving quickly to the right, positioning themselves directly to the rear of the fort.

Fitzwilliam smiled.

"All right, everyone. Time to get going. Remember, don't fire until you see the whites of their eyes. Make the shot count," he said quietly. This was it. "On my order," he warned. He felt the change in atmosphere as his men readied themselves for the action, tense and expectant. He felt that small, cold knot of nervousness in his own belly. Some would call it fear. Nothing wrong with that, as long as you didn't let it get the better of you. He raised himself onto his haunches and debated whether to draw his blade. No. Pistols today. He reached down to his belt, taking hold of the handgrips and pulling his flintlocks free. Holding both in the high port he moved his left hand over his right and pulled back on the striker, readying the weapon to fire. He then repeated the action right over left. Balanced on his haunches, he tensed his thighs and pushed up. He heard his men follow suit beside and behind him.

"Alright, lads. Lots of noise now. Let the buggers know we are coming."

Fitzwilliam bellowed, "For the King!"

His men responded with a range of shouts and curses and as one they went for the enemy. They covered the ground swiftly, accelerating all the way. Ahead, the Moors reacted with apparent confusion, their shouts merging with the English battle cries. Fitzwilliam realised, as they closed the distance, that there were rather more of them than he had first thought. It was too late to worry about it now. A Moor reared up in front of him, scimitar held high. Fitzwilliam skidded to a halt and pointed his pistols out before him. He pulled the left trigger. The time it took for the flint to strike the pan and the spark to ignite the powder charge was enough for the tribesman to move to striking range. As his scimitar began its downward slash, the pistol boomed and caught the growling Moor full in the face. The force of the shot threw his head back. The sword lost its forward momentum, falling from the hand and sweeping past Fitzwilliam's shoulder as he dodged away.

His arms were still outstretched and he pivoted towards another target. This one had a spear held at waist height, was moving left to right, seeking to take one of his soldiers in the back. Fitzwilliam tracked the Moor and moving his pistol ahead of the man, fired. His timing and placement was perfect, the ball catching the Moor in his side, the spear falling to the ground as the man spun away into the melee. Fitzwilliam took in the scene of battle. Red-coated soldiers grappled with the black-swathed Moors. Bodies already littered the ground from both sides. He kept his senses alert for danger as he replaced his pistols and reached for his sword. As he did so a great flash of light erupted before him. Out of the mist, musket rounds flew through the air striking men from both sides, the crack of igniting gunpowder following in their wake. Fitzwilliam swore, even as the enemy, flanked on two sides, gave up the ghost and fled the way they had come.

"Cease firing! Cease firing! English. English soldiers here!" he shouted. It must be Sergeant White, but what was the fool thinking? He knew that the rest of them would be in hand-to-hand combat. He should have sent in his men, not fired blindly. Even as he thought this, a command giving the order to stand down emanated from directly ahead. Ah, yes. Now he thought about it, that volley had come from the direction of the fort. White's position was to the right. The fort must have thought the sound of battle was in fact a headlong assault. That was a nice way to show their gratitude.

"Corporal? You still here?"

"Sir," responded Longshore.

"Casualties?"

"Just taking stock now, Sir. Saw one of ours drop from a bullet. Another took one in the arm."

"Right. Carry on." Fitzwilliam sheathed his blade and marched towards the fort. He was angry. He had had everything under control and now he had lost men through friendly fire. Someone was going to get it.

The low earthwork of the redoubt's back came into view. He could see men watching him.

"Ho the fort!" he cried. "So which bloody idiot gave the command to fire? Don't you lot know the difference between English and Moorish? We were shouting loudly enough for you to hear!"

He stomped up onto the top of the mound, folded his arms and glared down at a line of English troops, some of which had the good grace to look embarrassed. "Well?"

"Ensign Fitzwilliam!" He looked up to see Cobb walking toward him. He looked murderous.

"Ensign, get your arse off of my parapet and come here this instant."

Oh hell, now what? Fitzwilliam thought. The cold sensation had returned to his stomach, but this time, it really was unwelcome. He knew what was coming. He looked for a gap between two soldiers and motioned for them to make room. As they moved he leapt down into the fort. He landed heavily, stood, adjusted his belt and blade, and paced over to Cobb, aware that all eyes were upon him.

Cobb stood ramrod straight, his hands, balled into fists, rested on his sides. His face was set in an angry snarl. Fitzwilliam stopped in front of him and saluted. He made sure to make eye contact. He wasn't sure if he showed outwardly but inside he flinched. The man's eyes, dark and hooded, had murder in them.

"Sir, I have to report-" Fitzwilliam began.

"Shut up, Ensign."

"What? I-"

"I said shut up, Ensign," responded Cobb in a quiet voice.

Fitzwilliam closed his mouth and drew his shoulders back, holding himself to attention.

Cobb stepped forward so that their faces were but inches apart.

He stared into the Fitzwilliam' face for several moments, studying him like a predator. Fitzwilliam kept his gaze held high. This was going to go badly.

"What the hell do you think you were doing, boy?" screamed Cobb. Spittle flew from his mouth and sprayed over Fitzwilliam, He reared back as the Captain's hot breath blew into him. "What kind of idiot game were you playing? What part of my orders did you not understand?"

Fitzwilliam couldn't remember the last time he had faced such fury. In normal circumstances it was like water off a duck's back, but this was different. This was actually terrifying.

"Sir, you were going to be flanked. I had no way to tell, you. The fort was already engaged and locked down. So I decided I had to make provision to stop you becoming compromised."

Cobb spat.

"You think I didn't know that? You take me for a fool, boy? You think I didn't plan for that? That I didn't have men in position for such a feint?" He poked his finger into Fitzwilliam's chest, causing him to stagger back. "I have fought in more battles than you have ever dreamed about. I know my business and do not need lessons in war from the likes of you."

Fitzwilliam felt his face redden. It was one thing to be bawled out, but getting physical was not acceptable. He stepped forward, regaining his position.

"Then perhaps you might have told me and saved me the trouble of worrying about you, Sir." he responded angrily.

"I gave you your orders, Ensign. Hold the line. I don't expect to be questioned by subordinates. I expect to be obeyed." Cobb's voice had lowered in tone. Once more he sounded calm and in control. Then he leaned forward and whispered.

"And I don't expect Royalist scum like you to behave any better than you have. Incompetent and arrogant, the lot of you."

Fitzwilliam flushed once more and he balled his own hands into fists. He could feel his body start to shake and it took an effort of will to hold him back. Cobb smiled coldly. He stepped away.

"Ensign. You disobeyed a direct order and put the lives of your men in jeopardy. I shall be making a full report to the Governor. Now return to your men and take care of the casualties. I hope for your sake your actions today have not lost us valuable troops." Cobb motioned him away. "Now go, get out of my sight."

Fitzwilliam, mindful of the silent audience, saluted once more, turned and made his way to the rear. A soldier, face kept purposely low, moved out of his way. He climbed onto the firing step and hauled himself onto the top of the trench. As he walked away, commands were shouted and the fort broke its silence as the soldiers regrouped. Fitzwilliam took a deep breath. Wonderful, just wonderful. Instead of the heroic outcome to the affair he was expecting, he was instead firmly in the sights of a clearly insane Cromwellian and soon to be up for censure in front of the Governor. Things couldn't get much worse. His men stood in a tight knot as they approached him. Longshore stepped forward, a look of empathy on his face.

"Sir?"

"Corporal," sighed Fitzwilliam. "How do we fare?"

"Two wounded, one dead. Private Smith, Sir. As I thought, shot by one of our own by the looks of it."

Fitzwilliam nodded.

"Right. Get the wounded home and find a stretcher for the body. The rest of you go back to your positions. We still have a job to do until we are relieved." He looked up into the morning sky. "Shouldn't be long. I'll go and find Sergeant White."

"Yes, Sir."

Fitzwilliam turned to go.

"Sir?"

"Yes, Corporal?"

"We did a quick count. Reckon we took out ten of them ourselves. Not a bad score."

Fitzwilliam smiled weakly. He didn't have the energy or the impulse to celebrate that fact.

"Yes. Not bad at all." He looked over his command. The men held themselves well, still flushed with their success in battle. "Well done, all of you. Fine work. Carry on."

Longshore saluted and Fitzwilliam nodded in return. He commenced his journey, each step feeling heavier than the last. It was going to be a long day and he felt very bloody tired.

*

Drummond placed the sheet of paper back on to the firm surface of his desk and pinched the bridge of his nose between thumb and forefinger. He squeezed his eyes tight shut then opened them, allowing a few moments for his sight to refocus. He reached across, picked up his quill and dipped it into the inkpot resting to one side. Placing the quill on the bottom of the page, he countersigned the document, his name resting below that of the garrison quartermaster. He withdrew the quill and replaced it back on the desk next to the inkpot. He studied the document once more, although he was already satisfied with its contents.

At first he had been surprised by just how much administration was needed for the simple prosecution of the garrison's defence, but he had grown quickly inured to the endless lists, numbers and signatures that war required. Indeed, it was clear to him now that no victory could be won without the proper adherence to supply and shipments. The army might do the fighting but the secretaries were the real generals. The devil was in the detail, and laid before him were precise accountings of how many rounds were fired, how much powder was spent, what rations were used and how much of each was returned. No soldier could hope to retain any of his issued gear without a list of it existing somewhere. This report would be sent back to England, and used as evidence against them, or for them, depending on the state of things and how well disposed were the prosecutors to their current endeavours. It did not sit easily with him that casualties, thankfully minimal in this case, were placed well down the list. This was a sorry position that a man's life was attributed less importance than the proper conservation of powder and shot. He had remarked as much to the Earl, somewhat brazenly, who had thankfully concurred with his observation. The Earl had posited that in times such as this, England and its territories were awash with fighting men. The government had plenty of that particular resource and therefore was not concerned by the wastage. In fact, as cold and heartless as it may seem, he would not feel audacious to suggest that the powers-that-be would happily welcome a winnowing of the less able herd. It meant one less unemployed vagrant on their hands. It was a sorry situation indeed, but the State understood well that wars were won with money, not manpower. And so the Earl had patted him on the back and encouraged Drummond to continue with his diligent efforts to justify the King's continued expenditure on this most worthy of endeavours.

He blew over the page to dry the ink and shook his head, smiling. Fitzwilliam would die of fright and betrayal if he ever tried to explain the workings of a modern army. It just wouldn't sit with his world view. Speaking of which, his smile faded when he recalled who was waiting outside in the hallway. Fitzwilliam's world view might well be getting that much smaller if things went badly for him.

A door to one side of Drummond's small office space opened, a loud babble of voices entering shortly before Teviot. He glanced over at Drummond. "That's the staff off. I finished briefing them on last night's excitement. I must say, I have never seen them so cheerful. Now," he face took on a sombre caste, "I suppose we should deal with the ink stain on an otherwise successful engagement. Go fetch them in, if you please, Adjutant."

"Certainly, my lord."

The Governor closed the door as Rupert stood and adjusted his jacket. He exited through the hallway door and discovered both Cobb and Fitzwilliam stood to attention as the stragglers from the staff meeting wandered by. One of the majors reached over and slapped Cobb on the back.

"Bloody good work there, Captain. Bloody good."

Cobb nodded his thanks but remained stern faced.

"Gentlemen, his lordship will see you both now," Drummond announced. He walked towards the double doors that lead to the Governor's chamber, took a grip of both handles and pushed inward. Then he stood aside as the two officers strode in together and walked the short distance towards the table at the far end of the room. Teviot was stood, leaning over the table, his arms held out wide, supporting his weight. He was staring intently at a map spread out before him. The two officers stopped a few feet from the table and bowed. A few moments of uncomfortable silence followed as the Governor continued to focus his attention on the scene before him. Fitzwilliam eyed the map, a hand drawn representation of the town and the outlying lands. Marked clearly were the Lines and fortifications, notes and symbols were scribbled across the length and breadth of the sheet.

"The Moors just had their first taste of someone being as sneaky and cunning as them. Though I doubt they realise it yet," said Teviot. He placed a finger on the map, on top of the location marked *Catherine*. "What I do believe is that Guyland will try again. He will put their first attempt down to bad luck. If his men can't get Catherine, then one of these two will be next." He moved his finger along the map, following the line of the connecting trenches, first towards Pole then doubling back and finishing on Charles. Teviot looked up and frowned. He looked first at Cobb then at Fitzwilliam, studying both intently for a few moments.

"I have briefed my staff and senior officers on this morning's action. Captain Cobb, good work. You dispensed your duties perfectly."

"Thank you, Sir," said Cobb, inclining his head a fraction.

"Ensign Fitzwilliam. I understand that you lost a man due to friendly fire?"

"Yes, Sir."

"Yes, indeed. And the reason for that was you had deliberately abandoned your post and took your men into harm's way."

"That's not exactly..."

"It was a statement, Mr Fitzwilliam, not a question," said Teviot severely. "The facts are clear. Your role was to maintain the dispositions of your guard force, as much as you would do any other night. Instead you allowed the enemy free egress across the Lines and into our echelon."

"They were going to do that whether we had stood fast or not, my lord" responded Fitzwilliam tersely.

Teviot did not respond immediately, rather he fixed his gaze on Fitzwilliam and held it. Fitzwilliam decided to keep quiet, but he also refused to look away. He had marked his position and he would defend it.

"The point, Ensign, is that leaving an unguarded flank would seem, to the wise man, a curious position. Especially when an engagement was happening not a short distance away. It smacks of a ruse. We were fortunate that the Moor did not stop to think on this and continued with their scheme and walked into the waiting volley of Captain Cobb's command."

"I was not to know that, Sir," muttered Fitzwilliam.

Teviot raised an eyebrow. "Were you not? No, I imagine you weren't. Your absence was conspicuous from last evening's briefing. But the Captain did inform you of your role, did he not?"

"He did, Sir. It was to place my men along the Lines."

"And you did this?"

"Yes, m'lord. And dutifully so. Right up until the firing started and I was informed by Captain Cobb that I was not longer required and ejected me from the fort, Sir."

Teviot glanced briefly at Cobb who nodded his agreement.

"Why then, did you choose to take matter into your own hands?"

Fitzwilliam shrugged.

"I saw two things. Firstly, that the enemy would try encirclement and that our rear did not have the protection. Secondly, that my men were too strung out. I was confident that I would lose one, if not two of them when the enemy made their move. In this instance I had no desire to see my men taken down without a scrap. It's not right, Sir. So I decided that I'd take back the initiative and steal a march on them. They wanted to flank us. So I would flank them and pounce on the buggers."

"Well, you certainly did that," grunted Teviot. "But you did not see fit to inform the Captain, your commanding officer, that you intended such a move?"

Fitzwilliam shook his head.

"No, Sir. I did not. As I have already reported, I had been ejected by the fort and did not consider any approach would be listened to."

"Because you had your orders, Ensign," growled Cobb.

"Sometimes you have to go with your gut, Sir," replied Fitzwilliam evenly. "The situation demanded that I act. Yes, I lost a man and took two wounded. So you might say the cost was the same. But the outcome was different.

They died fighting and took ten of the bastards with them. A victory does wonders for morale, Sir."

Teviot raised an eyebrow.

"Indeed so. Yet we already had a victory in the bag, Ensign." He stood straight and tucked his thumbs into his belt. "Your actions contravened the Captain's orders and in so doing, your contravened mine. And I will not have that. By rights you should be stripped of your rank and cashiered. "

Fitzwilliam swallowed. He had been afraid of this.

"News of this incident has spread quickly. There was far too many a witness to Captain Cobb's remonstration of you. Your behaviour has soured the night's work. The men will talk to each other about what happened. So I find myself in no other position but to congratulate you."

"What? Uh, I mean, what, Sir?" Fitzwilliam stammered. He looked at Cobb, a shocked expression clear on the older man's face.

"I could punish you as I saw fit, including execution, if I so wished. I have that right. But that would only serve to exacerbate the situation. It would harm morale as much as it would send a message about my methods. And that is not how I do business. I want my men to respect me and follow me. Fearing me has its uses but is often self defeating. I would rather a man died *for* me than because of me." Teviot leaned over, picked up a goblet and sipped.

Fitzwilliam risked another sidelong glance at Cobb. The man was standing stock still, his face now a mask.

Teviot spoke up once more, holding the mug slightly to one side of his face. "My adjutant, a close friend of yours to be sure, has pointed out to me that you did in fact show a remarkable level of initiative and tactical thought. A trait that has been sadly lacking in much of this garrison's affairs up until now. I am minded to agree with him that a public recognition of such qualities be made, in fact I wholeheartedly approve. It would do much to lessen the impact of the morning's events. It'll give the men something to cheer about and the officers something to think about."

"Right, Sir. Ah, thank you." This was not going the way Fitzwilliam had predicted and he was in no way ready to understand it.

Teviot shook his head. "Don't thank me, young man. I don't do this for you. I do it for necessities' sake. Captain Cobb?"

"Sir?"

"You have kept silent but I have known you long enough to read that look. You don't approve."

"No, Sir. I do not."

"I understand. This would seem like a slight against you. But it is not. I know and value your quality and I do not believe your reputation will bear any grievous injury. You are still the man of the hour. I say this in front of Fitzwilliam so that he is under no misapprehension as to where my true appreciation lies."

"Yes, Sir."

Fitzwilliam was certain that Cobb's acceptance was little more than skin deep. The man's ego would be crying out for justice.

"So, I have already said as much to the staff. The word will go out about the 'official' view of what happened. It won't stop the men talking but it'll will take the edge off and draw a line under things. Now," he leaned forward and placed his hands back on the table. "I said Guyland would try again. And when he does, and fails, the lesson will sink home. They will begin to understand who they face. Ensign Fitzwilliam, as reward for your efforts you will be placed in charge of Pole Fort. It is some way off being finished and I do not doubt that our enemy will see it as a more inviting target. Captain Cobb will remain within Catherine and will be charged with maintaining overall command of the Lines and its men. Your soldiers will man these forts for the next week. Any longer and I do not think the Moors will come. That's it, gentlemen. Please retire and get some rest. I will see you back here one hour before dark for a more thorough briefing. That is all."

Both men saluted and turned to go.

"Oh, Ensign?" said Teviot quietly.

Fitzwilliam stopped. "Sir?"

"It is a fine line between brilliance and insanity. You are neither brilliant nor insane. I ask you to be competent and mindful of your superiors. That begins with Captain Cobb."

"I understand, Sir."

"Very good. Dismissed."

Drummond, on station by the doors, stepped forward to open them once more. As the two passed by, he winked at Fitzwilliam, closing the doors once more as they passed over the threshold.

Left by alone in the corridor, Cobb stopped and turned to Fitzwilliam, his face no longer a mask. Now it radiated scorn. Fitzwilliam tried to scotch any more antagonism.

"Captain, I-"

"Shut up, Ensign."

Fitzwilliam shut up.

Cobb folded his arms and looked him up and down.

"Aren't you the lucky one? Having the Adjutant as your guardian angel. You men of breeding always look after your own, don't you?" he stepped forward. "Don't expect any more second chances. I will be watching and waiting. Just one mistake, Ensign. And I'll make sure you pay for it. Am I clear?"

"As day, Sir" replied Fitzwilliam, firmly.

Cobb smiled thinly.

"Good. Then I will see you tonight."

With that he turned and strode down the corridor. Fitzwilliam watched him go, removed his hat and ran his hand through his hair. That was close. But now he knew what he was up against. Cobb was the devil's own bastard and no mistake. He'd be after him now, so he would have to be extra careful. Put not a foot out of place except where it trod on something smelling of roses. And who would have thought it? *Initiative and tactical thought!* By God but Drummond had a way with words. He vowed to buy the man a bottle or ten.

15 June 1663
The Jolly Sailor Tavern

"Good morning!" announced Drummond brightly as he entered the Tavern. He stopped, a slight frown on his face, and retreated back the way he had come. He held the door open and gazed quizzically into the sky. "Good afternoon!" He walked back in, letting the door close behind him. "I was slightly confounded by the sight of you taking breakfast. But, of course, your hours do tend to confuse the issue of meal times, do they not?"

"You can go off people, you know," grumbled Fitzwilliam, as he dangled a piece of bread in a bowl of stew which lay steaming merrily on the table in front of him.

"Though in my case, your levels of tolerance are exceedingly high. No doubt encouraged by my ability to get you out of the shit time and again," responded Drummond.

"Yes, well. You won't let me forget it, will you?"

"Not ever."

Drummond took a seat next opposite Fitzwilliam at

their favourite table, tucked away in one corner looking across the room and onto the entrance itself. He waved at Donahoe and pointed at the bowl.

The Irishman nodded and disappeared into the kitchen.

"The good captain keeping you busy?" asked Drummond, his face kept deliberately neutral.

"You already know the answer to that," replied Fitzwilliam, glaring at his friend. "He gives me not a moment of peace. I was supposed to be in charge of Pole Fort, but instead he has me as his errand boy. I am constantly backwards and forwards between the garrisoned positions and the main gate."

"There is a good reason for that," replied Drummond, evenly. "We have stepped up our observations of the enemy, looking for any sign of coordinated movements. The sooner we know there may be trouble in the offing, then the better prepared we are."

"Yes, I know all that," replied Fitzwilliam, waving the sodden bread in an arc. Rupert swayed to one side to avoid any rogue droplets of stew. "But surely an NCO can perform such a duty?"

"There is a lot of trust in you, Fitzwilliam, to be so delegated the role of liaison."

Fitzwilliam popped the bread into his mouth, chewed vigorously for a few seconds then swallowed. "Trust isn't the word I'd use." He sighed and stretched. "What with the increased manpower on the Lines at night, at least I have gotten to keep command of my boys. All of them are holed up in Pole."

"Interesting that Cobb did that. I thought he would want to split you all up."

Fitzwilliam shook his head.

"I think it's because he feels they like me too much,

and he doesn't want their words of praise spreading out to the rest of the garrison. Keep my good name contained, as it were."

"Hasn't worked though, has it?" asked Donahoe, placing a bowl of stew and a plate holding a large hunk of bread and cheese in front of Drummond. "I've heard the talk from some of the lads. They don't bear you any ill will," he said, nodding at Fitzwilliam.

Fitzwilliam frowned.

"Well, that's good. But I think Cobb is expecting me to make an ass of myself sooner or later and remove from my men any inkling of favour they may wish to attribute."

"Then don't allow yourself to be taken for one," suggested Drummond, forcefully. "Besides, I cannot defend you again. Teviot is possibly the finest man I have had the privilege to serve but he still has his duty and he must be seen to carry it out correctly. He won't think twice about hanging you from the gallows if garrison discipline requires it."

Fitzwilliam nodded, staring into his stew.

"Are you going to eat that?" asked Donahoe. "It's just that Siobhan does take these things personally. She gets very touchy about her food not being given the proper respect."

"What? Oh. Yes. I'll finish it up. Quite delicious," said Fitzwilliam.

Drummond laughed.

"You really are tired. Normally any chance to get in her good graces would be seized upon in an instant!"

"I must commend your unusually optimistic approach to wooing my daughter. You have shown remarkable patience with her charming nature," said Donahoe.

"Always the gentleman, sir," replied Fitzwilliam.

Donahoe nodded.

"Yes. And that is why I haven't thrown you out on your arse. There are many would-be suitors after my Siobhan and by the holy powers none of them will get near her. You I suffer, because underneath that roguish exterior, I'm thinking that there might just be a decent man." Fitzwilliam was taken aback, He was not entirely sure as to whether he had just been given a compliment or a telling off.

"Besides," said Donahoe, sniffing and rubbing his hands. "I get more business out of the pair of you than I do the rest of this god-forsaken colony put together."

Drummond leaned across and slapped Fitzwilliam on the back.

"I think I'll have some ale to celebrate the fact that finally someone else has divined your good qualities. I no longer need to consider myself a madman. Or at least I now have company in my madness. Have one yourself, my good man," he said to Donahoe. "Not for him, though. He has to go to on duty soon. He can't be seen to be condoning drinking."

Fitzwilliam pushed his bowl forwards and looked upon the two men in disgust.

"Go ahead, make me the butt of your jokes. I'll be your whipping boy. Just you remember who is the Scottish Wildman around here!" He pushed himself up and walked towards the door, retrieving his hat from where it hung on a nail. He stepped outside and jammed it on, the door slowly closing to the sound of laughter from within.

*

"What have we got here, then?" asked Swallow, as two

of his colleagues carefully lowered a wooden box onto the earthen floor of the fort.

"You never know, Simon, could be a crate of wine for us to sup away the long night with," suggested Blair.

"Or it could be food?" suggested Swallow, with genuine hope.

"Or, if you look at the big black cross on the side, it might tell you that whatever's in it is likely to be dangerous," said White, walking up to point at the box.

"Still could be food then," quipped Swallow.

"Afraid not," said White. "Sir, our package has arrived."

"Right you are, Sergeant," said Fitzwilliam as he wandered over. "Best we open it up and get acquainted with the contents whilst we still have some light. We really do not want to be doing this with naked flame."

"Here," said White, handing a small crowbar to Swallow. "Insert it there, and lever up when I say. And do it gently!"

Swallow took the bar and pushed it gingerly into the gap between the lid and the frame. Sergeant White did the same at the opposite end.

"Right, and together, now."

The two men leaned into the bars, the lid popping open with barely any pressure.

White pushed the lid of the crate and hunkered down. He swept away a layer of straw packing and studied the small spherical objects that lay on yet more straw. He reached in and picked one out, holding it up for all to see. There was a deeply concerned murmuring as some of the men recognised what he was holding. Fitzwilliam picked out the word 'grenado'.

"Here you are, Sir."

Fitzwilliam took the proffered object and twisted it

around, taking care to hold it tightly. The grenado was the size of a large pinecone, but rounder, like a small cannon ball. At the top, the hole was sealed with wax. This was where the fuse would go, fed deep into the object itself.

He had never seen these in action but he had been assured they were quite fearsome. They had arrived by transport just this morning and the Governor had wasted no time in issuing them to the forts.

Fitzwilliam looked at the soldiers gathered at a respectful distance from the crate.

"I understand the principle behind these things but have any of you men experience of using them?"

The fifteen redcoats glanced at each other and shook their heads.

"Very well, then, I would ask for volunteers. Specifically those with a steady hand and heart." He noticed the lack of enthusiasm that greeted his statement. "And if not, then I'll just pick some."

*

It was the sixth night after the attack on Fort St Catherine and the garrison were starting to think that perhaps the Moor had indeed decided against further aggression. They were wrong. The sentries at Pole Fort heard a low-lying thunder and felt vibrations through the ground. From out of the darkness, the noise grew and as it drew near, the sound resolved itself into the familiar drumming of a mass cavalry charge. This time the moor had decided to waste no time in a protracted fight. They wanted to take the fort quickly and by sheer force of arms. Cries went up from the cavalry as they drew within fifty yards of the English position.

"Steady lads!" shouted Fitzwilliam. "Remember, no one fires. Just stay low and wait." The troops crouched low on the firing step with the fort. In front of them, facing outwards, was a steep slope of some six feet that acted as a berm against any charge. Both cavalry and infantry would have to check their advance, allowing defenders time to respond, presenting a small target for enemy fire but maintaining the advantage of high ground.

The horsemen, sensing no defensive fire, urged on their steeds expecting a short fight. The lead rider lifted his blade high. Suddenly his horse reared its head and screamed. It checked its forward momentum as its hind legs collapsed. The rider was propelled onwards, arms flailing, his sword flung into the air. Along the line, horses whinnied in pain and terror, bucking and collapsing. Many swerved left and right, as their riders tried to avoid their fallen brothers only to collide with the next as the tightly packed formation started to fold in on itself. Horses neighed in terrified confusion and men shouted curses. All semblance of order was lost. A man stood up and howled in pain, a small star shaped object protruding from his hand. Caltrops or, as some called them, *crow's feet*. The land in front of all the forts had been seeded with hundreds of them during the first night after the failed assault. Teviot had guessed that the Moors would try a new tactic and so he had employed the ages old tactic. In the rough terrain the small, metal objects, little more than nails and sharpened spikes bent around each other, made a supremely effective counter to cavalry. Infantry could easily kick them away, but a horse at full stretch, its hooves slamming hard to the ground, could not hope to avoid impaling themselves in the wicked things.

"Right, lads. Give them a volley!" ordered Fitzwilliam.

The men stood up and from their position on the firing steps, took aim.

"Fire!"

A ragged line of flame spat out into the milling pack of Moors. The shots were indiscriminate, hitting both man and beast alike. That was enough. The rearmost cavalry, who had reined in before hitting the trap, turned about. Unhorsed riders and riderless mounts followed them. Some were able to grab the reins and guided the beasts out, quickly clambering onto saddles the moment they were able. Two or three horses were still alive but in pain, desperately trying to regain their footing. Fitzwilliam felt a momentary pang of regret. Such noble animals didn't deserve such a death, though he had scant time to dwell on it.

"Reload," White ordered. They men stepped back down and started to recharge their weapons. Fitzwilliam kept his position and squinted into the dark. A cry erupted from where the cavalry had headed, and then he saw them. A great body of men were charging towards the fort. Wherever a cavalry charge occurred, infantry was always required to hold the land taken. Their leader Guyland was certainly adept at the basics of war.

"Corporal Longshore, light them up, if you please."

"Yes, Sir!"

Fitzwilliam turned to watch as half a dozen men put down their muskets and retrieved grenados from waist pouches, each with a fuse already inserted. Longshore, a burning taper in his hand, moved along the line, applying it to each grenado in turn, moving on only once the fuse had fizzed into life. In the dim light Fitzwilliam could see the concerned faces of all, not just those that held the weapons. It only needed one of those things to go off within the confined space of the fort and if it did, well, he'd had Longshore describe to him what it was like to advance into cannon firing grapeshot. He turned once more to watch the progress of the infantry assault. They were just about upon the carnage of the stalled cavalry charge. Being in no way confident of the grenados' burn time he decided better to peak too early than too late.

"Throw 'em over, lads! And don't bloody drop 'em!"

Needing no more encouragement, the six grenadiers stood and threw their missiles into the night.

"Next batch now!" Fitzwilliam shouted.

Once more the men withdrew grenados and Longshore moved down the line. Fitzwilliam counted the seconds as the Moorish infantry picked its way through the minefield, slowed up in equal measure by the bodies of men and horses and the liberal scattering of caltrops that remained. As the first grenade ignited with a boom he ducked his head down below the parapet, not wishing to be hit by shrapnel. A sequence of five more explosions followed in quick succession.

"Again!"

Once more the soldiers stood and heaved threw their grenados into the night. Ragged holes had appeared in the line of infantry but they were at point blank range, still advancing toward them, just yards away. Fitzwilliam started to think he'd left the second volley far too late as he ducked behind the parapet once more.

"Ready weapons. Fire when you have a target."

The soldiers primed their muskets or hefted their swords but stayed low. Fitzwilliam saw a black shape sail overhead and land on the floor of the fort. A glow emanated from its top.

"Damn!" he shouted, realising that an enterprising Moor had quickly learnt the value of returning the favour. Before he could react, Swallow had flung down his flintlock and as fast a buck, jumped onto the grenado, scooped it up, and returned the throw. A moment after it had cleared the parapet, another series of bangs, much closer than before, lit up the night sky, illuminating the front of the fort in a red and orange flash. Figures were highlighted as they stood upon the parapet, their arms flung wide in supplication, caught in the blast of the explosives. A body was thrown into the fort, tumbling into the back wall.

"Now! Stand and shoot!" cried Fitzwilliam, an edge of hysteria to his voice. The enemy were upon them. He rose up from his crouch, both pistols drawn. Though the backwash of the grenados had affected his night vision, the enemy had clearly suffered worse. With their numbers reduced, they stumbled on towards the fort but lacked the motivation they had started with. Along the firing line, English soldiers took aim and let fly. Fitzwilliam shot a man directly to his left and pulled the trigger to take care of a second. The gun failed to fire.

"Bastard!" Fitzwilliam cried as the Moor batted his pistol aside with his shield and leaned into stab Fitzwilliam in the chest. He threw himself back from the step, narrowly avoiding the full extension of the blade. He landed heavily on the floor as the Moor leapt down after him. A musket butt slammed into the side of the tribesman's face causing him to spin round and collapse in a heap. Fitzwilliam regained his feet and withdrew his sword. Along the line his men were using their muskets as clubs, trying to hold back the Moorish swordsmen. In a melee like this, it was only a matter of time before his men were overwhelmed.

At the far wall, he spied Longshore lighting two more explosives. Fitzwilliam hurried over, took hold of one and nodded at the Corporal.

"These are the last two, Sir."

He held his hand up and watched the fuse burn down. He glanced at Longshore's face. It radiated a mix of panic and excitement in the dim, flickering flame. When there was but seconds left before the light entered the shell, he nodded. Together they ran forward and gently pitched their grenados over the heads of the struggling men.

"Everyone down!" he shouted.

In the swirling melee, those that could jumped away from the firing step, whilst others fighting in the fort simply threw themselves down to the ground. For the third time in the space of a minute, the flash of death illuminated the darkness. For the soldiers it was the closest they had come to feeling the deadly force of the grenades as the exploding cases turned into fragments of metal that shredded through flesh effortlessly. The Moors upon the parapet were ripped apart in a spray of blood.

Fitzwilliam's ears rang with the aftermath of the detonations. He pushed himself off the floor and started shouting at his men to regain their positions. As he ran back to the firing step his hearing started to return. He could hear the soldiers call to each other, as if from a distance, their voices returning to their natural pitch and timbre by the moment. Placing a foot on the step he pulled himself up to look out on the ground. At first he could see little but a pile of dark shapes gathered on the slope leading up to the fort. His eyes adjusted to the dark, revealing bodies everywhere. He fancied he could see a gaggle of Moors disappearing over the horizon. He was alerted to musket fire coming from the right and he turned to watch a second assault going in against St Catherine's Fort. It appeared to be entering its final stages. The firing was coming from the redoubt in an ordered regular sequence, while the Moors continued to draw closer. An explosion lit up the ground followed swiftly by another then a third, as St Catherine used up their supply of what Fitzwilliam happily reflected was a most wonderful weapon. And that was it, with that last barrage the game was up. From his elevated vantage point he watched the enemy retreat back into the ditches and gullies that lead up to the Lines. Fitzwilliam had to give it to the fort's commander. Cobb had conducted his second successful defence in less than a week.

"Sergeant White? What are our casualties?" he asked, turning to look back on his command.

"The Sergeant's had it, Sir. Took a thrust in the belly," responded Longshore.

Damn, that was a blow. He had liked the Sergeant. A far more amenable fellow he could not recall having at his side.

"Very well, Corporal. You are now my second."

"Right you are, Sir. We've got three others gone to meet their maker and two more in no fit state."

That meant he had eight men left. Damn but they had been close to breaking.

"Everyone back on the steps!" he ordered. Men doubled past him to retake their positions.

"Good thinking with the grenados, Corporal. And Swallow? You still alive?"

"Yes, Sir!" waved Swallow from further down the line.

"That was one of the maddest, bravest things I've ever seen. I'll be commending you for that."

"Thank you, Sir."

"Oh don't do that, Sir. I couldn't cope with his head getting any bigger. He'll be insufferable," moaned Blair.

As others laughed and traded insults with an indignant Swallow, Fitzwilliam grinned. It felt good to be alive.

"Corporal, we'll stand to for ten minutes. If nothing

more occurs, detail two men to help the wounded back to the walls. We'll keep Swallow here. He's our new lucky mascot."

"That's right, Sir. Stick him up on the slope so he can shield us from their arrows," laughed a soldier.

The night continued uneventfully. In the morning a tally was taken of the enemy and friendly dead. The Moors had lost almost a hundred men in their twin assaults. The English had lost five.

16 June 1663
Outside the Lines

Teviot sat on his horse in a deliberately relaxed pose and pursed his lips. He was surprised by the summons for a parley. Not that it *had* happened, but that it had happened so swiftly. He had thought the Moors might try one more assault. But, to give Guyland credit, he had decided to not waste more manpower on a strategy that had already failed twice before. Teviot had been impressed by Guyland's second try at Fort St Catherine. He had clearly thought that hedging his bets and going for two forts would bring success. Teviot had in turn outthought Guyland. If anything, Catherine was stronger than before; the intervening days between attacks had not been wasted.

And here came the man himself, Guyland, his esteemed enemy. Flanked by an honour guard of four men and a standard bearer, bearing a pennant of white emblazoned with a blue crescent moon, he looked quite the warlord. For his part, Teviot had but three men: a soldier bearing the Union flag, his adjutant and his translator. Whilst they were outnumbered he did not fear any skulduggery. They were well in range of the artillery upon the walls, and he'd had the guns sighted upon their position for such an eventuality. Besides, this was a meeting of two commanders and there was etiquette that had to be followed the world over. As the party drew closer, he acknowledged that Guyland looked quite fine in his own way, a true prince of Africa. He wore a chain hauberk and beneath that a robe of white and gold cloth, His headdress, whilst swaddled in the same cloth, was at its core a functional piece of metal, with long cheek guards and a wide nose piece. It put him in mind of the Muslim commanders of old who had fought against the crusaders. Teviot, in turn, wore his breastplate, grieves and gauntlets, and upon his head a rounded cavalry helmet with a faceplate of horizontal metal pieces, pushed back, resting against the top of the headpiece. Whilst those days were long past, the similarity of the scene with those of centuries ago, when Christianity warred with Islam, was not lost upon him. Here they were, playing out on the same stage once more. At least now the reasons were, in his mind, far more honest. This was about land, not belief. The world had changed, and the economics of governance and empire was, if not necessarily a finer cause, one that did not always need to end in bloodshed.

Guyland's party drew up a few yards from the English. Both sides took a moment to size each other up. Teviot wondered for a moment what protocol the Moors would follow. They had called this parley and it was he who had scored the victory. So by rights, they should begin the exchange. As if reading his thoughts he was satisfied to see Guyland raise a hand in greeting. Teviot elected to respond in kind, taking hold of his hat and sweeping it out in an expansive arc, inclining his own head briefly.

Guyland looked to his left and one of his honour guards walked his horse forward. The warrior also raised his hand.

"My master, Ghailan, greets you as an equal." The warrior spoke slowly and deliberately; his English was halting but clear as he moved his mouth around the words. "I can speak for him and for you."

Teviot nodded at the translator. Well, I should not have expected Guyland himself to learn our words, he thought. I wouldn't have wanted to, in his shoes.

He motioned towards Lieutenant Cooke, a bookish young man with an excellent command of languages, who had been sent to accompany the new Governor. Major Allinson had been most pleased to no longer have the role of interpreter.

"I have a man who can speak for your lord as well. But, I am happy for you to do so."

The warrior inclined his head.

"As you wish."

"Lieutenant?" said Teviot.

"Sir?"

"Do make sure to alert me if anything is... misunderstood."

"Certainly, Sir."

The warrior smiled and commenced the parlay.

"My lord congratulates you on your masterful defence. It was cunning."

Teviot smiled warmly. He allowed himself a moment to enjoy this.

"Lord Guyland's strategies have been most difficult to counter. He is a worthy foe."

The Moorish lord returned the smile. His eyes were fixed firmly upon Teviot. "And, it is with respect and honour that he would ask a...favour?"

Teviot arched an eyebrow.

"Go on."

"My lord has pressing matters to attend to in the south. They require his full attention and that is why he wishes to end this disagreement between us."

Hah! And there it is. The way to save face, thought Teviot. And so we have a negotiation.

He pulled a concerned face.

"Oh dear, is there a problem with the locals?" he asked.

The warrior pulled a confused face, and then spoke quickly to Guyland. The Moor moved his gaze away for a brief moment to reply. He maintained his composure but Teviot was sure he caught a flash of annoyance.

"No," responded the warrior. "There is nothing wrong with my lord's...people. There are matters to which he must attend. There are always those who disagree with a King's right to rule, is there not?"

Teviot nodded sagely.

"Oh yes, I completely understand your position. So," he leaned forward into the saddle. "This favour, I believe, would be regarding a truce of some kind?"

"Indeed, lord."

The sudden use of an honorific spoke volumes.

"Then what manner of truce would this be?"

"My lord Ghailan would like to offer you time, some six months. This would be enough for him to do his duties elsewhere. And then perhaps we return to discuss a better plan for our shared love of this land," he said, indicating in a broad sweep, Tangier.

Teviot sat back and stroked his chin.

"So you will not attack us for six months. In return for us doing what?"

The warrior shrugged.

"You may open your gates, gather wood for fuel, trade, plant crops. But do not extend your fortification further. Do not claim more territory than you have."

Teviot nodded and directed his gaze straight back at Guyland.

"Very well. I accept this truce of six months. I will not extend my fortifications any further than the Lines I have already drawn out. We will conduct ourselves peacefully."

The warrior started to translate, but Guyland had already shown his understanding with a slight inclination of his head. Guyland spoke once more.

"My lord is very pleased with this news. You are as wise as you are strong. He is looking forward to returning soon to talk with you once more."

"And tell your lord I likewise look forward to that day. Wish him the very best of luck over the coming months. I hope he resolves all of his, ah, duties, to his satisfaction."

The warrior nodded but did not repeat the message.

"Right gentlemen, time to head back!" he announced briskly.

The English party turned their mounts and walked at a gentle trot back towards the gate.

"Did we miss anything in translation there, Cooke?" Teviot asked.

"Surprisingly little, Sir," said Cooke. "But..." he hesitated.

"Out with it man!" admonished Teviot.

Cooke flushed. "I am sure that Guyland called you an idiot at one point, but I couldn't be sure, it seemed to be slang. I'm sorry about that, Sir."

Teviot smiled.

"Oh, don't worry about that. I'm sure it was nothing."

He turned in his saddle and watched the Moorish party disappear from view. "Your thoughts, Drummond?"

Drummond reached up and tugged at an earlobe.

"It was a rather brief negotiation I thought, Sir."

"Indeed?"

"Well, yes. He asked for some time off, you said yes, and that was the end of it."

"I suppose you are right, Adjutant. But I may say you did rather miss the point of it all."

"Would that be a clever ruse, Sir?" asked Drummond, with a hint of cheek.

Teviot glanced back at him with a stern face.

"Your consorting with the Scotsman has not improved your manners, Captain."

Drummond sat up stiffly.

"Sorry, Sir."

"But, yes, as it happens your second view of proceedings was far more accurate. That bastard is not going anywhere. We bloodied his nose and I think he is doing two things. Firstly, he didn't expect to lose as many men as he did and now he is summoning reinforcements. Secondly, he is saving face but making it seem like he has, through his wily ways, lulled us into inactivity. It'll prove to his men how much cleverer he is."

"But of course you expected all that," stated Drummond.

"A statement loaded with confidence, Adjutant. Thank you. He is afraid of our forts. He doesn't have the ability to neutralise them, his army just isn't up to it. They are still savages in the art of modern warfare. So he has no intention of giving up on destroying them whilst he has the chance. But what he has done is given us time. That is what we need, time. Time to finish our new fortifications. We need to be ready because the next assault will be the final throw of the dice. His gambit will be to surprise us by breaking the truce and catch us napping, then overwhelm us."

"But instead we are going to do that to them?" asked Cooke.

"That is what I intend to see done. I want to knock the stuffing out of them. Send 'em home with their tails between their legs, so to speak. This colony cannot hope to survive under constant threat. We must remove it for a time until it becomes too late for them to do anything about it."

"So how much time do we have, Sir?" asked Drummond.

Good question, thought Teviot. Guyland would not attack immediately. He would expect us to be wary. I must admit, he is a smart man.

"We are in a race, Drummond. Guyland will come when he considers us suitably convinced of a truce. So he will withdraw most of his watchers. We must finish the forts quickly whilst making it look like we are relaxing our guard. We finish them before he attacks, and then we may have the advantage. If he attacks sooner, then we'll be in for a fight."

"Well, I know at least one man who'll look forward to that," replied his adjutant.

"Good, but I want more than one. I want this garrison to be ready. We start preparations tonight."

*

Ghailan dismounted and walked into the shadows of his tent. The English commander was either a fool or he knew precisely what he was thinking. It was a gamble and a risk. He had been repulsed twice and the second time had shown skill. There was, he believed, something to be respected in the man who called himself, what was it? An earl? It had been explained to him that it was a mark of nobility, no doubt accorded through martial prowess. The truth of that matter was clear. There must be a swift conclusion to this affair; the English had to be ejected from his lands. He could ill afford to allow them time to finish their fortifications and entrench themselves like a tick into a camel. So let them think they had a truce, let them relax their guard, let them stop manning those accursed cannon. He had no intention of keeping to any truce. There was no honour lost when dealing falsely with an infidel. He had already given orders to withdraw his forces to make it seem they had truly left. There were a thousand places within a day's ride that could mask his men. Extra cavalry was already on its way, he had already laid out good hiding places from which to launch surprise strikes. And then it would be up to Allah, and the English, to tell him when he should strike.

16 July 1663
Upper Castle Ramparts

"Have you ever heard of the Roman Geese?" asked Teviot as, with one eye shut, he squinted through his spyglass.

"No, Sir," replied Drummond.

"Me neither," grumbled Fairborne. "But I warrant that it has something to do with the pack of hounds that we had the devil's own time rounding up."

"You have it, sir," replied Teviot as he swept his device along the meandering Lines. It was well into the dark hours and even from on high his sight was limited. He could spot the lanterns of the sentries well enough. What with the truce it made sense that they gave the impression of a relaxed stance. Lights bobbed along at a slow pace as sentries ambled along the trenches, other lights immobile and often indistinct, fixed the locations of his forts for all to see. They were almost finished. In the months since the truce was agreed, the forts had been improved, walls had been built higher and there were now berms on all sides. Firing ports had been added and the entrances to each one fort had been strengthened. They were still little more than blockhouses and did not possess any cannon, but each one could be expected to hold their own against a foe armed only with a few muskets. It would take a significant force to be able to break their way in. Any further conflict would likely descend into siege warfare now. Yet the enemy was not to know that and neither did Teviot want this to happen; a siege served no purpose for anyone. He still needed to beat them soundly, otherwise they'd just come back that much stronger than the time before.

"The Roman Geese were employed by Caesar to discover spies lurking within his lines. They became quite agitated when they caught wind of the unwashed barbarians in their midst and alerted the legionnaires with some insistent and sustained honking. We don't have geese in these parts, and I'm confident that if we had, the men would have caught and eaten them by now. But what we do have is dogs. Loud, boisterous and aggressive. If anything, I expect them to be even more energetic in their task than the geese ever were."

Teviot removed the spyglass and turned to look at the gathered officers.

"I believe the reports of our sentries are correct. I think that our friends the moors have returned and begun infiltrating our lines. So I suggest we release our chain of dogs and see what they can sniff out for us."

*

Two hours after midnight the gates were opened, and a pack of fifty or so dogs were shepherded out by soldiers wielding sticks and employing swift kicks to the rumps of the dawdlers. The whole affair was noisy, chaotic and

213

clumsy but after a few moments the dogs were off. Splitting into smaller groups, they dispersed into the undergrowth. Some did so in a desultory fashion, others showing more vigour as they caught wind of promising scents. It had taken the best part of two days to gather together all the strays of Tangier, a task that the hunting parties had taken to with a great deal of enthusiasm. It was a welcome change to their normal duties, though a few now bore teeth marks and a rueful lesson in how not to win a dog's favour. The more enterprising of the soldiers had worked out that rather than gentle coaxing or aggressive posturing, the animals were best encouraged by the provision of foodstuffs. The animals had been penned into a crude stockade within the courtyard of the main gate, a suggestion from the garrison engineer when he had noticed that no one had given a thought as to how to contain such a number of beasts. More food had been provided and after some excitement the animals had settled down into a dozing mass of fur and flies. Since then they had not eaten and now their need to hunt was driving them to action. Snouts lay close to the ground as the search for food began. Men watched with some amusement from their positions on the walls and posts within the Lines. Occasionally a dog would seize upon a small creature, no doubt a rat or rabbit, and a fight would break out as nearby mutts would try and gain their measure of the kill.

Twenty minutes into the hunt, the unwitting guard dogs finally earned their keep. A pack of seven animals entering a deep draw stumbled upon a party of forty Berber horsemen, gathered not fifty yards from the one of the forts. The dogs, in a mixture of anger and excitement, reacted to the tightly packed horses and men and began to bark and howl enthusiastically. The Berbers only succeeded in encouraging more dogs to join them as they tried to shoo the creatures away.

Teviot smiled to himself as he received word that the dogs had appeared to have found something of interest. The message hadn't been entirely necessary; he could hear quite well the racket coming from beyond the walls. As he lowered the helmet over his head, the sound of the barking became muffled and indistinct. It didn't matter. He would find his way to them. He turned in his saddle and raised his sword high, so all of the gathered cavalry of the Troop of the Tangier Horse could see.

"Follow the sound of the dogs, they'll guide us in. Keep close and keep discipline. Engage the enemy quickly. If they break and run, do not pursue. They are crafty and not to be trusted. One ambush could easily lead to another."

"We're ready, Sir," responded Captain Witham, now in command of the cavalry after his steady performance during Peterborough's disastrous sortie.

Teviot nodded with a satisfied smile. He turned back and shouted at the gate guard. "Open up!"

The men moved quickly to obey, and as the two heavy doors swung open, Teviot was through first and quickly brought his mount to a gentle canter. He would not risk increasing the mare's pace until he had a clear run at the foe. The ground was treacherous at the best of times and in this light doubly so. Behind him, the cavalry troop formed up in a tight wedge. Each armoured rider carried his sabre for the charge and two pistols for close quarters fighting, one to attack with and one to cover any retreat. Another legacy of Cromwell's organisation. He knew the men were eager; they had played little part in any of the engagements thus far and wanted to prove their mettle. That was good but he knew how even well-drilled riders could lose their heads and drive after a defeated enemy when their blood was up. He took a deep breath and savoured the familiar smells of metal and leather, tinged with a musty smell of stale sweat. Like the men that rode with him, it had been some time since he had been in such imminent danger. By God, he had missed it. There was nothing like it: at first the nerves in the pit of one's stomach, the sense of mortality as the realisation of what was to come hit home, then the thrill of the charge, the feeling of motion, a sense of strength as the powerful strides of the horses carried you into the fray. Then the swirl of swords, the grunting and cursing and the grim focus of survival as all about you men fell and died in a hundred different ways. And, if you were lucky, at the end of it you found that you were alive and whole.

Teviot spied ahead of him the guard trench. He raised his sword once more and kicked the flanks of his mount, its pace markedly increasing in response. Behind him the riders were responding in kind, the drum roll of the horses building in pitch. The trench was upon them and, at the last instant, Teviot kicked the flanks once more. The gap was not wide and with a shallow jump he was across, bouncing only lightly in the saddle. Instead of easing up, he kept the pace. The dogs were just ahead of him, he could see them gathered, some crouched low in an aggressive posture facing towards an unseen target.

He raised his sword to the horizontal, at shoulder height, its tip pointing forward. He felt the weight of it and his muscles tightened in response. Then he was through the dogs, the animals scrambling out of the way of the onrushing horses. The land sloped swiftly into a tight gully, and ahead of him the waiting Berber cavalry were in the process of turning and withdrawing. With a shout he urged his horse in between two Berbers. He pulled his blade back and swiped it across the back of the one on his right hand side; the blade trailed behind and he felt his shoulder wrench as momentum carried him beyond those two and into the press of riders beyond them. His mount slowed quickly and he brought the sword back in a wide sweeping arc, cutting left and right of him. The Berbers seemed more intent on escape than combat and gave little resistance. He buried his sword deep into the stomach of one who had turned to face him, twisted it savagely and withdrew, the rider falling forward as he did so. There were no more to replace him as the remaining enemy cavalry disengaged and withdrew along and out of the gully. The Tangier Horse swept by him whooping in delight. Teviot took a moment to look about. He could see at least half a dozen bodies on the ground. He had hoped for more but the enclosed space had worked in the retreating force's favour. The press of horses had slowed his rider's charge and given time for the enemy force to pull back. He urged his mount to follow in the wake of his men and quickly emerged out from the draw. He nodded to himself when he saw his men arrayed in good order.

"Well done, lads," he said loudly as he pushed through the line of horsemen. Ahead of them, the Berber cavalry had withdrawn and were now reforming. A quick count of both sides put the Moors at a slight disadvantage. So why had they stopped? A suspicion formed in his mind.

"Take a moment to recover yourselves men," he ordered. He wanted a moment to size up the situation. What were they waiting for? He squinted and took in the surrounding countryside. Above the noise of neighing horses and his own heavy breathing, he strained to hear something, anything.

"Damn it all!" he removed his helmet.

"Sir?" asked Witham, reining in next to him.

Teviot raised his hand angrily.

"Everyone. Be silent."

He tilted his head and closed his eyes. There! Voices on the wind. Distant, unintelligible but the tone was clear. He had heard it on a hundred battlefields. Men being exhorted, being commanded. This wasn't a test of resolve any longer. It wasn't simply probing. Guyland wanted to end this game. He was sending his entire army against them.

"Everyone back to the gates. Captain Witham, detail riders and send them to our forts. Stand them to. Let them know I am sending extra provisions and men."

"Yes, Sir."

As Witham barked out orders, Teviot glared back at the waiting enemy horsemen. They had no need to engage. Damn but he had wished to give them a hiding, to show he was wise to their game but Guyland had proven a far more wily and aggressive opponent than he had given him credit for. He yanked hard on the reins and spurred his horse back to the walls, his care for uneven ground forgotten in his haste.

*

The messenger bowed before Ghailan who sat astride his mount observing the distant lights of the colony. The Moorish commander listened patiently as the report of the cavalry action was delivered and then dismissed the man with a wave of his hand. It was becoming an interesting night to be sure. He found he was enjoying this action more and more as the time passed. It was truly a challenge to pitch his wits against the foreign commander, the man was no fool and it did them both honour. The Englishman had been clever to send dogs to scout out his hidden cavalry. That had been a shame. He had hoped to launch a lightning strike to take one of the forts before his main assault began. The English lines would then already be compromised even as they tried to reinforce their other positions. But no matter. Now he had to be quick. This was the moment to strike, this was his land and he knew that it was working with him. He could read the signs. The English would no doubt see it soon but he had already been sent word of a mist blowing in from the sea. Even now it would be creeping over their walls and a westerly wind was blowing across the land toward Tangier. He had several thousand men marching upon the outlying fortifications but their steps, god willing, would be hidden. The weather had been warm of late and this had dried the overgrown scrub and grass that covered the approaches. It was ripe for burning.

He turned to one his aides.

"Keep the army in position. Do not allow them to advance. Tell the commanders to send men forward to fire the grass. The wind blows from the west. The smoke will go before our men, shielding them from the muskets and cannons of our enemy. Go."

The aide nodded, kicked his heels into his horse and rode swiftly away.

Ghailan felt satisfied. Allah had given him this opportunity to smash the threat of foreign aggression and expansion. It should be quick. They would take the forts, bring them down and the English would sue for peace on his terms.

*

"Oh good God," muttered Blair. He turned away from his firing position and looked across at Fitzwilliam. "Have you seen this?" he continued jabbing a thumb towards the no-man's land in front of him. "Going to make the Moors bloody difficult to shoot at if we can't see them coming."

Others on the firing step muttered their agreement.

"Steady, lads. We'll still hear 'em coming," said Fitzwilliam. Though in truth they were far too adept at moving silently. He leaned forward and gazed into the dark. Dawn was coming but still some distance away. That was not the case with the wall of swirling smoke that glowed faintly against the dark background. That was coming towards them at a fair clip. The night was well lit and relatively cloudless but already the stars in the western sky were beginning to lose their brightness as the dense smoke climbed higher.

"Oh hell," cursed Fitzwilliam, a sinking feeling in his stomach. He had been feeling quite optimistic about being handed command of Pole Fort once more. He had thought the coming fight would be a chance to repair, at least in part, his reputation.

"See? Didn't I say?" said Jacob, nudging the newly promoted Lance Corporal Swallow, who could do nothing but nod grimly.

Fitzwilliam took a moment longer to gauge the pace of the smoke then glanced back towards the walls and the cannon emplacements.

"They'll be as blind as us," he said.

"No help from them, then?" asked Longshore.

"Lads," said Fitzwilliam, raising his voice. "Looks like we are going to be on our own for this one. The Moors will be on us before we can fire a volley. He glanced at the row of faces to either side of him. They looked worried; he needed to pep them up a bit. "It'll be hand to hand. Just the way I like it!" he said with a grin, drawing his blade.

This pronouncement was met with several groans and rueful laughs. The men were used to his predilections and were becoming fond of them, if not entirely sure of their wisdom. He could live with that, just as long as they followed his lead.

Swallow shook his head. "The bloody Scottish Wildman."

"Do you think we should let them buggers know who they are facing? Might give them pause. The lord God knows it does me," replied Jacob.

*

Teviot, now back in place on the ramparts of the Upper Castle, sighed and chew his lip. "The bastards have us by the balls, gentlemen," he announced to the assembled officers. He looked over the town, now swathed in the insidious mist coming in from the sea. "We are blinded in our rear and to our front. Soon there will be nothing left for us to observe."

He estimated that the smoke generated by the burning of the undergrowth was but minutes away from engulfing his forts. Once that happened, the Moorish thousands, and he had no doubt that the numbers were truly great, would swamp those positions and his cannon could do nothing. They would fire into the empty smoke or they would hit their own men.

Fairborne slammed a fist upon the stone wall and swore.

"Bastards! What shall we do, Sir? We have sent out half our men to hold onto the Lines. If they are engulfed by that, they will be lost."

"The forts are provisioned, they are set for a siege," countered Fitzgerald.

"Aye, Colonel," responded Fairborne. "But without cannon support, the lads cannot last for long. They will be fighting against swordsmen and we don't have enough scrappers like young Fitzwilliam."

Drummond, who had been listening quietly, started to hear his friend's name mentioned. "Fitzwilliam and his men in Pole Fort would be the most likely to withstand the onslaught."

"I am counting on it, Captain," agreed Teviot. He was pleased that his adjutant was remaining positive. He also approved of Drummond's loyalty to his friend; this time he hoped it would bear fruit.

"Captain Cobb will hold St Catherine's too," said Teviot with a deliberate firmness.

"That's two forts. And the rest?" said Fairborne.

Teviot gave him a sharp look.

"My apologies, Governor," responded the Major quickly. "I am frustrated."

"As am I, Major. But do remember your place in these matters." Teviot turned to Johnson.

"How long do you think these fires will last for?"

The engineer shrugged.

"It is a little out of my field of expertise, Governor. But I'd say that with this wind it could reach our walls within an hour and blow itself out."

"The forts would not have to fight alone for long," said Fitzgerald hopefully.

Teviot knew he had two options. Leave the forts to fend for themselves until the smoke cleared. Or order an immediate withdrawal, which would save lives but give up the ground they had fought hard to hold and handing the victory to the Moors. Neither appealed overmuch but he would trust his own counsel.

"Gentlemen. I believe we have done enough to ensure the robustness of our fortifications. That is why they are there. They will earn their keep and they will hold. We will trust to the engineering excellence of their construction and the spunk of the men that fight behind their berms and walls. As soon as the smoke begins to clear, I want the gun crews working themselves to exhaustion and the metal of their cannon glowing white-hot. We pour it on the Moors and make them pay for their audacity."

His staff nodded in agreement, their confidence buoyed by the resolve in his words. Teviot knew he was gambling and he secretly did not begrudge the look of concern that still clouded Fairborne's face. But he could not afford to show weakness. The decision was made and it was now down to how well his men would fight and how long they could hold against such a horde.

*

Fitzwilliam placed both flintlocks upon the ledge of the berm. When the Moors charged, he would discharge them at point blank range then withdraw back to give him room to swing his blade. There had been plans to erect a palisade wall along the berm's top, with a walkway for men to fire from an elevated position. But the truce agreement, for all that it had been a sham, had put paid to that. So he and his command found themselves in the same position as before. But this time he had no grenados, just a handful of extra soldiers, new to his command. The only thing they had going for them was, apart from these additions, that his men were more experienced in a face-to-face fight. They wouldn't break as easy. But break they would. This was not like the earlier engagements they had fought in. This looked like a full-scale attack. He was tempted to say 'Hang it all!' and lead a charge out from the fort. It would be quite a way to go and would be the last thing the enemy would expect. But he had had his fill of going against orders for a while. Best he suffer this one out.

"What do you reckon, Corporal?" he asked of Longshore, who was thoughtfully scratching his beard.

"I'd say that smoke is just about in musket range. You can make out something in there now. Just shapes, but you can bet your last copper there's a thousand of the bastards just waiting to charge right at us."

"You don't need to see 'em to hear 'em," added Swallow, referring back to Fitzwilliam' observation.

It was true. The approaching force was so close you could hear their footfalls, a muffled crackling sound as hundreds of feet crunched down on the blackened growth.

Fitzwilliam sighed. He reached out, picked up one of his pistols and cocked it. He replaced it and repeated the action with the second.

"Alright, lads, they'll be charging us in a moment or two, just as the smoke reaches us. On my command, give them a volley. Try and pick a target if you can, but more importantly, keep your aim low. There are enough of them out there that you'll likely hit something. Once you're done, make sure you grab something sharp and be ready to fight for your life. Anyone left standing at the end of this, I'll stand you a drink."

The men readied themselves and leant into their muskets. Swords, spears and long knives lay ready to be picked up for the coming combat. There would be no time to reload.

Fitzwilliam watched as the smoke, pushed along by the wind, came to within thirty yards of Pole Fort. He felt his breath quicken. Any moment now. He wiped his left hand, still clutching his pistol, against his forehead. He was surprised to find he was sweating. He shivered a little. The warm air coming from the burning vegetation had been quite pleasant if a little pungent. But now he came to think of it, that smell had gone....

"Wait!" he turned around quickly.

"What?" responded Swallow.

"The wind!"

"What about it?"

"The wind," said Fitzwilliam as he held up his hand and looked at where the moisture had gathered. His hand had been facing away from the smoke. Yet he had felt a breeze against his skin.

"The wind. The bloody wind has changed direction!" he shouted.

Fitzwilliam studied the advancing smoke cloud. Except it wasn't anymore. It had stalled and was swirling in chaotic eddies, struggling to maintain its form.

"The Ensign is right," shouted Blair. "Look, the wind has stopped from the east, it's being pushed back. It's going the other bloody way!

A ragged cheer erupted from the firing line as this became apparent to all. The smoke was being forced back, retreating away from them and losing its coherence. And in its wake, four thousand Moorish troops started to emerge from the gloom.

*

"Fire! All guns, fire!" shouted Teviot. All along the parapets and emplacements of Tangier the order was carried. Cannons fired as soon as the order reached them and in a ragged, expanding wave, the walls of Tangier glowed. In the clearing smoke, the shot cut swathes through the advancing Moors. A shudder swept through their advancing lines. Ragged volleys of musket fire erupted from the forts. And the shudder turned to a disorganised halt as Moorish commanders tried to make sense of this change of fortunes. Here and there groups started to move on but in an uncoordinated fashion. The gunners were already reloading and were guaranteed another shot before the Moors could get to the forts.

*

Ghailan looked on aghast. From his vantage point he could see the smoke clear and move away from his exposed forces. His men, large in number, were now easy targets for the cannon even though they still had the advantage of night. They were grouped too closely together, deliberately massed to attack the forts. The loss of life would be appalling even if they did succeed in storming those positions. This was too much. For some reason there had been an intervention. Today, it was not Allah's will that he should be victorious. Barely containing his shock and anger, he issues orders for a full retreat before the cannons could do any more damage. Flags waved signalling to the various commanders to commence a withdrawal. He quietly seethed as bands of cavalry cantered past, and large bodies of black robed warriors turned about and ran westwards.

*

It had been a gamble. But sometimes in war, luck, with a fair dose of preparation, was all you needed. Or perhaps, Teviot reflected, not normally a pious man, it was divine intervention. Around him his staff officers and the rank and file soldiers upon the curtain walls cheered. The Moorish lines were retreating. Exposed and outgunned, their massed groups would be torn apart by concentrated fire.

"Cease fire," he ordered

Fitzgerald looked at him aghast.

"But we have them on the run! Why stop now?"

"Because we want Guyland to withdraw without his men turning on him. He is defeated, but we allow him to retreat from the field with some modicum of honour. I have a feeling he will be far more amenable to a true peace."

"Very clever, Governor," said Fairborne with an appraising nod. "A politician too, eh?"

Teviot gave a quick smile and inclined his head.

*

The day passed quickly as messengers and envoys freely moved between both camps. Negotiations were energetic and swift, and as the sun sank behind the high ground to the west a line of thirty horsemen, framed against its fading rays, picked their way across the battlefield towards Catherina Port. At their head, flanked by black and white pennants, was Guyland, ready to make his peace with the English.

A banquet had been swiftly organised to receive the Moorish chieftain. Fitzwilliam found himself in the same chamber that the Governor had first entertained his new officers but now there were a number of tables set out on three sides of the room, all other furniture having been manhandled out to accommodate the English and Moorish leaders. He was rather surprised that he had been invited. He didn't think his rank would have warranted it. But he did see that almost all the garrison officers were present.

"He is very trusting," he remarked to Drummond.

"Who, Guyland?"

"Well it's not Teviot who is surrounded by his bitter enemy and has only seven men to call on."

"Good observation," Drummond shrugged. "He is here under a banner of truce and Teviot believes him. And it would hardly be fair if we were to take him hostage now. By all of us being here, we are showing him respect."

"Fair enough," said Fitzwilliam, draining his glass and motioning a servant to refill it. He waved his empty vessel at the Moors. "Have you noticed that none of them are drinking?"

"I believe it is a requirement of their religion."

"Lunatics," said Fitzwilliam, as his glass was recharged.

He took a moment to study Guyland and his captains. All of them were dressed in black robes and burnished armour. Some also wore large black clothes wrapped around their heads though their faces were uncovered. Their aspects were very strange to him, weathered and as alien as he had ever encountered. They carried small, stylised sheathed daggers tucked in the sashes across their wastes. Short, curved and vicious looking. They had not been allowed to bring any weapons into the room, although he had secreted a dirk within his boot. Just in case. Their leader, Guyland, sipped from a glass that contained water, his eyes straying around the room, taking it all in even as he listened to his interpreter as Teviot engaged him in polite conversation.

"That is no way to live. I fear I would not be a very good Muslim," said Fitzwilliam, shaking his head as he took another quaff.

Drummond laughed.

"You barely make a half decent Christian!"

Fitzwilliam shrugged.

"I should take offence but I dare say you are right. But God, so they say, loves the weak. And I am such a man when it comes to the pleasures of the grape and grain."

"Never a truer word have you spoken. Is it the drink that has made you eloquent?"

"I am practising my poetry to woo the fair maiden."

Drummond raised an amused eyebrow.

"Keep practising," he advised.

*

"Lord Guyland. Do you find the terms of the peace acceptable? They are reasonable, considering the circumstances." Teviot waited for his question to be interpreted.

Ghailan nodded and responded in kind.

"Six months of peace, where you will not extend your fortification beyond the present boundaries, is acceptable to us."

"Then that is good. We shall also open our gates for mutual trade. I will have a formal document drawn up to reflect this. Perhaps you have a scribe who would like to make a copy?"

Ghailan gestured to another of his men.

"He will write the document." Ghailan took another

sip of water, his eyes once more scanning the room. "Your men dress like women. They do not have the look of warriors about them. Except that one." He pointed towards Fitzwilliam, who responded with a raised glass.

Teviot coughed. He should bridle at the insult to his men but had to agree with Ghailan's notion. He still had too many officers who only played at soldiering.

"Yes, you could say that. Mr Fitzwilliam has Scottish blood, and displays much of their love of battle. He also has little affection for the more refined ways of his fellow officers. I believe he enjoys fighting you," Teviot added mischievously.

Ghailan smiled.

"That is good. He must be the one who carries a great blade into battle?"

Teviot nodded.

"His men refer to him as the 'Scottish Wildman', I believe."

"A warrior indeed." Ghailan's gaze continued onwards once more. He pointed his finger again. "And that one, that man has an air of violence about him."

"Yes. That is Captain Cobb. He held Fort St Catherine against you. He is very...capable."

Ghailan tilted his head.

"Your word for 'dangerous'? Tell me. What will you do with your peace?"

Teviot thought before he answered, but decided to be truthful. If he was allowing trade between Tangier and the local tribes, word would certainly get back to this man eventually.

"I am returning back to my country. I have an estate in Scotland that I have not visited in some time. I also intend to speak to my King, Charles II. He will want a report on what has occurred here."

"Indeed so. We all have masters. I am required to support my own lord, Mohammed, in defending his right to the throne. You will send my greetings and humblest respects to your king?"

Teviot inclined his head. "I will be honoured to do so."

"That is good." Ghailan studied Teviot closely and smiled broadly. "I have enjoyed the game we have played. You are a clever man and a foe to be admired. Perhaps one day you will visit me in my palace. Perhaps our roles may be reversed?"

Teviot smiled back.

"My lord, that day will be a very long time coming."

*

"Did you see him point at me and then at Cobb?" asked Fitzwilliam.

"Yes, I was forced to when you elbowed me in the stomach," replied Drummond.

"What do you think that was all about?"

"It is probably no coincidence that the pair of you are the most ill at ease in this room. You both happen to have reputations when it comes to fighting."

"There will be scant little of that if this peace holds. Think it will?"

Drummond took a deep breath and sighed.

"My concern is what will happen to this garrison if the peace holds."

"What do you mean?"

"Remember Dunkirk?"

Fitzwilliam was silent for a moment.

"Ah." Then he smiled. "But we have Teviot. He won't brook any mischief, even from the likes of me."

Drummond shook his head.

"I am afraid not. Teviot and, I don't doubt, a number of our fellow officers will be taking the next supply ship home and will be on leave for a few months. Fitzgerald will be the Lieutenant-Governor."

"Oh." Fitzwilliam hadn't expected that.

"I suggest, James, that you keep a low profile for a while. Boredom will make the men insolent and resentful. A lack of purpose will see them turn their thoughts to settling scores."

"It is a good thing we have our safe haven," Fitzwilliam raised his glass. "Here's to the Sailor."

He drank deeply and looked for the servant to refill his glass once more.

He chose to ignore the venomous look that Cobb sent his way.

Cobb left the residence at midnight. He was drunk, but it was a cold, focused drunk. He had spent the evening thinking of nothing else but that young upstart ensign. He despised the man. He was a waste of air and a disgrace for all that he had fought for. He wanted to see him humbled, to see him put in his place. The garrison would soon become quiet, the excitement of action forgotten. The soldiers would slip back into their normal state of sloth and laziness and they would quickly lose the edge they had finally honed in battle with the Moor. It made him angry. This was not like the New Model. There a man knew his place and understood the meaning of discipline. They were professionals, run by men who knew their business and didn't shirk from it. But this King's army, this Royalist force, was manned by nothing more than ne'r–do-wells and ruled over by privileged inbreds who thought money and titles bought respect. And Fitzwilliam was the worst of the lot. The rest drank and gambled and played at privilege behind the walls of their residence in the castle, but Fitzwilliam flaunted himself around town with no regard for propriety. He had his own drinking den as a residence, dressed as he pleased and ignored proper military conduct whenever it suited his fancy.

And his men loved him for it.

The man had to be brought down and quickly. He was a risk to the coherence of this force, where morale was shaky at best. Teviot did not approve of his officers engaging in private conflict, but he would soon be gone. And the Lieutenant-Governor, Fairborne, was not so diligent. He could easily engineer the ensign's downfall but for one thing; his friendship with the Adjutant. It was clear that the young captain had already interceded on his behalf at least once before. It would take a great deal to see Fitzwilliam humiliated but there had to be a means of getting to him, finding a way to see the Scotsman damn himself.

He stopped by an alleyway, undid his britches and relieved himself against the wall. As he did so, his thoughts drifted to the bar wench with the thick, jet-black hair, the daughter of the owner. My, she was a pretty one, with curves in all the right places. As he tucked himself back in, he felt himself grow hard. Yes, she'd be a fine ride. Intruding on his thoughts of passion, it struck him. Of course! He was blind to it before but now it was clear. There was the weakness he needed. He'd heard it said that Fitzwilliam was sweet on her but she had always refused his advances. What better way to rile the man but to steal the bitch from him?

A scheme formed in his addled mind. He'd need allies.

He couldn't do it alone. Not with Drummond around. Not with what he had planned. But he could do it. He could put that young bastard down. It would just take a little time.

18 August 1663
The Lines

"Do you think they are still out there?" asked Simon.

"Course they bloody are," replied Jacob, rubbing a hand over his head and slapping his cheeks in an attempt to keep himself awake. The dark hours before dawn always took a heavy toll on him.

"They are watching us, just as we are all up and about in the devil's own hours looking out for them."

"But what's the point? We are at peace. We've got friendly with the locals and they come in and out of the gates every day. The accord was signed. They had themselves a fancy do and everything."

Jacob glanced askance at Simon.

"You're the corporal now, not me."

"Just say your piece soldier."

"That's better. Think about it a moment. They've been treacherous before, we know it and they know it. Both sides are just biding their time. And you can bet me rotten left foot that half those locals are reporting back to someone. They'll know what's going on inside the walls better than we do ourselves."

Simon sniffed. He didn't like it. Blair continued.

"So we stand here in the mucky, sweaty heat of the night and in so doing we tell the Moor that we aren't bloody idiots and we aren't taken in by their smiles and their friendly waves."

"I don't get it. But then, I don't get paid to think," said Simon.

Jacob laughed.

"No, Simon, you really don't."

Longshore joined them on the firing platform and looked across the high ground ringing Tangier. In the months since the peace, whilst work on the mole had continued at a snail's pace, Colonel Fitzgerald had been more energetic in his desire to improve the defences of the Lines. Whilst the treaty had forbidden any new works, their current positions did not fall under that pronouncement. Now Pole Fort had its own palisade and was more akin to a blockhouse. The men were now required to climb up to the level of the berm. From there firing slits had been cut into the wood. It gave them far greater protection and meant any new assault could be far more easily repelled.

"How goes it, lads?" he asked.

"All quiet," responded Simon. "What's the news?"

"Nothing that you wouldn't know already. The Lines to either side are as quiet as here and inside the walls everyone sleeps like a babe."

"And we stare out into the dark, always fated to see the sun but for the briefest moment before we collapse on our beds," waxed Simon.

"That's what you are paid for," said Jacob.

"When they remember to," muttered Simon.

*

The day was hot and sultry as Siobhan made her way amongst the stalls and carts gathered around the square. The market was busy today, a consequence of the new peace between the local Berbers and the English. Finally fresh produce was available once more the like of which she had not seen since the Portuguese had left. It reminded her how much she had missed the hustle and bustle and being amongst her mother's people. She could tell her father enjoyed the company of the two English officers and she knew he didn't feel as isolated as he once had. Now that sense of isolation had passed to her, and it felt like she was the one who was out of place. There were other women about, some wives, a number of prostitutes, no one she could call a friend. It was hard on her but she could only tell her father so much, and she so longed to express how she felt. Yet she didn't want to upset him. She was all he had. The two officers that stayed with them were just...customers. Drummond was respectful and kind enough, she suspected he did so to balance out his annoying partner, Fitzwilliam. The man really was too much. He placed roguishness higher than maturity.

She spied a number of familiar faces amongst the Berbers and greeted them in their own tongue. She had learnt it made the difference between a fair exchange and a fleecing. The English soldiers had yet to learn that. She bought a sack of plums and another of lemons; her father would no doubt chide her for her profligacy then later thank her when he ate a hearty meal.

She hefted the plums under her arm and then bent down to collect the second, heavier sack.

"Madam, let me help you with that." She looked

round into the smiling face of one of the officers who had started showing up in the tavern in the evenings. What was his name?

"No, it is fine, thank you. I can carry them myself." She bent down to haul up the lemons but the officer was quicker, placing a restraining hand on hers.

"Please, I insist. What sort of gentleman would I be? It is the least I can do."

She stared at him hard then at where his firm, calloused palm rested on her hand.

He smiled once more, pulled his hand away and allowed Siobhan to release her grip on the sack.

"If it is no trouble for you?" she asked, dubiously.

"None at all. In fact I am on the way to the Tavern now. Things are quiet around the colony. I had hoped to partake of some of your cooking, it is quite delicious."

Siobhan felt a small measure of pride at that remark.

"Then, indeed, come along. Mister?"

"Cobb, Captain Cobb. At your service, madam."

30 August 1663
The Bay of Tangier

Fitzwilliam lay back against the smooth, bare rock and ran a hand across its milky white surface. It felt like marble though he had no knowledge of its true nature. It was very hot to the touch, almost uncomfortably so, having had its full face to the sun for the best part of the day. He withdrew his hand and manoeuvred himself back into the shade of the nearby overhang, enjoying the cooling breeze coming in from the sea. For all that the stifling heat of the summer months could drive a man crazy, he enjoyed this place far more than he ever did the seascapes of Dunkirk and northern Europe. It was... cleaner. He sighed and took in a long deep breath through his nose, drawing in the smells of the Mediterranean. It was warm, salty, fishy yet fresh, comforting and welcoming. He had to admit that since the peace, he had expected life to become increasingly unbearable. Yet as the summer months rolled on, the daily routine was relaxing, and he had no desire to seek excitement. Every day rolled into the next. As a reward for his efforts in action, he now had full command of Pole Fort and the connecting trenches in its sector, but it was still the night watch duty. Fortunately, Cobb had been moved to the day watch, but had been given complete control of the Lines. This was an important duty for just a captain, but with so many officers away on leave, the pool to draw from was much reduced. He hardly saw the man now. Out of sight out of mind, Drummond had advised. He was probably right. The man was a dangerous ass but if they didn't run into each other, there was no reason to seek out antagonism.

Fitzwilliam pushed himself up and located the sun's position in the sky. Looked look lunchtime. He rolled off the rock; collected his sword that was laid carelessly on the rocky trail, and made his was back towards the town. The path he was on followed the outer works of the walls as they paralleled the coast. It was a pleasant retreat to get away from it all and he was surprised that few others used it. He drew near to the beach that acted as the landing point for the supply ships and occasional fishing vessels that now visited the port. He inspected the work of the mole, that great enterprise for which they had been shedding their blood, and found that progress was slow. The garrison engineer, Major Johnson, had also returned home, and without his presence, there was little impetus to maintain any kind of urgency. A work crew of a dozen or so laboured in the sun, moving large rocks and boulders into place. Each one was a bugger to manhandle and had to be moved into position and dropped into the sea to build a solid breakwater. He found it hard to imagine what a grand harbour of Tangier would look like. He compared it to the likes of the dockyards he had seen in Kent and northern France. Tangier had some way to go before it was a force in the seafaring world.

He walked under the Watergate and into Tangier proper, working his way towards the centre of the town. The streets were quiet as they always were, especially in the stifling heat of the day. It had become apparent that the local custom of resting for several hours, from late morning to mid afternoon, was an eminently sensible thing to do considering how damnably unpleasant the heat was. Most of the garrison and locals would be turning in quite soon. He finally encountered some life as he walked into the market square. One of the benefits of the accord was the opening of trade links with the locals. They had arrived almost immediately after the treaty was signed, bringing with them fruits, breads, trinkets, carpets and pottery. Donahoe said that the local tribes had traded quite happily with the Portuguese. Fitzwilliam enjoyed browsing the market stalls for wares, finding the sights and smells quite wonderful.

Today, there were a dozen or so pitches, and he idled along, one stall catching his eye. Resting on a crude tabletop was a selection of sheathed daggers, similar in form to those he had seen worn by Guyland and his lieutenants. He had enquired after them, learning their name, *koummya*, being a traditional dagger of the Berber and Arabic peoples of the region, not unlike the Scottish dirk. He picked up one that caught his eye. He played his hands over the scabbard, made of two pieces of wood with exaggerated upturned tips, stained black with ornately curved metal worked around the wood halves, holding them together. Withdrawing the dagger itself, he studied the contoured handle, the pommel covered with an engraved metal cap, the sharply curved double-edged blade and compared the curve to the scabbard itself, noting how the weapon slotted together. It really was quite a wicked looking thing, but no doubt well suited to the existence of the tribesmen and herders of these lands. He ran his fingers along the edge and the tip – it was nice and sharp. Yes it would do. He made eye contact with the vendor and raised the weapon up, indicating interest. The seller, a swarthy-skinned man with a white beard and rheumy eyes, gave him a toothy grin and raised his fingers indicating seven. Fitzwilliam barked a laugh and shook his head. He held up three fingers.

"Three, and that is more than fair. Three."

The trader smiled and raised his hand once more. Six fingers. These Berbers did love to haggle.

"Alright, my dark skinned savage. I'll give you four and I'm paupering myself in the process."

Six fingers again.

Fitzwilliam pursed his lips. This one wasn't going to budge.

"All right, I give you five. Five. And that's it. I barely get paid as it is and you want to rob me of all of it."

The trader shrugged and shook his head, breathing in a deep sigh as he did so. Fitzwilliam smiled, it was quite theatrical. He nodded and held out his hand. Hah! Success. He dug into his pouch and handed over five coins. He held the dagger up in a victory salute, bowed and went on his way. He was looking forward to Drummond's outrage when he saw his friend sporting this new weapon.

He was also looking forward to a spot of lunch, a flagon of ale and a bit of a snooze before supper and another night of boredom. With thoughts of food inevitably came thoughts of Siobhan; she truly was a most talented cook. He had not given up harbouring thoughts of a romantic nature with her, but after more than half a year of trying, he was coming round to the idea that she really wasn't going to be interested in anything more with him. They had settled down into a relatively peaceful co-existence where she would tolerate his presence and he kept his suggestive remarks to a minimum. If anything he was starting to think of her now as more of a sister than a potential love interest. Which was, in the greater scheme of things, a shame. He arrived outside the entrance to the Jolly Sailor, his home, and entered.

"Afternoon, Donahoe. What's for lunch?"

*

Fitzwilliam squeezed his eyes tighter shut, pulled his shoulders back and then thrust his arms out wide, yawning as he did so. He then opened his eyes, gazed about his room and scratched idly at his beard.

"God, but I shouldn't have had that second flagon," he muttered. Sleep had been far too sound and his belly far too full. He looked out the window and judged by the lengthening shadows that he had overslept. He rolled off the bed, quickly pulled on his britches, boots and a new shirt. He splashed water over his face from the bowl on the small table in the corner and ran his wet hands through his hair, trying to dampen it enough so he could tie it back. Once done he grabbed his jacket and weapons and ran downstairs. He would be late for reporting if he had supper. But by the same token he would be bloody starving if he missed supper. He weighed the options as he entered the Tavern itself. Ah, no one would notice, the men knew their jobs. He'd just have a quick bite.

He strode in and as his eyes accustomed to the gloom he went straight for the bar. He could see there were a few drinkers in already. He nodded to Drummond, who was already perched on a stool, and dumped his gear on the countertop.

"Good evening, one and all. Bit late today."

Donahoe wandered over.

"You are indeed. What can I get you?"

Fitzwilliam tugged at an ear and pulled a face.

"Well, I cannot lie, I am mighty hungry."

"That is your own problem, Ensign." A stern voice cut through the gentle murmur of the tavern, stopping Fitzwilliam from finishing his request.

He stopped and turned, knowing full well whose voice that was.

Cobb sat well back in the darkened rear of the room, raised a mug to his lips and drank deeply before standing and emerging from the shadows. Fitzwilliam felt his spirits drop. He had forgotten. How could he have forgotten? For weeks now Cobb had been coming in, usually later in the evening. Drummond had told him of this and it had vexed him greatly.

He swaggered over to the two men at the bar counter. He nodded amiably at Drummond.

"Good evening, Adjutant. All done for the day?"

"Indeed so. And you too, by the looks of it."

Cobb inclined his head. He turned his attention to Fitzwilliam. "And of course, it is now time for others to take on the welcome burden of enforcing the King's peace and keeping us all safe in our beds. Is that not so, Ensign?"

His face maintained a friendly aspect but Fitzwilliam could see the challenge in his eyes well enough.

"Yes, Sir. Absolutely right. I will be on my way. I just thought to take a quick draft of water, to refresh myself for the work ahead."

"I'm sure you were. But no time for that. By my reckoning the bell will sound shortly and the guard must be gathered for inspection. It would be insubordinate of you to miss it. Is that not so, Adjutant?"

Fitzwilliam swallowed hard and bit down on any irritation. The man had him bang to rights and there was no way Drummond could turn a blind eye to this.

"Quite so, Captain. I am sure my friend knows his duties well enough to discharge them correctly," replied Drummond, perfunctorily, his eyes fixed on Fitzwilliam.

"I do indeed. And I must humbly excuse myself from you honourable company, sirs. My duties and the safety of the garrison demand it," he replied.

"Good lad," said Cobb, jovially. "Along you run."

Fitzwilliam swallowed his anger, gathered his weapons, stood to attention to both men in turn, and hurried out.

Cobb watched Fitzwilliam leave and in turn Drummond watched Cobb.

"Now I shall sleep safe at night," he muttered bitterly.

"You couldn't ask for a better man guarding your back, Master Cobb," said Drummond lightly.

Cobb shot him a hard look then covered it with a tight smile.

"I am sure, Adjutant. I am sure. Ah, Mistress Donahoe. It is good to see you." He stood and gave a bow as she bustled into the room carrying a tray bearing plates of steaming stew. She smiled as she moved past.

Drummond took a step back. Cobb's face had changed aspect in an instant, becoming the very image of good-natured civility. What was this about? Cobb had been buttering up Siobhan for some time now, he had told Fitzwilliam as much. This was not going to end well. As she returned, Cobb stood in her path. She reared back and folded her arms but did not look perturbed by his move. At least not in the way she often did when Fitzwilliam had tried it on.

"I was wondering," said Cobb, "if I might impose on you for a dish of that stew? It has been criminal of me to not try it earlier."

"That it is," laughed Siobhan, "but sit yourself back down and I'll rustle something up."

Cobb inclined his head and smiled warmly as she disappeared into the kitchen.

"I never put you down for a gentleman, Cobb," observed Drummond.

"Never make that mistake," responded Cobb, raising his mug to his lips. "But I can be civilised. When I wish to be."

The door opened to the tavern opened and in strolled Lieutenants Oates and Green. They swaggered over to the bar as if they owned the place, and it did not escape Drummond's notice that both had clearly been drinking already.

"Good evening, gentlemen. So glad you could join me here," said Cobb.

Oates scratched at the scar on his left eye and gave the tavern a squinting inspection.

"Simple place. Tidy enough, I suppose."

"Drummond," acknowledged Green. "Joining us for a drink? You seem lonely without your shadow around."

Drummond decided not to rise to the bait. He drained his mug, made his farewells and exited the tavern, having no desire to be amongst their company or return to his room. He wasn't tired so he might as well go back to his office; there was always more work to do.

*

"What an uptight arse," muttered Green.

"A wonder his only friend is the worst officer in the

garrison," observed Oates.

"Now, now, my friends. Don't speak ill of the Adjutant. Our Governor approves, and he is efficient enough," said Cobb.

"At least that distasteful excuse for an officer is kept well away from us. I see the man so rarely now, I can almost believe he isn't here," said Oates.

"Barkeep, do you have wine that is fit for officers?" asked Green, slamming a palm onto the counter.

"If you have the coin, I daresay I can find you something suitable" responded Donahoe, affecting an even tone.

"Then find it!" ordered Green.

"In all seriousness, Cobb. Why did you invite us here? This is not the place for the likes of us. We should be up with the rest of the officers," protested Oates.

"Because, it will do you good to get out more. See what the town has to offer," Cobb responded. "And look, here is a fine example."

Siobhan emerged from the kitchen carrying a tray upon which sat another bowl of stew and bread.

"Here you are, Captain. Where would you like it?"

"If you could place it over there?" he said, pointing an empty table at the far end of the Tavern.

She nodded and took the food over.

Cobb looked at his colleagues.

"Perhaps you begin to understand? Come along, join me and I will explain in clearer terms the reason for my invitation."

He stood up, gathering the wine bottle and glasses that Donahoe had placed in front of him, and walked towards the table. He smiled at Siobhan as she walked past. Once she was beyond his vision, Cobb's smile turned cold. He was looking forward to this evening; it was going to be a most entertaining affair.

*

As Fitzwilliam ran along the street towards the gate, he was fuming with rage. Cobb's presence in the tavern felt like a personal affront. It was his place and a Cromwellian devil had entered it. He knew he wasn't going to have a good night tonight. He wouldn't be able to get it out of his mind. Surely Cobb had better things to do with his time than bait him?

He met the rest of his men, who were stood in readiness as always by Catherina Port, and led them out towards Pole Fort. He brooded throughout the handover of duties between himself and the outgoing guard commander, allowing his Sergeants to conduct the normal dispositions. Once they had reported all was in good order, he bid them carry on and then took himself for an inspection beyond the Lines.

"Is that wise, Sir?" asked Longshore. "Standing orders are no one ventures out beyond the agreed boundaries of the trenches at night."

"Those orders are for the safety of the men, Corporal. If there is anything out there that shouldn't be, then they should be the ones to be worried about. I will be fine."

Once Fitzwilliam had gone Corporals Longshore and Swallow got their heads together.

"What's up with the Ensign, do you think?" asked Swallow.

Longshore scratched his head.

"Not sure but it isn't like him. The only time he gets like that is when he has had dealings with an officer above his rank."

"He gets that a lot, though."

"True enough."

"Think we should send someone after him?"

"No. Like he said. Who is going to have the balls to have a crack at him?"

*

Outside of the fort, Fitzwilliam paced along an unmanned section of trench. He looked out into the hinterland, assured himself that all seemed well, and hauled himself over the top. He tried to calm his mind and reason the problem through, not usually his strongest suit. Cobb had taken up residence at the Sailor. Each night he would be there, drinking but causing no trouble. It was clear he was deliberately trying to rub his nose in it. And worse than that, he had struck up some kind of friendship with Siobhan. From what Drummond had told him, he was nothing but a perfect gentleman towards her. A perfect bastard more like. Fitzwilliam wasn't a fool. A week previously he had approached Siobhan and tried to warn her, to tell her that the man could not be trusted.

"Do you think I care about the clumsy attentions of any one of you?" had been her angry response. "Do you think that I am not capable of seeing what is going on? I'll thank you to keep your nose out of my affairs. If any man wishes to flatter me they are welcome to try, because it is good for business. I suffer you because you pay us money for board and lodgings. I suffer him because he pays for drink."

Fitzwilliam had felt properly chastised and had swiftly departed from her icy presence.

On reflection, her answer had mollified his concerns

somewhat. He should have remembered the words of Donahoe; his daughter was far too smart and strong-willed to get suckered in by sweet words. Good god but he had learnt that the hard way himself! He laughed and his mood lightened. He had no need to worry about Siobhan; his gallantry was misplaced. Continuing to chuckle he wandered along the hinterland of Tangier.

A sentry patrolling the Lines stopped and tracked the sound. When he saw the figure picking its way idly and quite brazenly across the rugged country, he shook his head and let his tension ease. All was well. It was just the Wildman.

*

"Cobb, you know you are asking us to take part in a deliberate deception?" said Green, with a focus and intensity that belied his earlier lack of sobriety. In fact, over the last few minutes he had sobered up quite quickly. A glance at Oates had confirmed a similar disposition.

"I do," Cobb replied.

Green pursed his lips. It was a strategy full of risk but he did most wholeheartedly approve of the outcome. He looked once more at Oates who, after a moment's hesitation, nodded his head in agreement.

"Very well, Cobb. We are with you in this. Fitzwilliam is a disgrace. God knows what damage he is doing to the men under his command."

"Turning them into ill-mannered brutes like himself, I imagine," replied Oates.

Cobb sat back, satisfied. He had his associates. He had given them a bitter and heartfelt tirade regarding the unsuitability of the Scot for command. More than that, he had dragged the man's character through the gutter. With these two, it hadn't been a particularly challenging task. He knew them; he appealed to their arrogance and breeding and turned it to his advantage. They would give him the support and the cover he would need to keep from becoming a collateral victim in his own enterprise. Now he could start the final destruction of Fitzwilliam's career.

"What do you want us to do?" asked Green.

Cobb tilted his head towards the bar.

"Go get the father to fetch us another bottle from his cellar. Once he has gone I'll duck into the kitchens. When he comes back, engage him in conversation if you can. Keep his attention from wondering. If he asks where I've gone, just say I have gone to find an alleyway to piss in."

Oates grinned. "And then?" he asked.

"And then, you play the honourable officers. You say that I was simply...defending myself."

"Then we best be about it." Green stood up. He wanted to start the enterprise without further preamble. He strode up to the bar. Donahoe looked up.

"Sir?"

"Barkeep? I have to say, you have impressed me greatly with your wine selection. Perhaps I can trouble you for a further bottle?"

Donahoe nodded. He disappeared down the stairs leading from the back wall of the bar into the cellar. Green turned and looked at Cobb, who pushed himself off the chair and walked nonchalantly towards kitchens and the back of the tavern.

Siobhan reached the top of the landing and opened

the door leading to Fitzwilliam's room. Whereas she would turn down Drummond in the morning, Fitzwilliam's unusual lifestyle had to be accommodated. She sighed. The place was a state, as usual. How could one man be so untidy? Clothes and bedclothes lay scattered, plates of half-finished meals and empty mugs were occasional finds. She set about dealing with the mess. Then there was a gentle tap on door, and she turned round in surprise.

"Oh," she said, bringing a hand to her chest, "it's you. Gave me a fright, so you did."

"I humbly apologise," said Cobb, entering the room. He stood and appraised the space.

"So this is his lair? Typical of the man."

His scornful tone was not lost on Siobhan. She started to feel uncomfortable. This man shouldn't be here.

"Can I help you, Captain?"

"Oh, yes. I had thought to find you in the kitchen. I find myself hungry again and was going to ask for some more of your wonderful stew. I hope you don't mind me coming to look for you?" he said smiling. In the dimly lit room she searched for any warmth in his eyes. She found none.

"I may have some left. If you'll permit me?" she made to exit the room, but instead Cobb took a pace forward and blocked her way.

"You know, now that I find myself here, I realise that my hunger is greater than I thought," he said, his voice dropping low.

Siobhan knew what he meant and exactly where it would lead. But she was not going to allow it.

"Captain Cobb, perhaps you should just head back down?"

"No, I think I'd like to stay a while here. Don't you

want me to?" he reached out and stroked her hair.

Siobhan reared back in alarm.

"Don't do that, Captain," she warned. "I'll call my father."

Cobb laughed. It was an ugly sound.

"And tell me. What do you think he could do?" he stepped closer and ran a hand through her hair.

She slapped him hard. She hoped it would bring him to his senses. His face whipped to the side, but his grip tightened on her hair. He turned back to face her once more, a dark, dangerous expression on his face. His grip on her hair grew tighter still and he yanked her head back. Siobhan cried out in spite of herself.

"You like it rough do you? Good."

With his free hand, he slapped her hard. The force of the blow knocked her against the wall, her legs buckling. She raised a trembling hand to her cheek. It felt numb. Cobb closed the door to the landing then advanced towards her, grinning.

"Don't worry lass. Your very own knight in shining armour will no doubt be along soon enough."

Siobhan looked into his eyes. She wouldn't cry out again. She wouldn't give him the satisfaction.

*

A breeze had sprung up during the night, providing welcome relief to the stifling, stale heat of the fort. Fitzwilliam had returned from his wanderings to a good-natured ribbing from his men. He had promised next time that he would take out a torch or lantern so that the sentries would not shoot him for a Moorish spy.

"And what if I get taken for an English spy by the Moors?" he had asked.

"Aye, it's for their protection, too. Gives 'em a chance to get away if they see you coming, Sir," Swallow had replied.

As midnight arrived, Fitzwilliam hunkered down against the back wall of the fort and worked at his pipe, coaxing a gentle glow from the tobacco. He enjoyed working the pipe, keeping the heat going, savouring the taste of the smoke. What a marvellous thing Sir Walter Rayleigh had done on his return to Queen Bess, bringing with him this wonderful plant.

"Who goes there?" a voice challenged in the dark.

"Messenger from the town, for the Ensign," replied a breathless voice.

"Come in, then. You'll find the Ensign over there."

A dark shape moved toward him and as it drew closer, Fitzwilliam inspected the soldier, who must have run all the way.

"You alright?" he asked.

"Yes, Sir. Message from the Adjutant. He was most insistent that I make all haste to get to you."

Fitzwilliam stood up quickly. What was this?

"Speak up then, man."

"Sir. The Adjutant asks that you report to him immediately at your lodgings."

"Anything else?"

The messenger shook his head. "He won't say what it is. All I can say is that he looked very worried."

That didn't sound good.

"Very well. Corporal Longshore?"

"Sir?"

"Take over. I am called away. I'll be back as soon as I can."

"Yes, Sir.

He made for the exit of the fort, passing through the

low portal leading to the connecting trench and hauled himself out. Once onto level ground, he set off at a jog for the gate. If Drummond had sent for him to come back to the Tavern, it could only mean one thing. Cobb. What on earth had the man done? It took a few minutes to cover the ground and gain entry back into Tangier. The gate was shut as per standing orders and he had an impatient wait as they first confirmed his identity, removed the bar and pushed open the gate. As he drew nearer to the Jolly Sailor he pushed himself harder, a strange, inexplicable dread settling upon his mind. When he arrived, a soldier stood guard at the doorway. He moved to one side as Fitzwilliam rushed past and entered into the dimly lit tavern. Sat at a table was Drummond, sporting a deeply pensive face. He rose quickly to intercept him.

"What is it?" asked Fitzwilliam.

Drummond placed a hand on his chest.

"James, I...I don't know what to say. I wasn't here. I should have been. I should have seen this coming."

"What is it, Rupert? Tell me, for God's sake."

"It's Siobhan."

Fitzwilliam felt his legs go weak.

"No. She's not...?"

"She's alive. But she was beaten and I cannot tell if her injuries are severe. Her father is in her room."

Fitzwilliam growled.

"Who did this?" he already knew what the answer would be.

Drummond hesitated for a moment.

"It was Cobb."

"That bastard. He pays for this." Fitzwilliam tried to push past, but Drummond increased the pressure on his chest and held him back.

"It is his word against hers," he whispered urgently. "Donahoe was distracted by Cobb's accomplices, Oates and Green. There were no other witnesses. You know how this will play out. A serving wench makes a claim against a serving officer and I guarantee she will be hounded out. She has no voice, not here. Cobb's men will stand with him."

Fitzwilliam forced his hand away. "James. He cannot be touched," implored Drummond.

Fitzwilliam stalked past him into the kitchen and on towards Siobhan's ground floor bedroom. A single light burned through the open window. The door was shut. He made a fist to knock and found his hand was shaking. With rage or fear he could not tell. He rapped twice and waited for a few seconds for an invitation. None came, so he pulled the door open and entered.

It occurred to him as he surveyed the room that he had never been in here before. He would never have dared. A table sat tight to the right hand wall upon which was placed a bowl, an ornate mirror, a hairbrush and a jewellery box. The candle he had seen also rested there. Ahead, a single bed was pushed up tight against the far wall. She sat there, head buried in the shoulder of her father, who rocked her gently, whilst stroking her long black hair. As he watched the gently swaying movement, he spied the occasional shudder coming from her body. She was sobbing.

Fitzwilliam felt physically sick. His mouth was open, but he could find no words. He had no coherent thoughts, yet his mind was racing. His hands flexed and then froze into fists. His fingers growing tighter, his arms starting to strain as he put more force into the grip. His whole body started to shake. Siobhan lifted her head. Even in the gloom, the dark, swollen patches around her eyes and lips told him the story. She met his gaze, locking eyes with him for a moment. He saw the hurt, the betrayal and the accusation. She blamed him. He swallowed. His mouth was dry.

"I'm sorry. I'm sorry," he croaked out.

She turned away and buried her head back into Donahoe's shoulder. Her father locked at him, tears rolling down his eyes.

"You want to make amends? You go find him and kill him."

Fitzwilliam nodded. Yes, he knew what he had to do. He left the room and returned downstairs.

As he entered the bar room, he didn't even stop to speak to his friend. He went straight towards the exit. Drummond stood up and grabbed his arm, a look of alarm on his face.

"James. Don't."

"What do you expect me to do?" Fitzwilliam hissed. "He meant for this to happen. He did this!"

"I know," said Drummond, "but think about this clearly! Think about what he is trying to do. He wants you to react."

"Well he's going to see me react now!"

"James, stop. Don't fall into his trap. We can think of something. I can speak to Fitzgerald."

Fitzwilliam pulled his arm away.

"And what is that fool going to do? It's my word against Cobb's. Do you think he cares about a tavern wench? No, he'll do nothing. Cobb started this and he wants to see me try and finish it. I will give him that satisfaction."

Drummond stepped forward and grasped his friend's shoulders and held tight even as Fitzwilliam struggled.

"I can't protect you, James, if you charge in and start

swinging. There will be nothing I can do. Even Teviot, a more honourable man I could not hope to find, would not accept your reasons."

Fitzwilliam nodded. A small part of his mind, his common sense, knew that to be true. It didn't matter.

"I'll see you later, my friend."

He gently but firmly lifted his friend's hands off of him. He thought once more of Siobhan, her father gently stroking her hair and whispering. The look she had given him, the hurt in her eyes. His stomach tightened and his heart felt fit to burst. He turned and stormed out of the Tavern, slamming the door against the wall with shuddering force.

He marched swiftly along the streets leading to the Upper Castle, for where else would Cobb and his cohorts be? He held himself back from running for he wanted to conserve his energy. His focused on one simple task. Find Cobb. He'd find him and make him pay. After a few minutes he walked under the gateway and into the courtyard of the Upper Castle. The two guards stood to attention. He ignored them. Ahead was the Governor's residence, lights blazing from the lounge room. As he drew closer he could hear the hubbub of voices in jovial mood. Laughter boomed from an open window. No doubt the assembled officers would be well into their nightly ritual of drinking and gambling. He entered into the main hallway, it was gently lit with just a few candles to keep out the dark, not so the entrance to the lounge where light and noise tumbled out from the gaps of the double doors. He turned left and opened the doors. He stepped through, deliberately keeping an air of nonchalance. He didn't want to give any indication there was something wrong. As he expected, the officers of the garrison were gathered in groups, some dicing, others engaged in games of cards. He looked about the room and spied Cobb, his back to him, stood in discussion with his two cronies. Fitzwilliam strode over.

Fairborne looked up from a table, a clutch of playing cards in one hand and a glass of sherry in another. He took in the sight of the young man and raised an eyebrow.

"No swords in here, young Fitzwilliam," he said sternly.

Fitzwilliam ignored Fairborne and quickly covered the ground towards Cobb. Green glanced over towards him as the distance closed, alarm flashing in his eyes. Cobb turned just in time to meet Fitzwilliam's fist as it connected with his nose. Blood splattered as the gristle collapsed under the force of the blow. Cobb fell back into Oates even as he raised a hand to his face.

"Get up, you shite, and get what's coming to you!" shouted Fitzwilliam.

The place was suddenly in an uproar. Outraged shouting and exclamations of surprise mingled with the smashing of glasses as men stood too quickly from their tables to observe the scene.

"Come on!" Fitzwilliam too a step forward his fist raised to strike.

"Ensign!" roared Fairborne. "Stand fast! What do you think you are doing?"

"Ask him!"

Cobb propped himself up and ran a hand across his mess of a face and studied the blood he had gathered upon it. He looked up and smiled triumphantly.

"Unless the young whelp is planning on running me through at this very instant, I demand satisfaction."

"Oh I think I'll just finish you now," said Fitzwilliam reaching behind him and drawing his sword.

"Ensign. You will not," commanded Fairborne, stepping in between the two men. "There will be no blood spilt in the Governor's residence."

More officers surrounded Fitzwilliam, making it impossible to swing his blade. He looked about him, daring anyone to come closer.

Fitzgerald, the Lieutenant-Governor elect, stepped forward. His face was red, his anger palpable.

"There are military articles for this sort of insubordination. This is mutiny. A junior officer striking his better will see themselves hanged as soon as their guilt is pronounced by a court martial, which I am required to conduct. The Governor has no truck with his officers settling accounts themselves." He looked around the room, resting his gaze first upon Cobb then Fitzwilliam, a cold smile playing on his lips. "However, I also believe in the right of a man to defend their own honour. Captain Cobb, in the absence of the Governor, I command the garrison and am responsible for the enforcement of good discipline. In this instance, I leave it to you to make your choice."

Cobb stood up, his eyes narrowing.

"Thank you, Colonel. My demand still stands. I want to see this undisciplined whelp humbled and will meet him tomorrow morning."

A murmur of approval met his request. Fitzwilliam was taken aback. He could have been on his way to a pointless death on the gibbet but instead Cobb had given him a chance.

Fitzgerald nodded and placed his thumbs into his belt.

"Very well. Then the two of you will met and duel tomorrow morning. Captain Cobb, you may choose your seconds. Ensign, you may do the same. Though I doubt anyone here will wish that duty."

Fitzwilliam tilted his head.

"Aye, that'll do me." If Cobb wanted a crack at him, he would be welcome to it.

"Now, where shall we conduct this? Not inside the walls," said Fairborne. He was looking at Fitzwilliam intently.

"I know a place," suggested Fitzwilliam.

The Colonel raised an eyebrow.

"Outside the walls overlooking the sea. There is a flat spot. Quiet, away from everyone."

"Captain Cobb? Is that acceptable?" asked Fitzgerald.

"It is."

"Good, then you will meet one hour after dawn."

*

"What did I say? I warned you, didn't I?" demanded Drummond, continuing his tirade before Fitzwilliam could open his mouth. "Honestly, James. How did you think this was going to turn out? You stride in, gut the man and stride out? Everything sorted? Honour and pride revenged?

Fitzwilliam shrugged.

"Something like that."

"Bah!" Drummond threw his hands in the air, and paced up and down the length of the Tavern. The place was shut, Donahoe having turned out the remaining drinkers and returned to minister to his daughter. In the dim candlelight Fitzwilliam helped himself to ale from behind the counter.

"Look, it works out better this way. The idiot has gone and challenged me to a duel. Can you believe it? All I have to do is give that woman-beating arse the hiding of his life and break all his bones in the process. He submits and then I walk away, all charges dropped."

Drummond stopped his pacing and walked over to the bar and took the mug out of Fitzwilliam's hands. He took a long draft, his Adam's apple bobbing several times. Wiping his hand across his mouth he handed the mug back.

"Thank you. Now listen to me. It isn't that simple. This isn't a fight to the death, you know. It's one thing for Fitzgerald to allow this to happen against Teviot's wishes. It's quite another for him to grant no quarter. It'll be first blood."

"Then that will have to do, for now. I'm not letting that bastard get away with what he did. I'll make sure that when I draw first blood, I make it a really deep cut."

"No, you are still not getting it. Whether you or he wins, that is purely a resolution to your own personal grievance."

Fitzwilliam grunted and drank deep.

"And that is the real issue. James, you have broken military etiquette. You struck a senior officer, threatened him with his life and did it in front of a room full of witnesses who will be happy to testify against your actions."

That caught Fitzwilliam's attention.

"So, even if I win. I'm still getting court-martialled?"

"In short, yes. I explained to Fitzgerald about the circumstances. He did at least question Cobb. And you know what he said? He claims she attacked him! And Oates and Green corroborate his statement. He was simply defending himself from a wild woman."

"Didn't Donahoe approach the Colonel? Surely he would have asked for representation, for justice?"

"He did at that. But as I have said to you countless times, he did not witness the act. It is purely Siobhan's word against Cobb's."

"And that will mean my head on a stake?"

"Most likely. But I imagine you'll be held until the Governor returns."

"Then as his loyal adjutant, you'll smooth things over."

"No."

"Come on, Rupert!"

"It's way beyond me, James. I am just a captain you know, and I've used up any credit with the Governor already, as far as you are concerned. All I can do is my job, and that means being impartial and observing orders to the letter. You are on your own."

Fitzwilliam sighed and placed his hands on the counter. His anger at seeing Siobhan had cooled somewhat. He did not regret any of his actions, but he could understand the position he was now in and he realised there was nothing his friend could do for him.

"Tell me at least you'll be my second?"

Drummond shook his head and frowned.

"I cannot even do that. I told you. I'm the Adjutant. I cannot get involved."

"Wonderful news. Looks like I am on my own, indeed."

"I am truly sorry, James."

Fitzwilliam reached across the bar and put a hand on his friend's shoulder. "I know. Don't worry about me. I'll sort something out. Just try and get me some decent food when I'm in the gaol."

"I'll do what I can."

*

Fitzwilliam ambled up the pathway to his favourite

resting place. It had seemed like a good place to enjoy his last few moments of freedom. It was going to be another fine, sun-kissed day. The autumns here were nothing like those of home. He looked out across the sea to the east, enjoying the first warm rays of dawn. Get it while you can, he thought to himself. He passed a squad of six soldiers. His honour guard to the gaol, once this business was finished.

"I will be along in a minute," he said, nodding to the sergeant in command of them.

Trailing behind him, a little less enthusiastically, were Swallow and Blair, his two reluctant seconds.

"So, what do we have to do again?" asked Swallow, who was too tired to be sure of what was going on when the ensign had met them coming back in from their guard duty.

"We're his seconds," responded Blair.

"Seconds to what?"

"God above and the devil below. How come you get to be the corporal?" muttered Blair.

"It means that you're here to make sure the other side plays fair," said Fitzwilliam, without turning round.

"I thought it meant we had to fight as well," called Blair.

"True, but duelling is something for gentlemen only. Cobb's seconds would never even think of fighting you two."

"Well, that's a relief."

"Just watch what happens and if you see anyone trying something they shouldn't, tip me the wink, or just shout it out," said Fitzwilliam

"That we will, Sir!" said Swallow, happier now that his role was clear.

"Oh, and if something should happen to me, make

sure Captain Drummond gets the truth of it."

"Yes, Sir" said Blair.

Fitzwilliam smiled. It was highly irregular for common soldiers to be used as seconds, probably completely against the rules. But then, the Colonel had been right in suggesting no other officer would stand with him and besides, he could hardly generate any more disapproval.

Ahead of him awaited his opponent, and apparent nemesis. As he drew near, he noted that Cobb had already removed his red coat and was waiting, white shirt open and sleeves rolled up. He stood at the far end of the plateau, arms folded, watching his approach. Behind Cobb stood Oates and Green, the latter holding Cobb's sabre, still in its scabbard, in his outstretched arms. They were waiting on a small plateau of land that marked the end of the coastal path along the walls. It was no more than five yards wide, with a steep fall into the sea below. At least there were no rocks at the bottom of it to dash anyone unlucky enough to fall in.

To one side stood the referee. It surprised him to see Fairborne fulfilling that duty. He walked up to Fitzwilliam and fixed him with a hard stare.

"There'll be no nonsense today, understand me, Ensign?"

"Yes, Major. Clearly."

Fairborne turned his eye towards the two soldiers and tutted. He eyeballed Fitzwilliam once more.

"Get yourself ready. Once we're done here, I'll summon the guard to collect you."

He turned and walked to a mid-point between the two groups. Fitzwilliam pulled out his two pistols, handing them to Swallow. He undid his belt, removed his sword and took off his jacket, which he gave to Blair.

"Make sure you get all of that and this," he raised his

sheathed sword, "back to the Jolly Sailor. There's already a flagon waiting for the pair of you once it's done."

Swallow nodded.

"Give 'im a whippin', Sir" murmured Swallow, looking grim.

Fitzwilliam grinned, pulled out his blade and handed over the scabbard. He nodded to Fairborne that he was ready.

Cobb turned to Green, took hold of his scabbard and drew out his sabre. He swished it a few times in the air then stood legs apart in a position of quiet readiness.

"This is a duel of honour between two men of rank and breeding," pronounced Fairborne. "Conducted by gentlemen who shall observe the rules of the duel. Your seconds are here purely to observe and bind your wounds. Once first blood is drawn, that is the end of the duel and honour is satisfied. Do you both agree to this?"

"I do," said Cobb.

"So do I," responded Fitzwilliam, though in truth he'd rather it was a fight to the death.

"Then, you may commence."

Fairborne stepped well back.

Fitzwilliam took one step forward with his left leg and brought his blade up to a low guard, the tip dipping just below the horizontal.

Cobb, holding his smaller and lighter sabre in his right hand, came forward to close the distance to just beyond the claymore's range.

Fitzwilliam studied his opponent's face: cold, hard, calculating. He was not sure he had ever witnessed such naked hatred displayed toward him. Cobb stepped to his left, Fitzwilliam followed. Another step, one more followed, but Fitzwilliam wasn't playing this game; he was no master swordsman or duellist, better to batter the man into submission. As Cobb started to shift his weight for another step, Fitzwilliam lunged forward, his blade lifting to a horizontal position. But Cobb had seen it coming. He shifted back onto his right foot, swaying out of the way of the thrust, extending his own blade to cut down onto Fitzwilliam's outstretched arm. Realising the danger committed to his lunge, Fitzwilliam pushed out with his legs, pulling his blade back and upwards. The two blades met with a loud clang. Fitzwilliam fell to the ground, rolled twice and picked himself up, fully expecting to feel the sting of a cut as Cobb followed him into the roll. But instead Cobb had stepped back and allowed him to regain his fighting stance, a smile playing on the older man's lips. The bastard wasn't doing that out of any sense of fairness.

Fitzwilliam hefted his blade to a high port and stepped forward. As he did so, he tilted the blade to the left and swung a roundhouse cut over his head and diagonally down towards Cobb's chest, who reacted by bringing his blade up, and using both his hands to block the force of the strike, the shock travelling along Fitzwilliam's arms. Cobb, holding his position, raised his right elbow and jabbed it into his face. It wasn't forceful but it pushed Fitzwilliam a step back, and Cobb followed up with a left to right slash across Fitzwilliam's midriff. He pulled his stomach in as the blade swept past. He felt a tug on his shirt. He dropped onto his left knee and launched a powerful blow at Cobb's legs. Caught off guard by this move Cobb jumped back quickly, the blade sped past and Fitzwilliam tensed to slow the momentum as Cobb stepped forward once more to deliver a downward cut onto his right shoulder. Realising the danger he stopped applying the counterforce, commanding his arm muscles to support the travel of the blade, bringing it round behind him as he instinctively leaned back away from the sword coming towards him. The blade met just inches from his shoulder. He pushed upward with his legs, grunting with the effort, using the claymore to force the sabre away from his body. Both men stepped back, breathing heavily. Fitzwilliam wiped the sweat from his brow, then gripped the sword with both hands and readied himself for another charge.

"Stop! First blood is drawn!"

Fairborne stepped between them and pointed at Fitzwilliam. What? Had he nicked Cobb?

"Captain Cobb has drawn first blood. Honour is satisfied. The matter is settled."

Cobb spat and turned his back, taking a cloth from Oates that he used to wipe down his weapon.

"Where? I have no cut!" cried Fitzwilliam. This was nonsense they had barely started to fight.

Fairborne pointed at his shirt. He looked down and saw where he had felt the sabre cut through the cloth. A red stain marked the edges. He pushed his hand in and felt for a wound, a red smear coating his fingers as he withdrew them. He looked closer; it was little more than a scratch, two inches across.

He looked up. "This? This is nothing."

"It is blood. The duel is over," replied Fairborne. He leaned in close. "And so is your career, if you don't hang first, you bloody idiot. If you insist on fighting with that weapon you need to fight dirtier. He had the measure of you from the start." Fairborne stepped back and mentioned for the waiting soldiers to walk up.

"These men will escort you to your new quarters. The court martial will be scheduled on the Governor's return from leave."

"When is that?" asked Fitzwilliam.

"He returns in January. So you'll have plenty of time to think about your foolish actions."

Two months? The only good thing about his incarceration was that he days would get cooler the nearer to winter they got, thought Fitzwilliam. Cold comfort indeed. He sighed deeply, looked at his weapon fondly, and handed it over to Swallow.

"Like I said, to the tavern. They'll hold it in trust."

"Yes, Sir. For what it was worth. If the fight had gone on, you would have had him."

Fitzwilliam smiled. He knew, he accepted, how things were going to end, but damn it all, he had expected to leave with some dignity. The Major was right, he was a fool. Not for himself, for Siobhan. He had let her down. And there was nothing more he could do.

25 December 1663
Tangier Gaol

The door swung outwards with a squeal. The dim light coming in from the hallway framed a figure bearing a tray.

"Merry Christmas."

"And to you, Rupert," replied Fitzwilliam from his prone position on the bed. "Nice of you to drop by. And bearing gifts I see."

Drummond stepped across the threshold and placed the tray down on the small table in the far corner of the cell, walked back out into the hallway and returned with a lighted candle, placed it next to the tray and then took post on the available stool. The door stayed open. As the Adjutant, he could be trusted, and was a daily visitor. He had used his influence to make his friend's stay more bearable with proper bedding and furniture.

"Don't I always?" he replied, removing the cloth covering the tray. It revealed two mugs and a plate of bread, cheese, fruits and meats.

Fitzwilliam pushed himself off the bed and examined

the food with a keen eye.

"Ah, a Christmas feast indeed." He reached over and picked up a mug, it was empty.

"And to drink?"

Drummond reached into his jacket and withdrew a bottle.

"A gift from the Donahoes."

"Wonderful."

Drummond uncorked it, took an appreciative sniff, and poured its contents into Fitzwilliam's proffered mug, then poured one for himself.

His friend took a swig, washed it around his mouth, swallowed and sighed.

"This is decent wine. I would have been happy with the worst kind of dregs."

"See? You are still held in high regard in some quarters. Not many, just one or two"

Fitzwilliam leaned forward and started helping himself to the meat.

"How are they both?" he mumbled, through a mouth stuffed with boiled goat.

"They are well. Business has been good. Siobhan told me to send her best."

"Finally starting to warm to me, then?"

"I think that she is being charitable. It is Christmas after all." He leaned forward and broke off a bit of cheese.

"We have just negotiated another two months to the treaty. Guyland was quite amenable to the Lieutenant-Governor's request. That means we don't have to look to our defences before the real Governor returns."

"Oh?"

"Teviot is on his way back. I received a letter yesterday. He should be arriving sometime next month."

"My fate approaches," said Fitzwilliam. He took another swig of wine and leaned back against the wall thoughtfully.

Drummond studied Fitzwilliam closely. Perhaps it was the inevitability of it all, but the Scotsman was calmer, more relaxed and at peace than Drummond had ever seen him before. While he liked his friend's passion, this new element to his character suited him. Could it be he was growing up?

14 January 1664
The Governor's Residence

Drummond laid out a sheaf of documents ready for inspection upon the Governor's desk. They ran the spectrum of duties and considerations that the post held. Progress reports on the construction of fortifications and the lamentable state of progress on the construction of the mole. There were requirements for more building materials. Intelligence accounts of local Berber activity. Endless lists of requisitions and ration levels. The accounts of resupply that each ship was delivering, weapons held in storage, weapons broken, barrels of powder held, pages covering each fort, its stock and manpower. There were even a few requests from local chieftains who wanted greater access to the town and better taxation agreements. Naturally there were facts and figures of garrison numbers, the dispositions of the sick, the lame and the lazy. And finally there was the provost report. A long list covering all the miscreant deeds acted out by a garrison of bored and often fractious soldiers: drunkenness, brawling, damage to property.

An unremarkable set of narratives, where punishment was meted out either by the lash, or the more effective method of the docking of pay. It also furnished the names of all those currently detained at his lordship's pleasure, and attached to that page, was a personal note by Fitzgerald, telling his involvement in the settling of a certain deeply disturbing incident involving two officers.

Drummond put that at the bottom of the pile. He stood up, straightening his jacket and brushing it down. He waited for a few moments looking expectantly at the door leading into the Governor's office. He stole another look at the pile of papers, and then looked back towards the door. He looked again at the papers and bit his lip.

"Oh, bugger it all."

He stepped back to the desk, dug out the provost's report and put it just underneath the top few papers. There was no point in trying to bloody hide it, he thought. If he did that he would just get taken to task for trying to bury it. And it's not as if someone won't mention it at the very first opportunity at the welcoming drinks planned this very evening. Whatever happens, Teviot will blow his top. He might as well deal with it now.

He stood to attention once more, settling into a pose of calm expectation, as the doors were thrown open and Teviot bustled into the room.

"Ah, good morning, my lord. You look well rested!"

Teviot did not falter in his advance.

"I do not, Captain, we got caught in a storm and was I emptying my gullet every five minutes." He walked round the desk and settled himself into his chair and immediately started leafing through the paper pile.

"Ye gods. I thought Colonel Fitzgerald could have dealt with all of this."

"I thought it best you were kept fully informed, Governor," responded Drummond.

Teviot grunted.

"Quite right too. Well, I won't spend overlong on these. I understand from Fitzgerald that a meeting to report on matters will commence in one hour?"

"Yes, Governor. All the senior officers will be present."

"Good, good. They'll want to hear what I have to say. It would not hurt to tell you now that I was fortunate to have an audience with His Majesty himself before returning. Although his words were not entirely welcome. I informed him of the peace treaty we had signed with Guyland. He responded to this news by commanding me to agree to no peace that would halt our expansion of the defences. That rather puts us in a difficult position" He waved his hand dismissively. "I will deal with this later. And what about you? Anything to tell me? Any news of import?" asked Teviot as he rifled through the paper pile.

Drummond coughed and felt his mouth go dry.

"Well, there is-"

"Wait a moment. What's this?" said Teviot.

Drummond closed his mouth, Teviot had in his hand the provost's report. He was staring intently at the list of prisoners. He then pulled out the written note beneath it and scanned the page, his head moving quickly.

Drummond held his breath, he could see a stiffening of Teviot's back, the anger radiating from him was almost tangible.

"Adjutant?"

"Sir?"

"I presume you were just about to tell me about this?"

"Yes, Sir."

"Good. And is the Colonel's account accurate? I do

acknowledge that you likely have a personal stake in this matter."

"I believe the Colonel's report to be correct in its facts."

"And those would be that we have two of my officers brawling over a woman?"

Drummond licked his lips. It was unlikely he would get another opportunity to put across the truth.

"Those are the facts, my lord. And taken in those terms you would be right to assume both men are at fault. However the woman was but a pawn, a tool to drive one man to anger, to censure himself in the process. That man, Ensign Fitzwilliam, has now been incarcerated for several months for seeking to defend a woman's honour."

"An act of chivalry? Or foolishness?"

"Both, my lord. Captain Cobb has a hatred of Fitzwilliam that is unjustified. He harbours an ill whose source I cannot fathom. And he has gone out of his way to damn my friend. He pushed James to the edge of his reason; even trying to steal a woman he cared about. And when she resisted him, he beat her, in the full knowledge what it would make James do."

Teviot placed his hands on the table and clasped them together.

"And they went and fought a duel. Something I had expressly forbidden. Were you there?"

"No, my lord, I felt it would be impolitic of me to be anywhere near it."

"A wise decision." Teviot waved his hand, as if he was done with the discussion. "Very well. I suggest I work my way through the rest of these before the gathering."

"Yes, my lord." Drummond was confused. Was Teviot's dismissal of him a good sign? Was he that unconcerned by the news of the duel? He trusted the Governor and knew him to be the best man he had ever served under. But the Army could not be run on leniency. If you appeared weak, men would not follow you. Perhaps the best he could hope for was that Cobb would receive a belated punishment for his actions. He didn't expect anything for his friend.

Once Drummond had closed the door, Teviot stood up and swore. Cobb and Fitzwilliam again. Damn them! He did not need this stupid and idiotic distraction, now of all times. They had proven to be two of his most able leaders in a fight. And you couldn't find two peas looking so different in the same pod. They summed up everything that made managing this garrison such a challenge, representing the leftovers of the bitter years of division that had so riven the kingdom. He had given them a chance before and they had squandered it. He had no doubt that Cobb had egged Fitzwilliam on, though he could never hope to prove it. The sad fact was that Fitzwilliam had committed a heinous act, whereas Cobb had disobeyed a direct order. They had given him no simple solution. In fact, he should let them both hang.

*

An hour later, the senior officers of the garrison seated themselves before Teviot's desk. He himself sat patiently, greeting the men as they arrived. Drummond stood next to him, sporting a troubled look. Once they were settled he stood and walked around the desk to face them directly.

"Gentlemen, I bring word from His Majesty. He will

broke no treaty with the Moor that hampers our efforts in establishing a fixed and enduring presence in this region."

Fitzgerald stood.

"Lord Governor, I can assure you that I negotiated this extension with all the best intentions," he said defensively.

Teviot motioned him to sit.

"Colonel Fitzgerald. I understand why you felt the extension of the treaty by two months was nothing more than the proper maintenance of the status quo. You did what you felt was right. But I do doubt Guyland has any earnest desire to live in amicable co-existence. I am sure he was more than happy to prevent us from extending our fortifications during the best digging season of the year. It certainly didn't escape the King that this treaty was nothing more than a temporary suspension of hostilities. He expects us to be more energetic with our relations."

"Guyland isn't going to take this well," stated Fairborne.

"Indeed not. But it is only proper that we communicate this change of affairs to Guyland and then commence the extension of new works as quickly as possible. He will no doubt take umbrage and will seek to disrupt us and, if he can, try once more to bring about our capitulation. Gentlemen, we must not delay. Prepare the men for action and steel them for the fight to come."

The gathered officers nodded.

"I shall distribute your orders later today." He moved round to behind his desk and sat down, clasping his hands in front of him and leaning forward. "Now, there is one more matter I wish to discuss. I understand that, against my express wishes, a duel was consented to."

"Yes, Governor. I allowed this to occur." said Fitzgerald, a defensive tone to his voice.

"And I refereed it to make sure it didn't get out of hand," added Fairborne, with no sense of contriteness.

"Why then," Teviot was angry and made no effort to disguise it, "if you are so keen to see this kind of insubordination conducted in front of the soldiers, are you any better than the officer locked up in the cells right now? You could have dealt with the matter within our own circle but instead, you allowed a private disagreement to spill out onto our very streets!" he raised one hand, made a fist and banged it on the wood in an uncharacteristic display of emotion. "Our men must have confidence in us. We must be their betters in everything we do. How much damage do you think has been done? How much lower is morale because of it? This is unacceptable, gentlemen. He stood up and walked back round to his desk.

"Two of my best fighting officers are at each other's throats. A junior one striking a senior officer at that! And breaking one of our most important rules. Rules that bind us and guide our good conduct. Then that same senior officer decides to break *my rules*. And that, I will not abide. I am gone six months and all the good work that had been done is almost completely undone. All of your actions in this matter, your acquiescence, make you as guilty as they are. I cannot punish the lot of you but I must make an example. Captain Cobb will be demoted to Lieutenant. As for Ensign Fitzwilliam, he has served four months in a cell. That is sufficient. Adjutant?"

"Governor?" asked Captain Drummond, a look of surprise on his face as the news sunk in.

"Make sure he is released. And please inform him that he is stripped of his rank and that he is no longer a member of His Majesty's Army. He is a private citizen and must conduct himself accordingly."

"I will do so, Sir," said Captain Drummond. The man now looked positively relieved. Teviot could understand why, but the man had been honest and loyal in hid defence of his friend.

"One more thing, all of you. The next time any one of my officers decides to step out of line I will personally hang them from the ramparts myself."

30 January 1664
Outside The Walls

Ghailan reigned in and leaned back in the saddle. He reached behind him and pulled up a waterskin, pulling the cap out and drinking deeply of its lukewarm contents. He looked up into the sky; it was overcast and grey. Good weather for gathering water, replenishing stores for the year ahead and preparing crops. He understood that and welcomed it, but it was also the best time for digging. The ground was made sodden by the winter rains. And digging was something the English soldiers seemed to enjoy no end of, as once more they sought to fortify their position. Each day that they did so would make it that much harder for him. Even now they were building a new hornwork before the Upper Castle. Teviot had returned, and the garrison was infused with enthusiasm and energy once more. His spies had said as much, before Teviot had ordered the town closed to the local traders. Reneging on the agreement he had made with the man's lieutenant was galling and proved that Teviot had seen through his plan. Apparently the English King had forbidden any peace with the Moors that would have stopped the expansion he was witnessing now. For that foresight into the mind of Ghailan, he gave this distant ruler due credit. It would have been exactly what he would have done. But now he had to redress the balance. The slight to him in breaking their agreement had to be answered. His honour, his men and, more importantly, his reputation, demanded it. If he did not respond in kind he would lose credibility and support. It was a dangerous time for him. He could not afford to dwell here long. He and his army were required in the south, not here at the northernmost point of his lands. The Great Tafiletta, that treacherous scoundrel who believed himself fit to rule Barbary, was on the move against his patron, Mohammed. The prize was the throne of Morocco itself. Already he was trying to gather allies, seeding lies, spreading rumours and creating discontent. Ghailan needed to send his men to fight in the coming civil war, not waste time against the walls of Tangier. The enemies within were far more of a threat to him than the designs of these foreigners.

When he had received word of the Englishman's return it had pleased him in part. He looked forward to the coming clash of wills again. He respected this leader. He was a worthy opponent. And this was how he would defeat the English. Their commander was the key. He had to find a way to break Teviot, to outmanoeuvre him.

Ghailan replaced his waterskin and looked behind him. A line of horsemen and infantry snaked back into the foothills. He had brought his entire army to Tangier. Grim-faced swordsmen, strong-armed archers and light cavalry without peer. Experienced and hardy men, they had been well rested in the months following the treaty. He would remind them of what it was to wage war and then take them south to put down the pretender.

He signalled to his commanders. The action would begin immediately. It would be what they did best. Ambushes and lightning strikes; throw the enemy off balance and see what they would do.

29 February 1664
Upper Castle

Teviot sat at his desk, once more pouring over his plans for the fortification. They were so close to completion. It all came down to time. Every day would make it harder it would be for the English to be rooted out. Guyland knew that too. A horn sounded not far from his window. Another assault was underway. He stood up and walked towards his window, from which aspect he could see a section of the castle ramparts. Against a bleak, overcast sky, he watched gun crews rolling their weapons forward to fire. At a barked command, the cannons roared, the concussion causing the window to vibrate slightly. For the last three days, Guyland had switched his attacks across the Lines, bringing pressure to bear on one point, throwing large numbers of troops into a narrow front. So far the blockhouses and forts had held firm, helped in no small part by the concentrated artillery fire of the Tangier batteries. Concentrating their attacks meant his crews could concentrate their fire also, wrecking a heavy toll upon the waves of infantry. He was thankful there was no counter battery fire and feared the day when the Moors of Barbary advanced in their military tactics and technology. They had already taken a step forward; he had noted the small groups of Moors armed with muskets, dispersed around the battlefield. Not many of them and displaying very little if any skill, they succeeded only in disturbing their own men and mounts, positioned as they were far too far back. The rounds were barely making the distance to the English positions, their energy all but spent.

As it stood, for their part, his soldiers were performing admirably. They had correctly surmised the ineffectiveness of Moorish musketry and had not allowed it to interfere with their conduct. His return and the threat of Moorish aggression had quickly roused them all from their collective slumber. It was a pity that they had not been better handled in his absence. The standard garrison duty that comes with peace was a poison to the fighting man, making him slothful and petty. His mind wandered to the incident with his two officers. Such a shame. Well, he was doing no good here. He returned to his desk, collected a pistol, retrieved his sword belt from where it hung on the back of his chair and finally took his helmet from its resting place on the mantelpiece above the fire. He walked towards the double doors leading from his chamber.

"Captain Drummond? I'm for the walls. I'll be back when the excitement has died down."

*

The distant rumbling sounded not unlike thunder. But he knew well enough what it meant. This was the fourth day of battle and the sound of cannon fire was becoming commonplace. Fitzwilliam tied off the rope and checked it was tight around the barrel.

"Haul it up."

The rope was pulled taut and the barrel started to inch up the two parallel straight edges that ran up the centre of the cellar stairs. Fitzwilliam got behind it and began to push, markedly increasing its speed. After clearing ten steps, he was back on the ground floor, stood behind the bar. Donahoe dropped the rope and nodded.

"Right. That'll do us for today. If the Moors keep this up I can't imagine we'll get as much business as we'd normally expect."

"No. Everyone will be stood to."

Fitzwilliam gathered a cloth from the counter and wiped at the sweat at the back of his neck. Another volley of shots echoed into the Tavern.

"I can't say I've ever heard those cannon firing for so long before," remarked Donahoe, as he undid the knot on the barrel, pushed it into a gentle tilt and started to roll it back toward the bar. In response Fitzwilliam shut the hatch, allow the barrel to continue to its appointed serving station.

"They must be getting desperate by now," he mused.

Donahoe lowered the beer barrel into place and scratched his chin.

"What? You or the Moors?"

"Not me," protested Fitzwilliam, "I'm happy to be out of it."

Donahoe pursued his lips, his left eyebrow rising in surprise.

"Is that so? A greater conversion has not been seen since the apostle Paul himself swore his soul to God on the road to Damascus. You miss it, I can see that."

"Alright, yes. I miss it," Fitzwilliam conceded, "but I'm also thankful to be alive and with a roof over my head, thanks to you."

Since his release, he had wondered what on earth he would do. He had little money to his name, and very few skills. It was a great fortune that Thomas had not driven him out but instead had offered him employment and lodging within the Tavern. He had been forgiven for his part in Siobhan's assault; Thomas bore him no ill will. Instead he had suggested having an extra pair of strong hands would not go amiss. Fitzwilliam had been taken back by this generous act but had still been uneasy. He felt responsible, no he *was* responsible. At first he had refused, afraid to imagine how Siobhan would feel, afraid about how she might look at him, to even bear having him around seemed impossible. Yet she did the unthinkable. She had come to him, when he was still sat in the cell that no longer kept him imprisoned, and had spoken to him. She had thanked him for what he had tried to do, called him a fool to be so easily manipulated, and accused him of putting his childish sense of honour before his own life. But for all that she thanked him. He recalled her words, words he had never expected to hear: "Because, in your own way, you always treated me with respect. You never forced yourself upon me. And in this place, that is a rare thing. Both you and your friend are welcome here and always will be."

He had been speechless. It was more than he dared hope for. And the next day he had returned back to the tavern, more of a home to him now than it had ever been before. Siobhan, for her part, no longer treated him with disdain. For him, for now, it was enough.

"You don't need to thank me, Fitzwilliam. Just do a good job. Tonight, I think I'll leave you in charge. Sure,

I've not had a night off in years. You think you can manage an empty Tavern for me?" asked Donahoe.

"Thomas, I'll do my level best to not bring the house down round our ears."

"Best you don't. Or I'll set my daughter on you."

*

"Get down!" roared Swallow.

As Blair ducked, Swallow swung his blade round in a backhand swipe, slicing open the leg of the Moor who stood behind and above Blair, his own scimitar raised. As the man fell back, screaming in agony, Swallow stabbed forwards, driving his blade into the chest of a second Moor who had been grappling with Blair.

The older man looked up at his friend, with an expression of shock and awe.

"You been taking lessons from Ensign Fitzwilliam?"

"I can think of worse men to learn from," he responded, giving Blair a hand up.

"Our arses are in the wind here. We should try and get to Pole."

"Good luck with that," responded Blair. "Moors are crawling all over it."

"We can't get back, we can't get to a fort. We stay here," shouted Cobb, from further down the trench. He raised a pistol, firing it point blank into the gut of a charging swordsman.

"And if any man runs. I'll shoot him myself."

The entire garrison had been called to defend the Lines, but it was not possible to get everyone into the forts. Small groups of men were scattered along the trenches, fighting hand to hand against waves of screaming Berber tribesmen. And Cobb, in another humiliation, had been given command of Fitzwilliam's men.

"Everyone, stay close together, watch your mates," Longshore ordered. They had already lost five men to wounds. They were left where they fell, as much a hindrance to their fellows as to any Berbers who gained the trench.

Swallow looked out across the battlefield. The pressure had eased on this section, but through the smoke of countless bush fires and explosions he could make out skirmishes being fought left and right of him. Behind another cannon barked and he felt the rush of disturbed air as a cannon ball fly over his head, he ducked instinctively. A moment later a cloud of dirt, scrub and rock erupted just ahead of him.

"If you got muskets, reload 'em while you got the chance," Cobb shouted. "The bastards are coming again!"

Blair looked at Swallow and leaned in close.

"Do you reckon we might get lucky and some Moor will get Cobb?"

"Fat chance. The bastard fights like a demon," replied Swallow.

"Maybe we should...?" Blair left the question hanging in the air.

Swallow thought for a moment. Since that bastard Cobb had taken command, he had made life difficult for all of them and reserved a special hell for those he considered favourites of Fitzwilliam. It would not be the first time an officer got a knife in his back when he faced the enemy.

Swallow shook his head.

"I might not be the sharpest tool but I'm not going sign me own death warrant, Jacob."

"The other officers will never know."

"It's not that. Cobb would stick me if I even looked like having a go. He's too vicious a bugger."

"Good point," muttered Blair.

∗

Cobb dropped low onto the floor of the trench and recharged his pistol. Amidst the chaos of battle, he felt a sense of calm that had eluded him for many weeks. The reason was clear. As he fought for his life he finally had an outlet for the rage that had almost consumed him. He had held it in check as best he could, allowing it to influence his behaviour with the men who had once followed Fitzwilliam, but he retained enough good sense to realise he could not push his treatment of them too far, lest he get a knife in the back. He had to suffer the indignity of demotion quietly when in public or with his fellow officers. Privately, he drank himself into a stupor, letting his anger and sense of betrayal express itself in drunken bouts of aggression, shouting at the four walls of his room. At least now, in battle, he felt more alive, more clear-headed and more worthwhile than he had for a long time. Whilst that young bastard had been imprisoned, he had felt justified and righteous in his actions. He was a senior officer with more battle experience than all the officers present in this god-forsaken shithole. He deserved respect; he had fought for his country for more years than some of these bastards had been alive. Instead the Governor had seen fit to punish him, *him*! And that Scottish whelp had been freed when he should be hanging from a gibbet. Where was the justice? He could expect none except that which he took for himself. When this battle was done, he'd find a way to put things right.

"Sir, they are coming again!" called Longshore, breaking into his reverie.

"Then stand and meet them," Cobb snarled. He pulled back the striker of his pistol and pushed himself off the floor.

*

Two hundred yards away, a large company of Moors, at least two hundred strong, assaulted another section of open trench. They marched on the Lines in good order, wearing shining breastplates and helmets over their black robes. Teviot, watching from the ramparts, recognised these as Guyland's personal guard. Full-time retainers, they were the best of his soldiery. They smashed against the ragged English defences and quickly swept aside the beleaguered redcoats. Upon the shallow berm at the front of the trench they planted a standard, white with a blue crescent.

"By God. That's his personal standard!"

"Sir?" asked an aide.

Teviot beckoned him forward but kept his gaze fixed on the battle.

"Send word to Captain Witham. Order him to take the Tangier Horse and capture that flag."

"Yes, Sir."

The aide hurried off as Teviot bounced his fists on the parapet wall. The battle was reaching a tipping point. The Moors had a foothold on the defences, that banner was a rallying totem; from there they could spread out left and right, get behind the forts. If they did so, artillery support would be greatly neutered. But not yet.

"Gunnery Captain?" he called to a nearby soot-stained soldier, who stood directing the reloading of the Upper

Castle ordnance.

"Sir?"

"Direct your fire on that position, aim for the flag. You have at best two shots then switch fire, our cavalry is headed straight for it."

*

Captain Witham led his thirty horse out of the gates at a brisk trot. Above their heads and to the right, a number of cannon launched a volley against his target, the rounds kicking up great plumes of dirt and dust. Most landed just short of the Lines, one round hitting the trench some yards to the left of the standard. Casualties to be sure, but not enough to dent the large concentration of enemy troops who were starting to pour into and spread out along the cover of the trench, moving towards the forts to either side. They had to be quick. The Moors would dig in and be as devilish as a tick to get out.

"Horse! Wedge formation, on me. We charge right down their throats!"

He raised his sword high, then level, and kicked his heels hard into his mount's flanks. It responded smoothly, moving into a swift gallop. To either side the troop shook out into formation, a swift, fluid spear point, designed to penetrate deep into a defensive line. As the distance closed to no more than fifty yards, another cannon volley flew overhead, dangerously close to the English charge. This time the gunners found their range. A half dozen balls landed in the heart of the Moorish position, tearing into their formation in a red mist of limbs, armour and dirt. The line did not buckle. Instead, more men pushed up, trying to gain the protection of the trench. The Tangier Horse struck seconds later, leaping the trench and smashing into the infantry who had no time to form an adequate defence. The cavalry lay about them with brutal energy, their momentum carrying them right through the block of Guyland's soldiers. With a fighting wedge established, Witham directed his lead riders to start lapping round the rear of the formation. As pressure was brought to bear on two fronts, the Moorish soldiers were squeezed against the trench, the cavalry started to extend their wedge, parting the infantry into two fighting groups. Witham aimed an overhead blow of a charging swordsman, knocking him to the ground, blood flowing from a deep gash to the crown. He took a moment to review the fight. The English were holding their own. The enemy were still reeling from the charge, unable to bring their greater numbers to bear. A thin corridor had opened up between his men as they pushed the wedge outwards. Sensing his moment, he kicked forward and galloped back toward the trench. As he gained the lip he reached out, grasped the abandoned standard tightly and allowed the momentum of his horse to pull it from the ground. As his horse gained firm footing on the English side of the Lines, he raised the banner high and waved it backwards and forwards, his body turned toward the Upper Castle.

Barely visible, Witham spied Teviot, who leaned out over the ramparts, raising his arm, acknowledging the salute, and then dropping it away sharply. Witham understood the signal. He pulled his arm forward and threw the banner away from him. As it clattered to the ground with a hollow twang, a collective groan travelled across the battlefield. Their battle standard cast down, their morale damaged, Moorish troops lost heart, turned their backs and started to peel away from the engagement. Guyland's troops closed ranks and pulled back from the cavalry line, keeping their discipline, allowing the riders no easy way through their defence.

"Let 'em go boys," Witham ordered. His men were still outnumbered and the Moors were withdrawing in order. To pursue further would invite a counter charge by enemy cavalry that no doubt lurked nearby. Let the cannon accompany them instead.

*

Teviot grinned broadly. He had trounced Guyland once more. In committing his best, the Moor had thrown the dice and lost the bet. He didn't fault the man for trying. But losing his standard like that? Folly! A cheer erupted along the length of the walls as the gun crews realised the Moors were withdrawing for good.

"Keep pounding them, men! Don't stop yet. Break their spirits, my brave lads!" he roared.

The crews returned to their task, laughing and cheering as they did so. Before the cannons started up again, Teviot caught the sound of further celebrations drifting across the battlefield from the forts and watched the waving of swords and muskets from the men who had struggled in the trenches.

He laughed again. He turned and shook the hands of his staff. Receiving and sharing congratulations. The men had their victory and their fighting spirit was restored.

*

Three hours later, as dusk settled on the hinterlands of Tangier, a lone envoy, bearing a white flag, walked his horse slowly towards walls. He was met by sentries and escorted to the gates where Lieutenant Cooke briefly conversed with him. He was then taken to an audience with Teviot. Twenty minutes later, the envoy remounted and was allowed to leave without hindrance and in peace.

Guyland had informed Teviot that he could no longer conduct a military campaign against him. The month of Ramadan was fast approaching and his men must fast and worship. The time for war was over. To that end, Guyland and his Berbers were withdrawing back to their homes. He would no longer challenge the English.

3 May 1664
The Governor's Residence

"It's not a surprise I'm afraid, Governor," said Johnson. "We've had these problems countless times before," he shook his head in frustration. "In fact, I recall having this very conversation with the previous governor."

"But never this bad," replied Teviot.

"We are so close, it seems criminal," observed Fitzgerald

"It's the damned Spanish, you know," said Fairborne. "They've never been content with us being so near their shores. I'd wager they were the ones to give Guyland those muskets."

"That may be so, but there is little we can do about that," replied Teviot patiently. "The truth of the matter is, our fortifications are all but complete, and yet we find ourselves without the necessary materials to finish the task. We need building stone and lime. Drummond?"

Drummond stepped forward to stand next to Teviot.

"Sir, gentlemen. Though we have sent repeated

requests for materials, the promised resupply has yet to be dispatched. What ships we have that can be guaranteed safe passage through the straits are earmarked for other essential supplies. Parliament can spare us no more armed escorts and any ships carrying those construction supplies would be at the mercy of corsairs. In short, forgive my bluntness, we can sing for them."

Teviot coughed, Fitzgerald frowned, Johnson looked embarrassed and Fairborne laughed.

"Fitzwilliam is really starting to rub off on you, Adjutant," he said.

"Yes, Sir. I shall redouble my resistance to his charms."

"What are our options then, gentlemen?" asked Teviot, giving Drummond a disapproving look.

"Short of trying to purchase these goods from a friendly nation in the Mediterranean, I would suggest that we should look to our own lands. The eight hundred or so acres we have annexed since we took control of Tangier are nothing more than sand. Good for digging but little else," said Johnson. "But a mile or so further in, you can see the geography changes, the land rises, becomes rockier. That's where you'll find stone and lime aplenty."

"Then that is what we shall do," said Teviot firmly.

"Is that wise?" asked Fitzgerald. "That's Berber country."

"And you know they will be watching," added Fairborne.

"I understand that. But Guyland has been good to his word. There has been no resumption of hostilities. We need these materials. With them we can at last put the final seal on our position here. I believe a small foraging expedition will cause little consternation. And by the time word gets to Guyland, we'll be on our way back," he finished with a confident smile and looked around the group.

"Major Johnson, how many men do you think we'll need?"

The engineer thought for a moment.

"If you want to be quick, a few hundred should do it."

"Well, then. Let's call it a large foraging expedition. We'll march out in good order, armed and ready, just to be sure, conduct our business and return in the evening. Captain Drummond, you have spent far too long shut up in the town. Why don't you accompany me for a nice, bracing stroll in the country?"

"Sounds delightful, Sir," replied Drummond, carefully avoiding any sarcasm entering his voice.

*

"That sounds like a barrel of fun," replied Fitzwilliam, sarcasm dripping from his voice.

"I rather like being stuck in my office. I get a lot done and I avoid the whole unpleasant business of putting my life in mortal jeopardy," said Drummond, morosely nursing a mug.

"Indeed, usually the whole mortal jeopardy business would be my job. But in all earnestness, Drummond, it would seem to me that you are starting to get soft. I remember a time you would relish a fight. You were even quite good at it."

"A compliment from the master."

"A retired one. You going to drink that?"

"What, oh, yes. Sorry. I really have gone soft, haven't I?"

Fitzwilliam laughed. "You and me both. Hauling ale

kegs will keep me strong but Siobhan's cooking will be the death of me."

"I heard that!" called Siobhan from the kitchens.

Fitzwilliam grinned.

"So, what are you going to do, James?" asked Drummond. "Things will hopefully get very quiet here now. We may yet realise the King's dream of a thriving port."

Fitzwilliam leaned in close and placed his arms down on the counter.

"I had thought to head home, make that stomach wrenching trip across the seas. But, you know what? I'm actually quite content here. Thomas and Siobhan have been more a family to me than any I have known. Besides I owe them. And you're here!" he pushed himself off the wooden surface. "I couldn't forgive myself if you had no choice but to consort with your fellow officers. God knows what would become of you. Fighting duels would be next, I'd wager."

"My gratitude knows no bounds," replied Drummond. He drained his mug and wiped his mouth. "At this warm moment of brotherhood, I think I'll turn in. We have an early start. The Governor wants us marching out just as dawn breaks. It's going to be a long day."

"Then a good night to you. I promise not to cause a racket when I retire later this evening."

"That'll be a first."

3 May 1664
Catherina Port

"Good morning, Captain Drummond!"

"Yes, Sir, it is morning," responded his Adjutant.

Teviot laughed and clapped him on the back. He climbed onto his horse and looked behind him. The street leading to the courtyard was thronged with soldiers. Amidst the sea were a line of quartermaster wagons, bearing axes, picks, shovels, and sacks. It was quite a gathering. A low hubbub of voices, belying the early rising enforced on the troops, mingled with the snorting of the wagon mules. Though the men grumbled, it was good-natured. Teviot put that down to the high morale that victory had given them. The battalion-sized force was a composite, made up of different companies, some five hundred strong. It represented virtually all of the spare able-bodied men of the garrison. As always, there was a large contingent of sick, lame and cunningly lazy who could not work. Everyone else was on essential duties.

"Major Johnson?" called Teviot.

The engineer hurried over. He was weighted down with a number of satchels containing various implements and articles of his engineering craft. From one he dug out a crude sketch map of Tangier. "Good morning, Governor, Captain." He took up station next to Drummond and unfurled the map, holding it up so that both Drummond and Teviot could see. The Governor leaned forward in his saddle and squinted.

"Not a bad rendition, Major. Carry on."

"Sir. The area of land that interests us is west and north, a mile or so away towards the coast. I have marked it on the map. We need to head for the bridge over Jews River, up to and over Jews Hill and onto the higher ground that is called the Great Valley. It is there, I believe, we will find an adequate supply of stone and lime."

Teviot clapped him on the back. "Very good. Whilst we are heading that way I would like us to spend some time on the eastern slope of the hill, around the bridge. The brush and scrub is quite thick there and we know the Moors have used it in the past as a perfect spot to hide and launch ambushes from. A couple of hours conducting a clearance of the area would deny them a tactical advantage. What say you, Captain Drummond?"

"Quite so, Sir. With the manpower available, I daresay we'll make short work of it."

"If that is the case, I can use that time to conduct a more thorough survey of the valley to locate the best site for our digging," responded Johnson.

"Perfect. Ensure you take adequate protection. A half troop of the Tangier Horse should do it." Teviot had made sure that even though this was primarily a foraging expedition, he also considered it a reconnoitre in force. He did not doubt that Guyland had men in the high ground; how they would react to such a large foray he did not know, but he wanted to be ready. If it was one thing he had learned here, the Moor respected strength. He was quite sure Guyland would not want to start another fight so soon after his last humiliation, but it paid to be prepared.

He looked about the courtyard and nodded.

"Let's be off."

The gate opened and the force marched out.

*

Swallow thrust his shovel into the ground. "So, tell me again, Jacob, how our lot has improved?"

Blair rubbed his bare head and pinched his forehead.

"In two ways, Simon. Firstly, here we are digging out the undergrowth, unhindered I might add, some half a mile further inland then we have ever been before. It means we are finally getting the better of the locals." Pausing, he reached for his water skin, took a quick swig, washed it about his mouth and spat it out again. "And secondly, we are away from that bastard Cobb for a day."

"Ah, now I remember. And ain't it a surprise that he volunteers us to come out here after being awake all night and doesn't come himself!"

"Oh, he's a smart one alright. Keeps his favourite half of the gang back and gets to stay back in Tangier. Tucked up in bed, I'd warrant."

"Awaking fresh as a daisy and ready to berate us for being slovenly when we have to turn out for duty again tonight," added Swallow.

"Which is why it would go better for the both of you if you stopped jawing and got back to work," advised Longshore, who was engaged in dragging a large root down towards the river. "The quicker we get this lot cleared, the quicker we move on, dig out the treasure and get home."

"Never a wiser word spoken," said Swallow sagely.

*

Johnson crested the top of the rise known as Jews Hill. It had been a difficult climb and he did not have the convenience of a mount. Ahead of him, the English cavalry, twelve in all, waited patiently, the horses cropping on the low-lying vegetation that had already gone dry although it was only late spring. Below him, the rest of the garrison laboured on the northern bank of the river. They were making quick work of it. All the better, it felt strange to be this far outside the Lines. For the first time, they were actually seeing something of the country they had occupied. Speaking of which...

He strode forward across the flat plateau and past the waiting riders to survey the surrounding countryside to the west. Ahead of him, the terrain was a mix of heavily wooded hills, steep gullies and ravines. He spotted a likely outcropping of stone at the base of a nearby hill, only a short walk away. He was about to investigate further when movement in the treeline caught his eye. Someone was coming out of the trees, a local tribesman perhaps. Out hunting? His mouth went dry. The man was not alone. More and more figures starting to emerge, sunlight glinting off drawn blades. More bands started to appear from other nearby woods and copses.

He looked at the cavalry then back at the men. They couldn't hope to even delay this large a body. He grabbed the leg of the man nearest him.

"Quickly. Tell the Governor. The Moors are coming!"

*

The call to arms spread through the English troops quickly. Sergeants and officers bellowed orders, work tools were dropped and arms regained. Within moments the entire force was running up the hill. Teviot watched them from the top of Jews Hill. His decision had been swift. He would not allow the Moors the high ground. The hill was relatively free of cover and climbed in such a way that the summit was formed of a sizeable flat plateau on the eastern side but the western approach was sloping and rocky. By holding the plateau the men could deploy properly and fight as they had been trained. The Moors could try a frontal assault if they wanted. Then see what that would get them.

Johnson hurried over from his observation position on the far side of the hill. "Sir?"

"Major. You look worried."

The engineer put on indignant face on.

"Not at all. Just counting numbers."

"Excellent. What is your reckoning?"

"Some thousands, I'd say. Perhaps three."

Teviot shifted in his saddle and made a thoughtful face.

"Three thousand, you say? I think we can manage that."

Behind him the first of the English soldiers gained the crest.

Teviot sat straight and called out loudly.

"Right men. Get into your formations. Standard drill. Smartly now, present your best faces to the enemy."

The English soldiers were in their element, forming a battleline was second nature. Hours spent drilling for this kind of warfare was their bread and butter. Within minutes, blocks of pikemen were formed up, the long shafts held at the ready, presenting a solid wall of sharpened steel. Mixed within and to either side of the pikes, musketeers readied their weapons, loosening pouches and pockets containing shot, wadding and gunpowder. The cavalry posted themselves slightly further out on both flanks to protect the musket men from any enemy charges.

Teviot nodded in satisfaction. The men were winded from their sprint up the hill, but they knew their business. This was true soldering. The English had positioned themselves on the far eastern side of the hill allowing them possession of the entire flat summit. The Moors would have to funnel in towards them or have to work round and up the slope to flank them. He wouldn't give them that opportunity. Only fifty yards away, the enemy began to appear. A whole damn host of scimitar-wielding, bloodthirsty tribesmen. As they formed up he could see no discernable discipline to them. He spied officers and standards here and there but it seemed as if the commander had decided to just overwhelm them. Perfect.

"Battalion!" he cried. "Forward!"

As one, the English ranks stepped forward, the pikes lowered to the horizontal. The whole frontage moved slowly, keeping the integrity of the formation. Sergeants kept the dressing together, pushing and cajoling the men to keep the pace. Junior officers exhorted the men to fight bravely for King and Country. Teviot nodded; it was as fine a phalanx as any he had seen. The very Spartans themselves would have approved of it.

The Moors, if temporarily unbalanced by the English advance, recovered quickly. A battle cry was taken up all along the line. Swords and shields were raised high.

From the centre, an officer and his standard bearer leapt outwards, causing a wave of Moors to charge in their wake towards the English line. Volleys of musket fire rang out just as the two sides closed, tearing into the flanks of the enemy. And then, in a loud screaming crunch of steel tips against shields and flesh, the two forces met. And the Moors suffered.

Heavily outnumbered as they were, the English were still equal to the task. Finally, they were able to face the Moors using the tactics they excelled in. The enemy had no way to break the dense hedge of spears, no way to penetrate through to the men who wielded them. The front line of Moors died terribly, driven into the pikes by the press of men behind them. The fear of the muskets stopped any attempts at lapping round, sending volleys into the press. Inexorably, the English line started to push and the Moorish horde began to fragment. At first, like splinters, small groups of men peeled off from the rear edges of the mob. These splinters become larger as the mass lost its coherence and in seconds the whole force was moving away from the English line. Pikes dipped and wavered in the air as the blocks of advancing men picked their way over bodies, cheers and insults ringing out in equal measure. Teviot slapped the pommel of his saddle. Hah! In less than five minutes the enemy had been routed. A force six times their size at that. His staff officers gathered around him, faces flushed with success.

"We don't stop. Order the men to pursue," he commanded. "We give them no chance to regroup. We'll teach each Guyland a lesson by robbing him of his army. Deploy the men into companies. Hunt them down!"

His men acknowledged and ran to organise the force laughing and joking as they did so. Teviot saw his few cavalry haring off in pursuit, he was minded to recall them but it was already too late. Their blood was up. Instead he looked for his Adjutant.

*

"Drummond!"

Drummond stopped, realising he had charged off to join in the slaughter even though he had no troops to command. He had never seen such a fine display from the men. It was inspiring. The engagement had proven swift and sure and not for one moment had he doubted they could win.

Embarrassed, he sheathed his sword. "Sir. I'm sorry."

Teviot chuckled.

"Don't be, Captain. I understand exactly how you feel. But we mustn't lose our heads. Take fifty men, return to the bridge and hold it. That is our path of retreat. Not that it is necessary, I'm sure."

"Yes, Sir."

"Good man. Yah!"

Teviot urged his mount onwards to follow the battle.

Drummond looked about and ran over to the nearest block of soldiers and recognised a familiar face leading them

"Lieutenant Oates. Orders from the Governor. I'll need some of your men to help form a rearguard."

Oates looked at first to argue but then he nodded with a sly smile.

"Of course, Captain," he pointed to a group of a dozen soldiers. "These are Cobb's men, the night guard. They are far too tired to be of use anyway. You are welcome to them."

Drummond nodded. He recognised these men. They used to be Fitzwilliam's. He ran over and touched an

NCO on the shoulder.

"Ah, Longshore isn't it? Take your men and double them back down towards the bridge. We are the rearguard."

Corporal Longshore tipped his forehead

"Yes, Sir."

As the soldiers detached from the formation, Drummond ran to the flanks and took further groups of soldiers and moved them into the wake of Fitzwilliams' old command. He did a quick count, twenty musketeers and thirty pike. He ran on and overtook the slower moving pikes on his way to the front of the column, joining Corporal Swallow.

"We winning, Sir?" he asked.

Drummond smiled.

"Yes, I believe so."

"Pity Mister Fitzwilliam missed it, then," said Swallow.

"Yes, a pity indeed."

Behind them, the English force spread out in pursuit of the retreating Berbers. The cavalry and infantry ranged wide, whooping and hollering, charging into the nearby tree lines of the Great Valley.

*

Lieutenant Green led seventy soldiers in between two steeply sided hills. The trees loomed large on either side but they were focussed on their quarry. Thirty or so Moors were just ahead, forming up to charge. Green grinned. Don't they learn?

"Pikes close up. Muskets form a line behind them. If they want to charge we'll meet them in this gap."

His men reformed into a tight wedge, weapons ready to meet the assault. Green was alerted by the shouts of the musket men who had moved to the rear. One pointed his weapon up the slope to his right and fired. Green followed the shot. Gathered by the edge of the trees, a mass of Moorish swordsmen were emerging, shouting and wailing and waving their weapons. He looked left and yet more appeared upon the other hill. In moments the Moors were eagerly charging down the slopes towards them. Green swallowed. It was too late. They were trapped. The enemy tore into them, cutting the redcoats to pieces.

*

Johnson ran into a lightly wooded copse, chasing down a half dozen Moors. He had attached himself to a half company of pike and was happily allowing its sergeant to conduct the hunt. He wasn't really a professional fighting man. His rank gave him authority to command, but he used it to build, not kill. Today, however, the sword in his hand felt good; he felt like a true soldier. He was swept up in the excitement and loving it. His group quickly moved through the copse and emerged facing a slope on the other side that had been screened by the trees. He was lagging slightly behind and was pleased when he saw the rest slow to a halt. As he emerged to join them, he stopped and looked aghast at the slope ahead of him. It was covered with Moors. He knew then it was over. The men were too tired. They could never hope to outrun the lightly armed Moors. The English soldiers, fearful and already resigned to their fates, readied themselves. It would be over quickly.

"Oh, God."

He gripped his sword tightly. He wasn't bad with a blade. Perhaps he might take some of them with him.

*

Teviot watched from the northern edge of Jews Hill as the terror unfolded. From his vantage, he could see his men, broken into small, uncoordinated groups, facing waves of newly emerging Moorish warriors from their hiding places further down the valley. In the enclosed, wooded spaces, English fighting tactics were useless. Behind him, the wagon train had finally gained the hill, mules and drivers waited patiently, ignorant of what was happening just ahead of them.

"Damn it all!" he cried. They were being ambushed and by a massive force. The realisation hit home; this was Guyland's entire army. He had been suckered in and ambushed. The bloody Moor had been waiting!

He shouted to a nearby mounted staff officer.

"Pull them back, pull our men back. Get them to the hill."

As the man rode off to make contact with the nearest embattled soldiers, Teviot feared it was already too late. The Moors continued to grow in number, and they had plenty of cavalry to chase the English foot down. There could be no one left to make a stand with. He turned to the wagon train.

"You, drivers, bring your wagons forward and make a semi-circle. Here."

*

A horseman tore down the hill towards the bridge. Drummond waited on the western side to meet him. He had placed his rearguard on the eastern side of the river. A wall of sharp pikes blocked the exit from the bridge and on either side of them, muskets covered the flanks, ensuring any charge was winnowed before it struck.

He held a hand out and the rider yanked savagely on his reins, the horse whinnying in protest.

"What is it? It sounds like chaos out there."

The rider, a look of panic in his eyes, nodded.

"Sir, we are overrun. The Moors have ambushed us. I am sent to warn the garrison and fetch the rest of the cavalry."

Drummond didn't hesitate. "Go. Go," he ordered, slapping the horse as it passed by. "Make way." he called back to his men. "Make way!"

He ran back across the bridge as the horseman dodged through a gap in the pike wall and headed east toward Tangier.

"Sir?" asked Longshore.

Drummond unsheathed his blade and turned to face his men.

"The Moors have attacked in force."

A murmur ran amongst the gathered soldiers.

"What should we do, Sir?" asked Swallow.

Drummond desperately wanted to march back up the hill, to rejoin Teviot. But he had his orders.

"We hold the bridge."

If the English had any hope of escaping, the bridge must be held. Minutes later, his decision was proved right. A hundred Moorish horsemen rounded Jews Hill from the west.

"Men!" he shouted. "They want to cut off our line of retreat. We will not let them."

Stood together next to the pike wall, Swallow looked at a grim-faced Blair and laughed.

"That worried expression makes you look ten years older."

Blair spat.

"If I was ten year older, I'd likely be dead of some palsy or flux."

"Barrel of laughs, you are."

"Hold fast, men," called Drummond, taking his place to one side of the pikes.

As the first group of cavalry mounted the bridge, he ordered the muskets to fire.

∗

"Stand fast, men, form on me!" shouted Teviot. He was still astride his horse, sword waving high in the air. He positioned himself in the middle of the plateau desperately trying to organise a defence. Before him stood only fifty or so exhausted men, mostly pike, some cavalry, some muskets, and a few staff officers wielding swords and pistols. He had them positioned facing north, ready to receive the first charge. To their backs, the wagons had been corralled to give them some protection from becoming flanked, the drivers stood atop them, armed with axes and hammers. He called towards more scrambling redcoats as they reached the top. "Here! Form here!" As the panting soldiers struggled to reach him, the first Moors came into view. They were right behind them. He watched as Lieutenant Oates was cut down, his hands flying into the air in supplication as he fell to the ground.

The men watched quietly as the small group of their comrades were cut down to a man. Teviot wanted to swear, to curse God, to curse Guyland, to curse himself. It was his pride and overconfidence that had led to this. After twenty years of war he had grown used to reading his foes, understanding the tides of battle, the intrigues of war. This time, someone had used that against him. Damn him, but Guyland was the most tenacious man he had ever fought. And what would happen to Tangier now? Teviot and his command were finished, that much was obvious. But would Guyland try again for the prize? Trust in the walls and the cannon, Andrew, he told himself. They can't get through that.

"Sir!"

He turned as Lieutenant Cooke, his sword held ready, ran towards him from the eastern edge of the hill.

"The Moors are sweeping round the flanks. Their cavalry will soon block our retreat."

"Thank you, Lieutenant. Take command of our rear defences." Cooke nodded and ran back toward the wagons. Teviot returned his attention to the enemy at his front.

"Steady lads," he spoke with as much confidence as he could muster. It was too late to make a run for the bridge. Already the tribesmen were massing just yards away from the redcoats, hundreds of them were reaching the summit and spreading around the edges to envelope them. Bloody scimitars and gore stained shields were held ready. Dark, yellowing eyes regarding the desperate English with a mixture of eagerness and hatred. A mounted warrior, an officer resplendent in armour, rode out in front, raised his first high and yelled.

The Governor pursed his lips and nodded. This was it. It was over. A young, remarkably fresh-faced pikeman looked towards Teviot. The look of panic on the soldier's face struck his heart. The Governor smiled down at him.

"Give them hell, lad. Give the heathen bastards hell!" he roared, as a wave of black-robed warriors swept in towards them.

*

Drummond wiped his blade free from blood and sheathed it. He ran a hand through his hair, realising he had lost his hat sometime during the melee.

The bridge was a mess of men and horses. The English had wreaked havoc and the enemy had taken a terrible toll. The first charge was nothing short of a slaughter. At least twenty cavalry had died, either impaled against the pike wall or hit point blank by musket fire. Such was the devastation upon the bridge it had become effectively blocked to any coordinated charge. Then the Moors had changed tack. The cavalry split and started to work their way some fifty yards up and downstream from the bridge and began to cross the river. It was quite fordable if one had the leisure to do so, even more so if one was on a horse. A third group of thirty or so riders remained to threaten another head on assault. He had ordered his muskets back onto the bridge against that threat, lined up in three tight ranks. Even so, it was clear they would be surrounded. He ordered the pikes to turn about and reposition themselves on the bridge facing east. The cavalry had quickly made the crossing to other side, gathered and charged. As they did so, the cavalry on the western side of the bridge dismounted and ran at the musketeers. They unleashed another volley, taking down more swordsmen, but not enough. Drummond fought with the gunners whilst the pikes held off the mounted charge from the southern bank.

The fight had been frantic, short and bloody. In the aftermath only half of the musketeers were left standing. The pikes had fared better, driving off the cavalry on the eastern side. Corporal Longshore, his throat torn open, lay amongst the dead.

"Sir, what do we do now?" asked Swallow, his hands and face splashed with blood. Drummond looked back up toward Jew's Hill. He saw flags and pennants, Moorish swordsmen and cavalry. He heard cheering.

Drummond turned to Swallow, to all of them. The day was lost. There was no one left to hold the bridge for. He had to save who he could.

"Run. Leave your weapons. They are no use now. Run for the Lines, before the Moors gather again and ride us down. Run!"

The men looked at each other for a moment but didn't need telling twice.

"C'mon lads, you heard the Captain. Move your sorry arses," ordered Swallow, chivvying the men along as his stepped across the bodies.

"Simon!"

Swallow stopped. Drummond stopped as well, watching the advance of the Moors.

Blair was on the ground, his head a bloody mess.

"Jacob, quickly. I'll get you up."

Blair smiled, his teeth stained red.

"No point. I'm dead and you'll be too if you don't get out of here. Just wanted to say goodbye,"

"Jacob, I can," said Swallow, kneeling down next to his friend.

"No, you can't. Here," Blair raised a shaking hand. Swallow clutched it firmly. "Have a drink for your old mate once in a while, alright?"

Swallow squeezed his friend's hand and nodded solemnly.

"Corporal. Come on!" shouted Drummond, pulling at Swallow's shoulder. They had to move.

Swallow nodded and looked at Blair. His eyes were closed. He was dead.

He stood and started to run. Drummond fell in behind, covering their retreat. He looked back towards the hill and spied another group of horsemen picking their way down the slope. "Dear God, let us make it," he whispered. But he knew they had too far to run. Someone would have to slow the cavalry down. He eased his blade out of its sheath once more and prepared himself.

*

Fitzwilliam looked up and toward the door when he heard the peeling of the bells. It was midday, and for a moment he confused the ringing with the noonday chimes. But they continued, on and on. An alarm. He shared an anxious glance with Donahoe and started towards the door. The sound of hurried footsteps preceded the door opening and a breathless Siobhan halting at the threshold, looking first at Fitzwilliam then her father.

"What is it, daughter? Why do the bells sound?" Donahoe asked.

"The garrison is under attack. The Moors have returned!"

Fitzwilliam took another step toward her.

"The foraging party? Teviot? Rupert?"

She shook her head.

"I know nothing more, I'm sorry."

He gripped her arm, squeezed it gently in gratitude and turned to head for his room. Taking the steps three at a time, he gained the landing quickly, entered and went straight for his sword, hanging from a large metal hook on the back of the door. He buckled it quickly, cinching the belt across his waist, the scabbard hanging almost to the floor. He then turned towards the chest at the end of the bed and retrieved his two pistols. He spent several precious minutes ensuring they were primed and ready to fire before tucking them into his belt. As he made to leave he thought for a moment about putting on his redcoat. No, that wouldn't be right. He wasn't a soldier anymore; his stained white work shirt would have to do.

Siobhan and her father were waiting for him downstairs.

"Be safe, James," said Donahoe.

"Thank you, Thomas," Fitzwilliam clapped him on the arm and looked at Siobhan. Her face was a mixture of concern and confusion. He had no time to dwell on it. He was out of the Tavern and on his way, pounding along the streets of Tangier. He kept his hand on the pommel of his blade, using the pressure to keep the weapon from dragging along the ground. The bells were still ringing, a discordant tempo that could not keep time with the speed of his steps. For all of the urgent cacophony, the entire town seemed deserted; he was alone as he proceeded west toward the walls, with no sign of any soldiers. Every man jack of them must have already been summoned and what few townsfolk there were would have taken refuge in their homes. He passed by an alleyway, registering it only for its proximity to the gates. He was almost there.

"Fitzwilliam!" a loud commanding voice made him slow up, taking two more stumbling steps before he could halt and turn. He wasn't completely at rest as he twisted round to see who had called his name.

Cobb had emerged from the alleyway and stood not ten yards from him. He had a raised pistol. Fitzwilliam barely had time to register the look on Cobb's face. The man was already pulling the trigger. Fitzwilliam used the remaining momentum he had to allow the twisting motion to veer his body into the wall on his right. He crashed into the fading white plaster with a grunt, feeling the bare skin of his arm scratch savagely against the rough surface. No more than a foot ahead of him, a bullet embedded itself in the wall. Cobb had over corrected in trying to follow his movement, the shot kicking up a plumb of dust and chippings. Fitzwilliam felt the sting of several on his face. Allowing instinct to take over, Fitzwilliam grabbed his pistols and fired in Cobb's direction. Cobb stepped back into the side alley as the pistols barked.

Fitzwilliam swore and dropped his guns onto the floor. He drew his sword and took up a two handed fighting stance. Cobb re-emerged, his own sabre carried low in his right hand.

"One more lucky escape, eh, Fitzwilliam?" snarled Cobb.

"I thought you would have gotten the message by now," Fitzwilliam replied breathlessly.

"What? That you are a worthless piece of shit who weaselled out of every deserved punishment awarded him?"

Fitzwilliam smiled grimly.

"That's one point of view. Cobb, we are under attack, my friend is out there as well as Teviot and hundreds of English soldiers. They need us. Whatever you say, we are the best at what we do."

"Being killers you mean?" replied Cobb. He took as step forward. "Yes, I'm a killer. I don't know what you are." He paced forward once more, closing the distance to almost a sword's length.

"I don't want to do this, Cobb."

"I do."

Cobb lunged forwards, his blade straight and level. Fitzwilliam twisted to one side, bring his blade round to parry the sabre away even as Cobb stepped past. Cobb used the force of the parry to turn, raise his blade high and launch a vicious backhanded downward swipe that Fitzwilliam barely stopped. The two men disengaged.

Fitzwilliam held his sword out in front of his body and looked left and right. The street they were in was only eight feet or so across. Wide enough to wield a blade but he had to be careful about trying any wild swings. Cobb beckoned for him to come forward, his sword hanging loosely by his side. Fitzwilliam was wise to that one; he had had plenty of time to think about Cobb and their previous contest. He had been too quick to charge before; it had meant he was off balance and the older man only had to move his feet. Cobb was a good duellist, Fitzwilliam had to admit it. So, maybe he should give Cobb exactly what he was expecting. He wanted this finished. Fast. He had somewhere he needed to be.

Raising his blade high above his head and shouting a battle cry, he charged recklessly towards Cobb. Smiling, Cobb dropped into a crouch as Fitzwilliam neared, planning to let the claymore whistle over his head. It was exactly what Fitzwilliam wanted. As he closed, he let the sword fall in an arc behind his back and towards the ground, its tip inches from the cobbles. Keeping a tight grip, he threw it upward. The blade, like a windmill sailing past his right leg, headed towards Cobb's head at a terrifying speed. Cobb reacted just as swiftly, throwing himself backward, landing on his rump, his sabre clattering to one side. Fitzwilliam was upon him in an instant, coming at his left side, weapon poised to strike down. Cobb kicked out with his legs and swept Fitzwilliam from his feet. He landed on his back with a loud "oof" as the air was knocked form his lungs. Cobb scrambled toward him, climbing onto his chest and raining down blows against Fitzwilliam's unprotected head. He raised his arms to block the blows but they were pushed aside.

"Thought you could outwit me, boy? You don't fight dirty enough."

Fitzwilliam felt his focus begin to go. He knew that within moments he would be too senseless to stop. Perhaps that should be the way? He allowed his arms to go limp, his body to give up on its struggling.

He gazed through blurring vision upon the triumphant face of Cobb.

"Finally learnt your lesson, whelp? Your king was weak and stupid and so are you. That's why you'll always lose."

Cobb grabbed the sides of Fitzwilliam's head, pressure tight on each side, the pain excruciating as his hair was yanked savagely. Cobb raised Fitzwilliam's head lifting it high off the ground, making to dash it against the floor until the skull cracked.

Cobb leaned in close. "Good riddance, Royalist scum," he whispered.

Cobb was too busy to notice as Fitzwilliam moved his right arm along the ground and behind his back, his hand searching for his belt. He found the metal handle of the Moorish blade, its ornate markings pressing against his skin. He yanked hard, drawing the sharp, curving blade out of the wooden sheath. Once clear he rammed it deep into Cobb's neck. A look of surprise passed across Cobb's face and his grip lessened. Then the confusion passed, replaced with a feral anger. His grip strengthened once more and he pushed hard and down.

Fitzwilliam's head cracked against the ground and his vision swam. He retained his grip on the knife and pulled it free. His head went down again. Another sharp blow and Fitzwilliam's world went black

How swiftly consciousness returned, he could not say. He opened his eyes and found no black shape of vengeance above him, felt no weight upon his chest. He turned onto his stomach and pushed himself up. A wave of nausea rolled over him and he groaned pitifully. Its passing was replaced by a sharp ache coming from the back of his head. He reached behind and felt the wound. The hair was matted, sticky to the touch. Withdrawing his hand, he studied the blood covering his fingertips.

He had seen men die of such wounds, hours after the battle. They'd just keel over, where seconds before they had been upright and chattering.

"I don't need hours," he muttered to himself, hoping that his much remarked upon thick skull would actually come in handy, just this once.

Opposite him, Cobb sat with his back to the wall. His neck and chest was a mess of red. He had bled out. The Moorish knife must have severed an artery on the way out. Fitzwilliam grunted and went about gathering his collection of fallen weapons. Once his sword was sheathed, pistols stowed and the knife in his hand, he went and knelt next to Cobb. His mouth was full open, caught as if in surprise or mid scream. Fitzwilliam wiped the knife blade against Cobb's trousers, removing the sticky congealed blood. Then he leaned in and whispered into Cobb's deaf ears.

"God save the King."

Fitzwilliam stood once more and walked swiftly towards the gate. He did not have the strength to run and doubted he would stay upright if he tried. As he neared Catherina Port a growing hubbub of voices filled the air, shouted commands, barked replies and the occasional, jarring scream.

He emerged into chaos, there were ragged looking men gathered everywhere, many of them wounded. He saw troops run to secure the gate, more positioning themselves on the ramparts above. Several horsemen were trying to calm their mounts and lead them away past Fitzwilliam.

He pressed himself tight against the wall as the harassed steeds cantered past; he then entered the square. The place was in an uproar, he saw Fairborne clustered with Sergeants and other officers. Along the walls exhausted men lay in breathless heaps.

He made for the gate.

"Sir!"

He looked about him and saw the familiar face of Corporal Swallow, waving at him from the wall just to the left of the street from which he had entered. Fitzwilliam hurried over.

"No, stay down," he ordered, gently pushing Swallow back as the man tried to rise. He looked the corporal over, his face was covered in dust, and he sported a cut to his forehead, the congealed blood mixing with the dust into a thick, lumpy mess.

"What happened, Swallow?"

The soldier looked distraught.

"Sir, they're all gone. We got jumped on, bad. They were all over us,"

"Swallow, where are the others? Longshore, Blair?"

Swallow shook his head, his eyes shining.

"They fell. Captain Drummond, he told us to run for it."

Fitzwilliam felt a surge of hope.

"Drummond, he's here?"

"Sir, I'm sorry. I haven't seen him. We were strung out. The Moors were right behind us, on horses. I could hear 'em. If it hadn't been for our boys riding out to help, none of us would have made it. I never saw him make it back to the gates. I'm sorry."

Fitzwilliam gritted his teeth and gripped Swallow on the shoulder.

"It's alright. I'll go and find him."

He stood and pushed his way through the press and walked toward the gate.

"Ho! Open this bastard up."

He reached the wooden portal and pounded his fist against it.

"Sorry, Sir. Orders says no one goes out," replied a sergeant.

"And I'm telling you to let me out."

"Fitzwilliam!" barked Fairborne, marching over to him. "What on earth do you think you are trying to do?"

"Rupert is out there. He needs my help," replied Fitzwilliam.

"If he is out there then he is dead," the Major said firmly.

"It doesn't matter, I am a private citizen. I can do what I damn well please. Now, open up this bloody gate and let me through."

"You might not be recognised as a soldier anymore, Fitzwilliam, but this is still a military garrison, ruled by a military governor. The rules apply to you just as anyone else."

Fitzwilliam beat his fists against the gate in frustration. Fairborne stepped in close.

"Lad, I know you are hurting. You've lost, we all have. Teviot is out there, likely dead. You know how many I have counted back through these gates? Thirty. Thirty out of five hundred. The Moor has horsewhipped us. No, he's massacred us. And don't think I haven't noticed the bloody shambles you're in. That's blood, I warrant." He placed an arm round Fitzwilliam and took him away from the gate and unwelcome listeners.

"Right now you look just like every other survivor from this sorry mess, and no one will ask why that is. Yet. I don't want to know what you've done, but I can guess. You've picked the best time to settle a score but don't let yourself stand out any more than you have to. Now, listen to me. We are battening down the hatches until nightfall. The Lieutenant-Governor is summoning every last man who can wield a pike or aim a musket. By God, we'll take anyone who can lift a rock and drop it from the walls. If the Moors are coming, they will have to come soon. So," he jerked Fitzwilliam's arm, "stand by the gates, and try and look useful. When dusk approaches, we'll look to gather our dead and re-establish contact with the forts. If you have a sensible bone in your body, you try no adventures by yourself. Wait 'til dark. Then go and find your friend."

Fitzwilliam closed his eyes, took a breath and gave Fairborne a nod. He had no choice, unless he was going to try and fight his way out. And that would achieve nothing.

*

Ghailan walked his horse to the centre of Jews Hill and dismounted. He removed his helmet and handed it up to one of his bodyguard. He looked about him, at the red-coated soldiers scattered in great numbers upon the hilltop and then breathed deep the smells of war, of death and victory. They were so familiar. He drank in the stench of sweat and blood, the stink of voided bowels and the bitter, acrid odour of gunpowder. Today was a great day, Allah be praised. His patience had been rewarded, his cleverness vindicated. The English had suffered their greatest defeat and yet they had fallen for the same trick twice. He had used three thousand men to pull the English into the waiting arms of ten thousand. He appreciated the irony that it was exactly a year before that the English had marched out, in their arrogance and confidence, and had been humiliated. Then, it had been a harsh lesson. But he had learned it. This time was sweet vengeance. His plan to feign a withdrawal and subsequent indifference worked perfectly. Teviot would never have thought he would be so committed to his task. He had been wrong. He picked his way over bodies, wrecked carts, slaughtered mules and abandoned weapons to a large concentration of redcoats and Berber warriors. This was where they had made their final stand, and there was Teviot. He lay next to a fallen horse, his body cut to ribbons by countless scimitar strikes. His men had not been kind to his body. Ghailan spied the English commander's sabre, laying inches from his outstretched hand. He knelt down, picked up the blade and examined it. It was not unlike a scimitar though not bearing such a pronounced curve. The hilt was still tacky from the blood that coated it. He placed the weapon back into Teviot's hand. It was fitting that such a worthy opponent should die in such a manner.

One of his captains approached him.

"My Lord?"

Ghailan looked up at the man. His breastplate was battered and bloody, but he carried himself well.

"My Lord. What do you command? The army has tasted victory and wish to march upon the walls."

Ghailan reached down and scooped up some dry earth, rubbing it between his hands.

"No."

"Lord?" asked the captain uncertainly.

"We will not march on the walls. The day is fine, their cannon no doubt primed and ready. They are waiting for us. Why waste men when the infidel is already beaten?"

No, he thought to himself, the English have lost too much. Half their army and their leader lie dead. It will take them a long time to recover. I have what I came here for. I have beaten Teviot, and regained the respect of my men. That is enough for one day.

"We have our victory. Send word to all my commanders. Ready the men. We march south. We march for home."

*

As dusk settled, the gates to Tangier opened. The remaining half troop of the Tangier Horse cantered out, spreading into a wide formation and moving off towards Jews Hill. Captain Witham held back a moment with two of his men and allowed the rest to gain some distance. When they were perhaps two hundred yards away he waved at the gates. A small force of twenty musketeers hurried out and took up a loose skirmish formation. Twenty pikemen followed them out in a column. Once clear, they were followed by a train of six wagons, and trailing behind them, another score of musketeers.

No one spoke for fear of alerting watchers to their presence, only the footfall of the draft mules and the creaking of the wagons disturbed the brooding silence that had settled upon the town and fortifications. The garrison was emptied of all able-bodied men. All that remained were the gun crews, watching grim-faced from the ramparts, those who stood by manning the gates and the few survivors from the first engagement; an exhausted force who nevertheless stood ready as a final rearguard if needed. In the distance, those garrisoning the forts looked on. They had been sent orders not to withdraw, not to assist. If the treacherous Moors tried another assault, they had to hold or there would be no territory left to defend.

Once the last of the company were out, the gates started to close. One more figure slid through the gap and stepped into the night. Fitzwilliam fell in behind, keeping his distance. He was not part of the recovery force. His task was his own.

The redcoats took their time, hampered by the slow creep of the wagons and their oft clumsy manoeuvring over the trenches. Witham ensured his riders conducted a full sweep of the area, spreading them wide, searching every nook and cranny on their route and then pushing them on across Jews River and another half mile beyond the top of the hill and into the Great Valley. He knew it was a risk. If Moorish cavalry was lying in wait, his men could hope to do little more than provide a warning to the rest. As the column made its way along the trail beyond the fortifications they started to encounter the line of English dead. One wagon hung back, two men jumped off it and started to load the bodies on. Fitzwilliam slowed and began to inspect the corpses. He moved along the trail, counting bodies: six, seven, eight. And there he was. Lying on his back, gazing sightlessly into the night sky. Fitzwilliam knelt beside his friend, inspecting the body. A long ragged slash from the shoulder blade to the stomach was his death wound. Fitzwilliam reached out, placed his hand over Drummond's eyes and forced them shut. He stood up, straddled his friend, reached down, and got his arms underneath Drummond's shoulders. He pulled up and leaned back, Drummond's stiffening body protesting. He grunted as he finally got Drummond resting over his shoulder, the bulk causing him to stagger a few paces. He righted himself and set off.

Fitzwilliam carried Drummond's body all the way to the walls. The weight of his friend became uncomfortable not far into the walk, the pressure on his shoulders went from dull to sharp, but he refused to stop and ignored the offers of assistance from the wagon crew as he passed them by.

When he reached the safety of the small courtyard of Catherina Port, he halted and looked about, confused as to what he should do next.

"James?"

Fitzwilliam couldn't respond. He had no rational thoughts left.

"Fitzwilliam!"

He shook his head, turned to the source of the voice.

"Lad, it's me. Major Fairborne."

"I had to get him back, I had to get him home."

Fairborne nodded and placed a hand gently on his shoulder.

"You've done that. He's home. Well done. Now, let us take him."

"But I've-"

"You've done enough," said Fairborne kindly. "Let us take care of him. He's home and he deserves a proper burial."

Fitzwilliam nodded, the man's words barely penetrating his fugue.

"His family. He has family. They need to be told."

"They will be. I'll write to them myself."

"He died doing his duty. He died a hero."

"That he did. Sergeant?" Fairborne beckoned to a group of redcoats standing to one side. A burly looking man stepped forward and saluted smartly.

"Sir?"

"Please take this officer to the infirmary. Treat him with dignity."

"Yes, Sir." The soldier turned to two of his men and motioned them forward.

"We've got him, Sir," said one of the men, pulling the body from Fitzwilliam. The wave of relief was immense. His tired muscles felt a wave of warmth spread through them.

"Now, lad," Fairborne placed a hand on his shoulder. "Get you home. This day is done. The Moors aren't coming back."

Fitzwilliam looked at him and cocked his head to one side. It was still hard to understand what he was saying. He felt a gentle push on his back and he was propelled towards the lane leading away from the gate. He didn't struggle, he just placed one foot in front of the other.

"James?"

He stopped, turned and looked back.

"Go home and mourn your friend. Then come back tomorrow. We have lost too many men tonight, some of our best. I need you back in the colours," Fairborne folded his arms. "Go home and I'll see you tomorrow. We've got a lot of work to do."

Fitzwilliam didn't reply, instead he resumed his walk. He wasn't sure where he was supposed to go, wasn't sure what home was. Drummond was his home, the finest friend, his brother. He was cast adrift, directionless. It was his fault. If he had been there he could have protected him. He had thrown that away when he had allowed his own emotions to get the better of him. It was his stubborn, pig-headed attitude that anything could be solved by a strong arm and sharp sword. It had gotten him nothing but an ill reputation, months in a cell and stripped of his rank and place. And now, he had been absent when Drummond had needed him the most. His dear friend who had stuck by him through all the foolishness and stupidity, the one true friend who had seen something in him, more than Fitzwilliam had ever seen in himself. He had defended him, covered for him, stood with him through all of it, and now he had not been there for his best friend, his only friend. He had not been there the one time Drummond needed someone to back him up, the one time, that one single, solitary time. And now it was too late. Despair flooded his soul, threatening at any moment to overwhelm him.

He stopped. Before him stood the Jolly Sailor Tavern. He had not known where to go yet his feet had brought him here. He took a deep breath, and stepped forwards. The door opened, Donahoe stepping out to greet him.

He reached out a hand, squeezed his shoulder then guided him across the threshold and into the gloomy interior. Familiar smells of clay, ale and cookery penetrated his reverie, giving him a warm remembrance of comfort and companionship. Donahoe let him go and alone once more he continued through into the kitchen, out to the back yard and slowly up the rickety wooden steps to his room. He put a hand on the latch and pulled it up. He glanced to the left, to the door that led to Drummond's room. He would have to go in there, sort out his effects. But not today. He pulled open the door to his room, let go of the latch and stepped up to his bed. He sat down, rested his hands on his thighs, let his eyes wander aimlessly around the room and took a deep long breath. As he released the air, his body began to shake and the tears came.

*

Siobhan stood by the door, the cooling night breeze bringing goosebumps on her neck. She watched Fitzwilliam, as she had been for some time. He had not noticed her; he was lost to his misery. She stepped inside and walked wordlessly towards him, sitting down on the bed. He reacted to the movement, his head whipping up to meet her, eyes wet, a look of confusion on his face, then recognition. He started to speak.

"I swear. I swear to you. Never again. I will never be the foolish boy. I cannot. I will be better. Every day I will try to be better. For Drummond, I must be a better man."

The hope and the fear of failure that flowed within his words moved her. She had never heard him speak like this. He had aged, matured in the space of one day. He reached and grasped her hand, held it desperately. She did not withdraw it. She understood all too well the need for human contact, for something safe to latch on to.

The tears began again.

Siobhan reached out and pulled his head to her shoulder. As he wept, she gently rocked him back and forth. One of his pistols dug into her side, it was uncomfortable, but she could bear it. She would always bear it. For him.

4 May 1664
The Walls of Tangier

As the sun rose in the east, a gentle sea breeze blew into and over Tangier. It whistled around the flagpole overlooking the Upper Castle and the lands beyond. The wind caught the thick cloth flag that hung limply against the weather-beaten wood of the pole. The wind blew harder, whipping the flag up, giving it life.

From his silent, lonely vigil on the walls Fairborne looked up at it and growled.

"We're still here, you bastards."

The flag of St George waved vigorously. It snapped and strained against the Moroccan winds that sought to rip it from its ties. But the flag held firm.

TANGIER
BOOK TWO: BATTLE HONOURS
Coming 2015

AUTHOR's NOTE

The major events in this book are, by and large, historically accurate. I have, of course, taken some dramatic license with my main characters and their adventures. That said I have always placed their actions within the actual historical context and outcomes. The loss of Teviot and a large part of the fighting force of Tangier did indeed deliver a significant victory to Ghailan, but he was never able to breach the walls. Yet he would not be the only lord who would seek to force the English from Africa...

ABOUT THE AUTHOR

Alex is a ex-Regular Army officer having served in both the Royal Engineers and the Education and Training Services. He is now in the Army Reserve. A fantasy author, he has also written for computer games. Unsurprisingly he is a self-confessed geek. Those who witnessed his lightsaber battles, late at night in the Hohne Mess, can attest to this.

34116966R00202

Made in the USA
Charleston, SC
01 October 2014